tHe ivy

WEST HOLLYWOOD HIGH

CLASS OF 2010

Callie,
You're a skinny bitch
but I love you anyway.
Have a great summer!
xoxo Samantha

Hey Cal,
Thanks for always having
my back in Calc. Without you,
I don't think I'd be graduating.
Good luck next year! Kevin

Dear Legally Blonde:
(Seriously, it never gets old!) They
say you're a mega-genius and all,
but I don't hold it against you
because you're smokin' hot. If you
ever get bored with Evan, you know
who to call—Jerry

Callie,
Don't forget us
when you're famous!
Best, Lisa

Hahvahd,
Ditto what Jerry said - Ted, 555.3621

Callie.
Four words: Game Three. State Championships. Your header off of
my corner kick = EPIC. I will remember it always. along with all the
practices.all the sleepovers. all the pranks (the boys' team
STILL doesn't know who dyed their uniforms purple!). and of course.
all the games. Even if you hadn't scored the winning goal at State.
you'd still be my Number One. Knock 'em dead at Harvard.
Co-captains 4eva.
Mellissa

Cal,

Oh the irony, oh the cliché. What's a best friend to say here in a yearbook anyway? It's not like I'm not going to see you every day this summer (if I can separate you from Evan for two seconds, that is). But in all seriousness, I wouldn't even know where to begin—so many things that I'm going to miss . . . Tuesday night fro-yo, Thursday morning "study" hall, working on the homecoming float, losing to you for homecoming queen!—still pissed btw ;)—staying at your dad's and pretending we go to UCLA, pretending we go to UCLA so we could sneak into frat parties (definitely having a repeat this summer), using Ted and Jerry to meet older varsity athletes (oh wait, that one was just me), your first <u>real</u> bra, my first kiss, 7th grade gym class, auditioning for that reality show, The Secret Notebook, July 19th 2006, poolside BBQs, beachside bonfires, "Mani-WHAT? Why are you touching my FEET?!?," Fashion Police!, the real police (don't blame me if that gets out when you're Mrs. Davies, Esq., and Evan's running for office), the night we "accidentally" locked ourselves in Bryan's bathroom. . . . Wow. There are just too many memories . . . and it's summertime now, biatch, so let's go make some more. Not going to say I'll miss you . . . Not going to cry!

💧←(OK, so maybe you're worth it)

xxx Jess

Miss Callie Andrews:

Well, I must say it's been a real pleasure competing with you over the past twelve years of our academic careers. The title of valedictorian was truly up for grabs toward the end, and I want to thank you for abdicating so gracefully. It cannot have been easy. They say the only reason one chooses Harvard over Yale is because one was not admitted to the latter, but I'm sure that's not the case with you.

Best of luck,

scott Hamilton Wentworth

VOLUME ONE

the ivy

BY LAUREN KUNZE

in collaboration with

RINA ONUR

GREENWILLOW BOOKS
An Imprint of HarperCollins*Publishers*

We'd like to thank all of the people who helped make this book happen: each other; our agent, Rosemary; our editor, Virginia, and everyone else in the Greenwillow family; our parents, Susan, Fritz, Hermine, and Mihran; our brothers, Michael and Remi; and, last but not least, Blocking Group # 49 and all of the other campus characters who may or may not have had a hand in inspiring this story.

The Ivy

For information address HarperCollins Children's Books, a division of HarperCollins Publishers, 10 East 53rd Street, New York, NY 10022.
www.harperteen.com

The text of this book is set in Adobe Caslon.
Book design by Christy Hale

Library of Congress Cataloging-in-Publication Data

Kunze, Lauren.
The ivy / by Lauren Kunze with Rina Onur.
p. cm.
"Greenwillow Books."
Summary: When Callie arrives for her freshman year at Harvard, she encounters her three vastly different roommates, new friendships, steamy romance, and scandalous secrets.
ISBN 978-0-06-196045-1 (trade bdg.)
[1. Universities and colleges—Fiction. 2. Roommates—Fiction. 3. Interpersonal relations—Fiction. 4. Dating (Social customs)—Fiction.] I. Onur, Rina. II. Title.
PZ7.K94966Ro 2010 [Fic]—dc22 2009042525

10 11 12 13 14 CG/RRDB 10 9 8 7 6 5 4 3 2 1
First Edition
Greenwillow Books

To José Félix Alegría,
for making it worth writing about

"I don't want to repeat my innocence.
I want the pleasure of losing it again."

—F. Scott Fitzgerald, *This Side of Paradise*

ONE

move-in day

PARK YOUR CAR IN HARVARD YARD

Dearest Froshlings: peons and future leaders of America,

Move-in day is officially here, and the upperclassmen cannot wait to welcome you to Harvard: our humble abode. Working tirelessly for your benefit as usual, I have compiled a list of the five *crucial* things you should know before you set foot in the historic city of Cambridge. These are the rules. Your homework: memorize.

1. what to read

Ladies, for your BA: *Vogue, Vanity Fair*, and *Hello* magazines; read the *New York Times* in public and *Star* in private.

Gentlemen, for your BS: the *Wall Street Journal* and the *Economist* are the bare necessities.

Gold diggers, for your MRS: *Forbes* 500, aka the Bible. Looks like at least three members of your newly admitted class are from families that made this year's top 100.

2. what to drink

Anything to keep those baby genius neurons firing fast: Red Bull, Sugar Free Red Bull, or my personal favorite, a Venti Caffé Mocha from Starbucks. Better make it nonfat, sugar-free, no-whip if you plan to avoid gaining the Freshman Fifteen.

Also, please keep in mind: Beer is for middle schoolers and football players. You're an adult now, kiddo: imbibe accordingly.

3. what to eat

Nothing. Seriously, do not eat. Especially not between the hours of 6 P.M.–3 A.M. Unless, of course, you'd like to gain fifteen pounds. Or, according to recent trends, what is fast becoming the "Freshman Twenty-five." Damn you, inflation.

4. what to wear

I generally rely on a little something I call the "Three Ps." That's pearls, Prada, and La Perla. Of course, I understand that for some of you, this may be a little too much to ask. My only real request, then, is that you shower–daily. You'd be surprised how difficult most Harvard students seem to find this one easy task.

5. who to meet

Some like to limit their social milieu to the people whose last names are the same as the major buildings on campus, or to those admitted due to their God-given talents in crew, squash, or equestrianism. My advice, however, is to put your Socially Darwinian attitudes aside, and get out there and meet some genuine Harvard dorks. They may look and smell a little different from the rest of us, but without them, Harvard wouldn't have nuclear weapons, MIT wouldn't have a weather machine, and I never would have made it through Math 21a.

Armed with these five simple rules, you stand a chance of surviving your first semester (don't worry, most people do–with exceptions).

And oh, I almost forgot: the Unspoken Rule–Rule #6. Since you're new, I'll give it to you straight: Freshmen girls, stay away from the upperclassmen boys. They only care about only one thing, and it doesn't involve your perfect high school transcript.

Welcome to life in the Bubble,
Alexis Thorndike, Advice Columnist
Fifteen Minutes Magazine
Harvard University's Authority on Campus Life since 1873

Callie Andrews struggled under the weight of two enormous cardboard boxes which, in a typical move, she had stacked one on top of the other, confident that she could handle the load. She was wrong. As her foot edged over the final step of the staircase leading up to the second floor of Wigglesworth Dormitory—her home at Harvard for the next year—the top box, the one her mother had insisted on labeling "INTIMATES" with a huge permanent marker, started to slip.

"Here, let me give you a hand with that," said a voice from over her shoulder.

"No, that's all right I've got it—" she began, but before she could say that she was stronger than she looked, thank you very much, he stepped into view. She gasped and both boxes plummeted to the floor, flaps flying open and contents scattering everywhere.

Under normal circumstances spilling your INTIMATES, OLD SOCCER STUFF, and other items of a highly personal nature all over the hallway on this day, move-in day, the very first day of college, and—if the cheesy graduation speech by Scott Wentworth the nose-picking, perpetually sweating valedictorian of West Hollywood High who beat Callie out by an infuriating fraction of a grade point average were to be believed—the "First Day of the Rest of Your Life," *could* be a bit embarrassing. Callie, however, was completely distracted.

Once during her junior year at semifinals for State, a soccer ball had hit her squarely in the solar plexus. That was sort of what she felt like now: unable to breathe or speak as she struggled to remain upright. Recovering her balance, Callie ran a hand through her post-red-eye airplane hair, cursing herself for neglecting to brush it that morning or bother with any makeup. She could almost hear the voice of her best friend, Jessica, who had already started at Stanford two weeks ago, saying, "I told you so, Cal—doesn't matter if you're going ten miles to a party or ten feet to my pool. You gotta get your face fully on before you leave the house because you never know when you're going to have a date with destiny."

For a moment she could see nothing but his eyes. The color was irrelevant (blue, if you must know), but the expression was magnetic: intensity masquerading as indifference, the look carrying a challenge: *Entertain me, or I will entertain myself at your expense.* His mouth twisted in a smirk so natural she had to assume that this was its default expression. Even in silence, he appeared to be mocking her.

Callie felt her cheeks grow hot. "Oh—uh—yikes," she stammered, bending down and shoving her bras and underwear back into the box, cringing as she reached for her smelly shin-guards and wishing, for once, that she had listened to her mother ("The doctor said no more soccer for at least a year; do you really think your shins are going to need guarding in college?"). Instead Callie had insisted, a tad bit dramatically, that they were the closest thing she had to a teddy bear (seeing as she slept with them on the night before every big game) and without them she was like a warrior without her armor, at which point Theresa Frederickson-Andrews—no, make that Theresa Frederickson (it'd been three years since the divorce but Callie still had to remind herself) threw up her hands and shook her head, muttering the oft-repeated phrase "just like your father."

In a way, though, it was true: without soccer—a busted ACL had put Callie out of commission at the end of last season for possibly forever—she wasn't quite sure who she was anymore. Thankfully as the rapt—raptly asleep, that is—audience had lapsed into a collective heat coma on graduation day, good old Scott Boogers Wentworth had also promised that "college is a prime time for reinvention." So far it was looking like she had a jump start on redefining herself as the dorm klutz.

"I'd offer to assist you," said the box-droppingly handsome Reason-for-the-mess, still watching with poorly concealed amusement and looking like help was the furthest thing from his mind, "but usually I like to buy a girl dinner or at least a drink before I handle her undergarments."

Callie froze over a ratty pair of white boy shorts—observing, with a frown, that this particular color and style seemed predominant—before she stood up and said: "Thanks, but I have a boyfriend."

The smirk on his face faltered for an instant but then expanded to a smile. "What makes you think I was asking?"

Oh. What *did* make me think he was asking? she wondered, mentally kicking herself and trying not to let that smile distract her . . . or that thick, dark brown hair . . . or the way his upper arms were straining against the fitted sleeves of his *Harvard Squash,*

Class of 2014 polo . . . or—*Crap—stay focused!* She bent down, stuffed the last of her old soccer shorts into the box, and jammed the cardboard flaps shut.

Straightening, she met his eyes. He stared right back. For a moment he was silent: she a deer; his gaze the headlights. Then his eyes danced wickedly. "I'm flattered," he said, taking a step forward, "but you should know that you're really not my type. I wonder, though . . . how would your *boyfriend* feel if he knew that it's only the first day of school and I've already seen your underwear?"

The perfect comeback was right on the tip of her tongue—really it was—but for some reason when he was standing this close to her, it became difficult to think or, for that matter, to even remember that she had a boyfriend whose name was . . . *uhm* . . .

Beep, beep, beep!

1 NEW TEXT MESSAGE
FROM EVAN DAVIES

Ducking her head, she flipped it open and read:

HEY BABE! SO SORRY BUT
I'M GONNA HAVE TO BAIL
ON OUR PHONE DATE
TONIGHT. INITIATION
FOR THE FRATERNITY I'M
RUSHING STARTS TODAY
AND THEY'RE ABOUT TO
CONFISCATE MY CELLULAR!
LOVE YA THOUGH, MISS
YOU CRAZY!

Evan, her boyfriend of two years, who could, she decided, definitely take this jerk in a fight, was currently about a billion miles away (okay, two thousand nine hundred and ninety-six, but who's counting?) probably cleaning toilets in the soccer fraternity he was rushing at UCLA. They had promised to call each other every single day.

No PROBLEM, she texted back, meaning it without pausing to dwell on how quickly the promise had been broken or why she didn't particularly care.

"Was that him?" This guy's voice was so deep and alluring that it almost made her want to lie and say it wasn't—that, in fact, she had made up the whole boyfriend thing on a crazy whim in the first place. . . . His smile grew even wider as if he could read her mind. "The so-called 'boyfriend'?"

"No," snapped Callie. "I mean, yes it was him but no, he's not my 'so-called boyfriend.' He's my real boyfriend, like, he actually exists. . . . His name's Evan and he's great," she blurted. "Really great and really . . . tall."

Dammit! Sometimes her brain said STOP TALKING but her mouth just didn't listen. At least this was better than Dual Mouth-Brain Failure, which she also suffered from. This involved a tendency to respond out loud to things that she had only imagined people might have said: the consequence of an overactive imagination and lack of what her mother called "a filter." Her dad, a mathematics professor at UCLA, claimed that this tendency to be "too in her head" was the reason behind her "brilliance"—a "brilliance," her mother joked, that she had inherited from her father and that most people had another word for: neurosis. That was, of course, back in the day when there were still jokes. These days, it was mostly fights: the kind where people loved each other so much (or so Callie chose to believe) that they couldn't stand it—or each other.

"Well, I'd better get these to my room," she finished vaguely, gesturing toward her boxes.

"And you're sure you don't want me to help take your 'intimates' off . . . your hands?" he asked, his eyes laughing as she stacked the box in question back on top of OLD SOCCER STUFF.

Yes—no—YES, I'm sure that NO, I don't want you to! she miraculously managed to think without verbalizing. Then, taking a deep breath, she smiled sweetly. "Thanks, but I'm just down the hall in C twenty-four," she said, nodding at the door that presumably led to her new home.

"What a coincidence, I'm—" he began, but before he could finish, that same door flew open and a girl stepped into the hall.

For the second time that day Callie felt her jaw drop.

The girl—with her straight, dark hair, impossibly high cheekbones, and huge gray eyes—was undeniably gorgeous.

As she moved closer, she lifted her fingers in a wave. Callie was halfway into waving back when she realized it wasn't meant for her but rather for the ~~beautiful~~ *mean* boy standing by her side. *"C'est absolument horrible ici,"* the girl murmured, smiling at him. *"Je ne peux pas vivre une minute sans une fumer. Tu veux une cigarette, mon chérie?"*

"Oh—hello," she added as if seeing Callie for the first time. She spoke English with an accent that sounded partially French, partially British, and definitely snobbier—ahem, more sophisticated—than anything Callie had ever heard. She was waif thin, like a model, and her long, flowing dress, embellished with endless strands of funky jewelry, wouldn't have been out of place on a runway in Paris.

Suddenly Callie's white cotton tank top seemed too plain, her grass-stained jean cutoffs too short, and the doodles on her battered, beloved Converses dirty and childish. She'd spent her high school years not caring that her old ripped jeans cost twenty dollars while the "destroyed denim" preferred by her classmates sold for two hundred bucks a hole. Her wardrobe—along with the cell service package for her "grandma phone," as Jessica affectionately called it since Callie was "literally the *only* person left in LA without an iBerryBlackPhone"—had simply been another casualty of *Le Divorce*. It sucked, sure, but Callie wasn't one to whine. She was much more of a picture-your-problems-(or-enemies'-heads)-on-the-face-of-a-soccer-ball-and-just-kick-the-shit-out-of-it kind of a girl.

So why all of a sudden did she care? Perhaps it was the way *he* was treating the new girl: like she was a peer while Callie was a Space Alien from Planet Klutz, which was totally unfair because she was actually very coordinated—at least she was when it came to her feet.

She turned to the girl. "Hi," she said. "I'm Callie."

"And I am Marine Aurélie Clément. You may call me Mimi, if this is easier."

The name, for some reason, sounded strangely familiar. Callie tried to place it while Mimi read the labels on her boxes. Suddenly Mimi's eyes lit up. "You are Callie Andrews, no?" she cried, leaning in to kiss Callie once on each cheek. "We are to be roommates!"

Ohhh right, Callie recalled, picturing the "Housing Assignment" e-mail she'd received over the summer listing the names and hometowns of her future roommates: Dana Gray from Goose Creek, South Carolina; Vanessa Von Vorhees from Manhattan, New York; and Marine Aurélie Clément, from a town in France whose name Callie could neither remember nor pronounce.

"I see you have already met Gregory," Mimi continued, smiling indulgently. "He is *such* an asshole, no?"

"Watch it, french fry," he retorted easily, "or my last cigarette's going down the gutter."

"You would not dare!" Mimi gasped, hands flying to her cheeks in mock horror.

Meanwhile Callie hovered over her boxes while her brain's internal iPod Shuffle (Playlist: The Soundtrack of My Life) selected a song by The Clash: "Should I stay or should I go?"

"Care to join us?" Mimi asked sincerely, or with an excellent imitation of sincerity.

Callie stole a look at Gregory, but he ignored her.

"No thanks," she said, and then, as if her mother, longtime attorney-at-law for the California Public Health Department, were watching her, she added, "I don't smoke."

Mimi shrugged and Gregory turned without so much as a sarcastic remark or even a glance in her direction, leaving Callie to wonder which unfamiliar sensation she liked the least: being embarrassed or being ignored.

Frowning, she waited until they had disappeared down the stairs before bending over to drag her boxes along the floor. She lugged them across the hallway and came to an abrupt halt in front of room C 24. A metal drop box and a whiteboard with four names on it were bolted to the battered brown door: DANA, CALLIE, MARINE, & VANESSA.

She stared at the names for a second, trying to conjure images of their owners. . . . There was Dana, the heavy metal goth rocker and terror of Goose Creek; Vanessa, the prim, bookish type who sometimes slept in the New York Public Library; and Mimi . . . well, clearly she was a Russian spy pretending to be a supermodel.

Smiling a little, Callie breathed in, and then flung open the front door.

"Hell-o-o! Anybody home . . . ?" she called.

No response. Instead she was greeted by a tangled mess of furniture, half-empty boxes, and suitcases. Two of the suitcases were unremarkable and black, but they stood out amid a sea of luggage splashed with the label LOUIS VUITTON, which may as well have screamed "too much money" or "too much bad taste." In the corner of the room under the windowsill sat three enormous, Old World European–style trunks covered with colorful labels.

There was a tearing sound as the bottom of the INTIMATES box caught on something and split open: once again her underwear spilled out onto the floor.

"Oops," Callie muttered, laughing as she stared hopelessly at the ground. "Note to self: buy better boxes." She paused. "Also: look into purchasing some sexier underwear. . . ."

"*Excuse* me?" a severe-sounding voice demanded from behind her.

"Ohmygosh—I'm so sorry—I had no idea somebody else was home!" Callie shrieked, wheeling around. A short, squat girl with slicked-back, plaited brown hair emerged from one of the bedrooms.

"Neither did I," the girl said stiffly, wrinkling her nose as she surveyed the mess. A formless figure was concealed beneath a conservative white blouse—buttoned to the neck—and a black, ankle-length woolen skirt, under which Callie detected pantyhose of the ancient dinosaur variety. The room behind her was meticulously clean, empty of any decor save for an enormous, wooden cross hanging on the wall above the bed. Squinting, Callie could make out the bold lettering on the sticker on the girl's laptop: CHASTE FOR CHRIST: PREMARITAL SEX IS A *SIN*.

"Greetings," the girl said. "I am Dana Gray. You must be the one from California. Callie. Callie from California. My parents told me they might look like you. The ones from California, I mean," she finished, eying Callie's bare knees and arms. "I was wondering: do you come from the north or the south?"

"South . . ." replied Callie, wondering wildly for a moment if Dana Gray from Goose Creek, South Carolina, knew that Dixieland was dead.

"Oh, good," she said. "Father told me that Southern California is the political salvation of the West, even though Hollywood is a cesspool of sin. Northern California is worse, though. There's this place called Berkeley and it's full of dirty . . ."

". . . hippies?" Callie asked, trying not to smile.

"Yes! Hippies," Dana said. "Dendrophiliacs," she added in a whisper.

There was an awkward pause, and then, just as Callie was about to ask Dana what she liked to do for fun down in Goose Creek, the front door burst open and in pranced roommate number three, who, by the process of elimination, could be none other than Vanessa Von Vorhees.

Stilettos high enough to strike fear in the heart of a pigeon clicked rapidly across the floor, no doubt designed to make their owner's legs look thin enough for her skin-tight "skinny" jeans. It wasn't really working.

But if her hips were a little generous, they were nothing compared to her chest, which looked even more buxom due to the word *Juicy* emblazoned across it in pink rhinestone lettering. Her long, strawberry blond curls bounced as she walked. In one hand she clutched the purse that matched her LV luggage; in the other, an iPhone that looked like an unfortunate superglue accident had left it permanently attached to her ear.

"Oh my god, like, *I know, right*—wait—seriously? *No—he didn't!*—wait, shut up—no, wait, seriously, *shut—up*!" she cried.

Callie stole a glance at Dana, whose mouth had silently formed the word *Juicy* and then apparently gotten stuck.

Paying them no heed, roommate number three flung open the door to her bedroom—nearly blinding them with a nauseating flash of pink, PINK, *PINK!*—and then bounded inside, chattering all the while: "You bitch! No, seriously, you are *such* a dirty whore! Oh, shut up, you know I love you. . . ." Slam went the door, the huge Marilyn Monroe poster on the back of it rattling ominously.

Dana stood stock-still for a moment: eyes bulging and mouth opening and closing like a hungry goldfish. She experimented with making a smile, failed, and then also retreated to her room.

Callie was wondering if she should knock and introduce herself so that she too could one day hope to earn an endearing nickname like "you bitch" or "dirty whore" when suddenly the girl popped her head back into the common room, one hand covering the mouthpiece of her phone.

"Hi, sorry! I completely forgot to introduce myself. I'm Vanessa Von Vorhees, from New York. I'd love to stay and chat, but I'm in the middle of like, a *super* important phone call. You understand."

"Uhm, of course, I'm Ca—"

Slam.

Strangely the closed door had little impact on the noise level of Vanessa's conversation.

". . . living with a pack of . . . yeah, no, of *course* not, ha-ha . . . The competition? Yeah, it's looking pretty slim. . . . No, not totally hopeless. The non–Jesus freak is super blond and pretty hot, actually, but, uhm, can you say, *fashion disaster*? . . . LA, I think. . . . No, more like Elle Woods meets *Trailer Park Boys* . . ."

Callie decided that she had heard enough. Abandoning her boxes with the rest of the suitcases in the middle of the floor, she opened the door to the bedroom on her left. The inside looked like it had been hit by a hurricane of fabric and jewelry. Strings of beads and bangles overflowed from an antique-looking trunk. The floor was littered with magazine cutouts, old copies of *Tatler*, and piles of books in foreign languages, packs of Virginia Slims, perfume bottles, and paintings waiting to be hung.

Closing the door quickly before Mimi—whose room this surely was—could walk in and catch her spying, Callie crossed the hall and opened the door to the last empty bedroom: a space so tiny and bare that it had probably been uncomfortable even for the monk who lived there back in 1636.

Home sweet home.

Barely noticing the incredible view of Harvard Yard with its majestic brick buildings, winding walkways, and towering trees, she plopped down on the flimsy mattress of her twin bed and breathed an enormous sigh.

At the beginning of the day when she'd stepped out of Logan Airport and hailed a cab, asking for "Harvard Square, please," in her very best "grown-up" voice, she had felt nine years old rather than eighteen. On the morning of her ninth birthday her parents had surprised her with a brand-new writing journal. The leather was soft, the pages thick like parchment, and it was blank in a way that felt alive with possibility—like with the help of a pen she could make *anything* happen. Her nine-year-old self had stayed awake all night, fantasizing about the stories and plays she would write. Unfortunately, however, the journal had remained mostly blank, for that was also the year they had discovered that she was something of a ball-kicking prodigy, at which point writing had taken a backseat to soccer.

Unable to sit still as the taxi navigated the streets of Boston, she had pressed her nose against the window, trying, for the sake of the driver, to limit the questions about Cambridge that were flying through her head at a million miles a minute.

As they crossed Anderson Memorial Bridge, she had literally shrieked with glee at the sight of eight powerful figures rowing in unison down the Charles River. Their oars made strong, deliberate strokes, their uniforms marked by the distinct shape of a large, crimson *H*. Suddenly it had all started to feel real. Harvard. She was really here, really stepping through an ivy-encrusted archway carved into the face of a massive brick wall and whispering the words of the famous inscription as she passed through Dexter Gate: *Enter to Grow in Wisdom*.

Right now, lying in her jail cell of a bedroom, she felt like the only wisdom she had procured thus far was the first-hand knowledge that there is such a thing as *way* too much underwear talk before teatime. That and she had a dynamite idea for a new sitcom called *The Freak, the Foreigner, and the Fashionista*. Why, yes, Oprah, my crazy college roommates *were* the inspiration—loosely, of course—for my new television sensation!

It sounded more like a crappy MTV reality show than a hit sitcom . . . or actually more like her life. She groaned. She had only been at college for an hour and already it felt like a month. It was going to be a long year. . . . A long *four* years without any friends or at least a soccer ball and a functioning knee so she could kick it really, really hard.

She was halfway through dialing Evan's number when she remembered that he was busy all day with his fraternity initiation. "Needy girlfriend" was the last persona she wanted to project right now, so she set her phone aside and closed her eyes.

They flew open as she heard a male voice calling from the common room: "Hello . . . is anybody in here?"

Rolling over, she pulled a pillow on top of her head. The voice went away, but it was replaced by her dad instructing her: *If at first you don't succeed, try, try again.*

Groaning once more, she forced herself off the bed. "Coming!" she called, opening her bedroom door.

Hovering outside was a tall young man with glasses and a kind face.

"Finally—another person in a T-shirt and jeans!" she blurted without thinking.

At that, the boy broke into a huge, goofy smile. "You can say that again." He chuckled, eyeing her with similar relief. "I must have missed the memo that said move-in day is supposed to be dress-to-impress."

She gasped, feigning serious offense. "You mean you're not impressed by my box-moving finest?"

"Oh, I'm impressed," he said a little too genuinely as she stepped into the common room. "I'm Matt, by the way," he added. "Matt Robinson."

"Hey, Matt; I'm Callie," she said.

"Callie Andrews, right?"

"How did you—"

She stopped midsentence as Matt held out a piece of clothing. It was her high school soccer sweatshirt: C. ANDREWS was written above her lucky number twelve. She must have dropped it earlier during the Great Underwear Debacle of 2010.

Uh-oh . . . A lump was forming in the back of her throat. Swallowing, she stared at the floor. She was weird that way: if people were mean when she felt vulnerable, she got angry; whereas, one kind word or gesture in the same situation sent her to the verge of tears. Just the verge, though. She (or really, her dad) could almost always trick herself out of crying by trying to factor a three-digit number into primes, say, two hundred and forty-five, which is five times seven times—

"Uh . . . I should probably get going," Matt said, starting for the door.

Nodding, she followed him, holding it open. He was halfway across the hall when he turned and offered, "I felt pretty homesick yesterday after my mom dropped me off, but it gets better fast. I'm right across the hall in C twenty-three if you need anything."

Callie smiled weakly but didn't trust herself to speak.

"In fact," Matt continued, his gaze lingering on her shiny hair and glistening green eyes, "my brother who graduated last year gave us his gigantic flat screen. You're welcome to come by and watch TV or movies anytime."

Now her grin was genuine, and Matt was openly staring, his suitcases sitting abandoned in the hall.

"Thanks so much, I . . ."

What the hell was I talking about?

Gregory, sweaty and shirtless, was laboring up the stairs under the weight of a ginormous box.

Callie stepped out into the hall, forgetting, along with the end of her sentence, that he was the devil incarnate.

But then he opened his mouth: "Yo, Matt. If you feel like taking a break from flirting, let me know because your TV is a little heavy. Plus, you're wasting your time anyway since apparently she's got a boyfriend. . . ."

Boyfriend—what boyfriend?

I mean, put a shirt on, you jerk!

Matt's smile did not quite conceal his embarrassment. "See you later?"

"Sure," she said. She looked at Gregory. He ignored her.

Whatever, she thought. It's not like I'll have to see him all the time or anything. At least he doesn't live—

Matt grabbed the other end of the box, and both boys walked into C 23: the suite directly across the hall.

The door swung shut. The names on the whiteboard read: ADAM, MATT, OKECHUWUKU, and, in indelible ink, GREGORY.

What fabulous luck.

As Callie turned to go back into her own suite, she noticed something inside the door's metal drop box that hadn't been there before. It was a glossy magazine: completely black except for the words *Fifteen Minutes*, which were written across the top in white curly lettering.

Curious, she grabbed it. Perching on an overturned box, a desert island in a sea of underwear, she opened the magazine and began to read.

Dearest Froshlings: peons and future leaders of America,

Move-in day is officially here . . .

TWO

orientation,

OR THE WEEK OTHERWISE KNOWN AS "CAMP HARVARD"

http://fm_homepage/advice/topics/freshman_year/blogspace

Dear Alexis:

I already finished moving in, but there's still a week left before classes begin. We haven't gotten any homework yet, so I'm at a loss for what to do!

—Grays Resident, Class of 2014

Dear Quintessential Harvard Student:

Welcome to "Camp Harvard": the week you should use to gain that mythical knowledge they call "real life experience." (FYI: in the real world Common Sense is typically defined as street smarts, *not* "an influential pamphlet written by Thomas Paine in 1776.") Now is the time to learn the definitions of some pop-culture, non-SAT vocab words like *hangover* and *hookup*. I imagine some of you will discover that booze and sex are almost as fun as solving differential equations and conjugating Latin verbs. . . .

(And of course, for those of you who prefer to learn about sex in the classroom instead of doing the fieldwork yourself, stay tuned for the University Health Services' "Practice Sex—Safely" initiative: a mandatory "wellness" seminar you'll all be attending sometime this week.)

—Alexis

Dear Alexis,

I walked into the freshman dining hall and was surprised to see just as many cliques as there were in high school, if not more. Where do I sit? Where do I belong?!

—Hurlbut Resident, Class of 2014

Dear Ms. Identity Crisis:

You are obviously one of those unfortunates who thought that college would be a golden opportunity to "reinvent" yourself free from the social disasters that characterized your high school experience. Oops, wrong! Instead of asking yourself where you belong in Harvard Society, ask yourself this: *What did I score on my SAT?* The answer will help you figure out where to sit in the dining hall: with the Recruited Athletes (lowest scores), the Affirmative Action Discretionary Slots (low scores), the Aristocracy (low scores; big donations), the Meritocracy (high scores; no donations), or the Asians and Indians (2400).*

Additional opportunities for soul searching: this Thursday at 2 P.M. is the Annual Harvard Activities Fair, where you can sign up for information on an array of extracurricular activities. If that's still not enough, visit Mental Health Services and their team of world-renowned therapists for free lollipops, happiness (Prozac), study buddies (Adderall), and advice.

—Alexis

*While there is a kernel of truth to most stereotypes, please take these with a grain of salt! ;)

Dear Alexis:

What sort of schedule can we expect to have in the coming months?

—Pennypacker Resident, Class of 2014

Dear Control Freak:

Sunday–Thursday: Work, Class, Work, Nap, Work, Eat (if time), Nap, Work, Class, Sleep (4 hour maximum), Caffeinate, Class, Paper, Test, Work . . .

Thursday (evening)–Sunday (mid-afternoon): Drink, Eat (if time), Drink some more, Binge Drink, Party like a Rock Star, Party like a Senior, Make Out with a Senior, Try not to Puke on a Senior, Sleep (14 hour minimum) . . .

(There's a reason they call us extreme.)

Welcome to college,

Alexis

"Hi, my name is Callie. I'm from California and uh . . . let's see . . . I played soccer in high school, I drive a 1967 red Mustang convertible, and I've never been arrested."

"Thank you, Callie," said the senior sitting at the head of the circle, leading the new residents of Wigglesworth Dormitory, entryways A–F, in a rousing game of "Two Truths and a Lie."

"Now, which do you guys think is the lie?" he prodded.

"Soccer?" Gregory asked in a bored voice from the other side of the circle. "When you have so much trouble staying on your feet?" Callie glared. He was sitting next to Matt, alongside what must have been their other two roommates, Adam and Okechuwuku. One of these guys was a tiny white man; the other, a huge black man. In the spirit of being a color-blind narrator: it was *impossible* to guess which was which.

"You don't look like the type who knows how to drive a stick shift!" another boy, from entryway B, called.

"Do too!" Callie insisted. "But I don't actually drive a Mustang. You got me."

"Great, wonderful," the senior said. "Now next up we have . . ."

Callie turned to look at Mimi, who was seated directly to her right.

Mimi had fallen asleep.

"NEXT UP WE HAVE . . ." the senior repeated louder.

Callie nudged Mimi.

"*Qu'est-ce que tu f*— Oh!" said Mimi, blinking rapidly. "*What are we doing?*" she whispered at Callie.

"Just say your name, then two truths and a lie," Callie whispered back.

"Hi, my name is Mimi, and I'm an al—Ah, ha-ha," Mimi gave a nervous giggle as she looked around the room. "*Pardon, je veux dire*: Hi, my name is Mimi and . . . my two truths are . . . I have been kicked out of two boarding schools in the past four years, and I speak five languages. And my lie is I have a tiny tattoo *sur mon pied*."

The senior at the front of the room stared as Vanessa and Callie started to snicker. Mimi shrugged and closed her eyes once more.

"All right . . . thank you, Mimi," the senior said, looking put out.

Callie tucked her hands behind her knees, locking them together in an effort not to be rude even though she was dying to check her cell. It had been three days, and still no word from Evan.

"Next?" said the senior, turning to Dana. Dana looked up from the pad of paper on which she had been furiously scribbling notes, almost like there was going to be a test later.

"Dana Gray. Goose Creek, South Carolina. And I'm really not comfortable with lying."

Vanessa's hands flew to her face in an attempt to stifle an embarrassing whoop of laughter, and it was all Callie could do not to break down herself as the senior leaned in to peer at Dana, no doubt searching for some indication that she was kidding.

"You know, I'm not sure that you guys quite understand how to play this game. Why don't I go ahead and take my turn, show you how it's done?"

"By all means, enlighten us," Gregory said, smirking.

"Hi, my name is Charlie Sloane, I'm from Auburn, Massachusetts, and in case you were wondering, I'm your prefect: that guy you call when you get into trouble and need someone to get you out of it. Not that you guys will be getting into any trouble," he added, his eyes traveling around the circle from Callie, who had cracked and pulled out her phone, over to Mimi, who had started to snore. Dana nodded emphatically.

"Wait a second," the ebony-skinned boy sitting to Matt's left (Okechuwuku, Callie guessed) leaned in and addressed his roommates in a BBC British accent. "Which part of that was the lie?" He looked genuinely confused.

Vanessa started to laugh again. Charlie Sloane, prefect, turned bright red. "No, uh, sorry—I was just explaining my job. Anyway, my name is Charlie Sloane, I'm a senior in Mather House, I study mechanical engineering, and . . . and . . . Oh, never mind. Why don't we just call it quits? After all, you guys have a whole year to get to know each other, right?"

"Right," said Vanessa, standing quickly.

"Now, hang on just a second. Before you leave, I have some very important literature that I need to pass out," he said, handing them each a pamphlet as they stood up to stretch. "My contact information is on page three: please don't hesitate to get in touch with any questions you have or advice you might need.

"Seriously, guys," he continued as they began to file out of the room. "Freshman year can be tough. It's all right to ask for help when you need it. And it's also okay to have some fun!

"Not too much fun!" he added nervously as he watched Mimi slip the leaflet he'd just handed her on the university's Drug and Alcohol Policy into a nearby trash can. "And don't forget: our 'Practice Sex Semin'—I mean, our 'Practice Sex *Safely*' Seminar starts tomorrow at 4 P.M.!"

"Whaa-AT?" Dana cried as they headed for the stairs, wailing like a police siren in response to the word *sex.* No doubt tomorrow would be her first foray into the world of awkward educational videos.

What's another name for students who undergo Abstinence Only sex "education" programs? Callie thought. Oh, that's right: parents.

"Well, Dana," Vanessa began, interrupting Callie's thoughts. "Tomorrow you are going to learn that, contrary to popular belief down in Goose Creek, babies do not actually come from the stork. . . ."

Callie frowned. Dana may be naive, she thought, but she's not dumb. . . .

They had reached the room. With the recent addition of a futon couch and a big overstuffed armchair, it was beginning to look more like a common room, less like a disaster zone. Mimi, Callie, and Vanessa settled onto the couch, but Dana headed straight for her bedroom, closing the door behind her.

"So what's next for us today?" Mimi asked Callie, stifling a yawn.

"The Activities Fair!" Vanessa shouted before Callie could open her orientation packet. For some reason Vanessa seemed abnormally anxious to please—but only when it came to Mimi.

"What's it like, having an ambassador for a dad?" she had asked Mimi on the morning after move-in day, when they were all sitting together in the common room getting to know one another for the first time.

"Meh," said Mimi.

"I mean . . . you must get to hang out with famous people, like, all the time!"

"Yeah . . ." said Mimi.

"No need to be humble. I saw that picture of you in *Hello* magazine at the beach in Monaco with Andrea and Charlotte Casiraghi. Tell me, are they really as gorgeous in real life?"

"They are trolls."

Despite her apparent background as some sort of European tabloid sensation, Mimi had given Callie the distinct impression that she was weary of the limelight.

In contrast, Vanessa couldn't wait for her opportunity to shine. "We have to be careful what we wear this afternoon," she was saying, "because the Activities Fair will be our first chance to really show ourselv—" Pause. "I mean, our first chance to really scope out the competit—" Pause.

"You mean to say that the Activities Fair is our first chance to meet new people, no?" asked Mimi, rolling her eyes.

"Exactly," said Vanessa, grinning. She twirled a finger through her curls. "Think of all the gorgeous upperclassman guys who will be standing out there in the middle of the Yard, asking us to join the crew team. . . ."

"You're planning to join the crew team?" Callie asked, shooting Vanessa a suspicious glance. The girl looked like she had never thrown a ball in her entire life, let alone rowed a boat.

"Lord, no, not me—though my mom would be thrilled to hear I was getting some exercise. She's always trying to drag me to the gym, but the one time I actually went, she spent the whole hour sitting in the steam room drinking cucumber water and gossiping with her friends. . . ."

Trailing off, Vanessa made a face and looked at her lap, pinching her love handles absentmindedly. "People always say I got my father's brain and my mother's hips," she continued, forcing a smile. "Thanks a lot, Mom, but do these come with a return receipt?"

As Callie and Mimi laughed, Vanessa glanced down at her watch. "Oh my *god*, would you look at the time?" she yelped, leaping to her feet. "Why didn't anybody *tell* me that it's already a quarter to two?" Then she sprinted toward her room wailing something about "how can I possibly?" and "only fifteen minutes!" Callie and Mimi exchanged a look.

"So, planning to sign up for any—what do you Americans call them?—'extracurricular activities'?" Mimi asked.

"Yeah," said Callie, leaning back. "I think I'd like to write for a journal or a magazine. I was really serious about soccer in high school, but I tore my ACL at the end of last season and my doctor says I need a break. What about you?"

"Well," said Mimi, wiggling in her seat as if personal questions made her physically uncomfortable, "I used to play tennis during secondary school, but it was always Renee who . . ." she paused, frowning.

Callie tried to smile encouragingly.

"She was top twenty at Wimbledon when she was only sixteen," Mimi offered as though that explained everything. "They all said she was 'the youngest star in the past fifteen years.'"

"So that means that you couldn't play anymore . . . ?"

"No," said Mimi, frowning again. "Well, actually, yes. I mean, what is the point to really trying when anything I can do, she can do better?"

At that moment Vanessa erupted from her bedroom and began sauntering down the hallway like it was a catwalk, pausing to strike a pose in front of their new full-length mirror.

Towering imperiously in her four-inch heels, she turned to Callie as if her roommate were a charity case on a makeover show and lectured: "The *only* time it is appropriate to wear flip-flops is when you're trying to avoid contracting foot diseases in a public shower."

Callie stuck out her feet and wiggled her toes. Her flip-flops looked just fine to her: convenient, affordable, the perfect polyurethane blend of rubber and foam.

Mimi slipped away to change. Vanessa magnanimously called, "Here, try these," tossing a pair of Tory Burch flats in Callie's direction. Callie made no move to catch them. They landed next to her on the couch.

Vanessa didn't notice. "Your earrings," the lecture continued as she slipped on a pair of gold hoops, "should *always* complement your purse," she instructed, gesturing toward a matching clutch.

"Marc Jacobs is a staple," Vanessa explained, twirling to show off her purple jumper. "And last but not least," she concluded, slapping a pair of Prada sunglasses onto her head, "always wear sunscreen."

"It's not even that sunny today!" Callie cried. Vanessa looked cute, but as Mimi might say, *C'est ci too much!*

"Callie dear," Vanessa retorted, "the sun never sets on cool." She paused. "So, what are you going to wear?"

"Uhm . . ." Callie stared down at her jeans and simple cotton T-shirt. "This?"

"You're kidding. No, you're not kidding," Vanessa corrected herself. "Callie, you can take back a lot of things in this world, but you can never take back a first impression. Now, hurry up and change so we can leave before Lady Madonna sees us!"

Callie felt stupid following Vanessa's advice but wondered if there wasn't a little something to it. After all, who knows who a girl might run into at the Activities Fair?

A wave of guilt washed over her as Gregory's face swam through her imagination. "Asshole," she muttered quietly, hoping that if she said it every time she inadvertently pictured his face then eventually, like Pavlov's dog, she would come to associate one with the other. "Asshole, asshole, asshole," she breathed. Then, satisfied, she glanced at her phone.

No missed calls. Well, how on earth could she expect her mind *not* to wander when she hadn't heard from her boyfriend in . . . one, two, and now three and a *half* days. Maybe the brothers had locked him in a dungeon. Or while cleaning a fungus-ridden toilet, he had accidentally fallen in.

WHERE THE HELL ARE YOU?!?!, she texted as she traded her jeans for a green camouflage-print skirt. She put on lip gloss—cherry ChapStick counts, right?—gave her hair an extra brush, and returned to the common room, where Vanessa was ready and waiting.

Vanessa jumped up immediately. "Come on!" she ordered. "Mimi already snuck out without us!"

Callie hesitated, standing outside Dana's door. "Maybe we should—"

"No time!" Vanessa interrupted, grabbing her hand and pulling her out of the room. "Let's hit the road!"

It was Indian summer in Cambridge, and the air felt warm as they stepped outside. Harvard Yard: an architect could draw your eye to buildings that had been erected as early as the eighteenth century; a botanist might describe the majesty of the trees and tell you exactly which week the yellowy green leaves would fade into the crimson golds of fall; and an annoying Crimson Key Society tour guide could tell you all about the amusing quirks of the student body—how they run naked and screaming across the winding walkways right before their final exams, and believe that it's vital to have sex in Widener Library and pee on the foot of the John Harvard statue before they graduate.

But that's all wash. To the average Harvard freshman (oxymoron—ha!), every musty old brick building looks like every other musty old brick building, every tree the same as its neighbor, and every confusing pathway just another opportunity to get utterly and completely lost.

"I thought you said you knew where we were going!" Vanessa cried, halting in front of a large statue of a man with a big golden foot. Some Japanese tourists were snapping pictures and rubbing the foot for good luck. Hey, isn't that the same foot that your annoying tour guide told you . . . Oooh, bad idea.

"Did I?" asked Callie, raising her eyebrows. It was entirely possible she had proclaimed as much without thinking.

"Excuse me, you there!" Vanessa called suddenly, and Callie's stomach plummeted as she watched her detain a tall, handsome upperclassman.

Biting her lip, Callie tried to shrink into the ground, reminded powerfully of the month Jessica had taken "revenge" on her for spending too much time with Evan by stopping every guy that crossed their path and demanding, *Excuse me, but have you met my friend Callie Andrews? She's a cheerleader, and she can do the splits!*

"We were wondering," Vanessa pressed on sweetly, flirting like a pro, "if you could point us in the direction of the Activities Fair? We're only freshmen, and my friend Callie Andrews here has gotten us very, very lost."

Callie smiled ruefully.

To her surprise the handsome stranger smiled back, breaking into an enormous grin when she met his eyes. His shaggy, light brown hair ruffled in the early autumn breeze.

"Not to worry, Callie Andrews and friend," he said, speaking only to Callie. His voice had a slightly southern lilt: relaxed and charming, just like his smile.

"It's Vanessa," Vanessa said.

"Vanessa," he repeated. "It just so happens that I'm heading there right now, and it would be my pleasure to escort you . . . both."

Vanessa beamed and started chattering away as they began to walk. Callie kept silent, stealing a sidelong glance at their escort and noticing how when he smiled, tiny crinkles formed around the corners of his eyes.

"I was in Wigglesworth when I was a freshman, too," he explained while Vanessa nodded eagerly. "You're really lucky, you know," he added, glancing over his shoulder at Callie. "They say it's the best freshman dorm on campus."

Callie blushed.

"You should have seen her the other day," Vanessa said. "She was just too cute! Jumping around asking everyone if 'Wigglesworth' didn't sound *just like it was straight out of* Harry Potter!"

Callie's eyes narrowed, and she waited for the upperclassman to look at her like she was an overgrown eleven-year-old. Instead, if possible, his smile grew even wider. "I love *Harry Potter*."

I love you, too. I mean . . . "I love it, too!" Callie cried.

"Hmm." Vanessa shrugged. "Maybe the two of you should get together and read it sometime. . . ."

Callie froze. Keep feet planted on ground, she instructed herself.

"I'd love to . . ." the upperclassman started.

You would?

". . . but unfortunately my girlfriend gets very jealous."

Girlfriend? What girlfriend! Oh, Callie realized. Jealous? she wondered. Did that mean he viewed Vanessa's proposal as a *date* rather than an unpaid baby-sitting venture or—

"Too bad." Vanessa interrupted her thoughts. "Well, thanks for walking us over!" she added, at which point Callie realized they had arrived. Hundreds of booths and swarms of students were everywhere, and giant Welcome banners flanked the Yard.

"No problem," he said. "I'd stay and show you two around, but they need me over at the squash booth. You should stop by later—you know, if you're interested in signing up for the sport." Then with a wave he was gone.

"Holy moly, what a *fox*!" Vanessa exclaimed all too audibly at his retreating back.

"Vanessa . . ." said Callie.

"And that voice! I wonder where he's—"

"Vanessa!"

"What? He, like, totally loved you!"

"No he didn't. He—"

"He totally wants to geek out with you and have babies named, like, Harry, Ron, and Hermione!"

"Does not!" Callie shrieked. "Hey wait—I thought you said *Harry Potter* is for kids."

Vanessa shrugged. "I dabble. Anyway, I cannot *believe* that I forgot to ask his name. No worries, though; we'll find him on Facebook. Until then I shall call him . . . Foxy McFoxerson."

"You. Are. Too. Much," Callie said, laughing in spite of herself.

"I know, right?" said Vanessa. "Now, come on," she added, linking their arms. "Let's go get active!"

Callie spent the next twenty minutes enjoying Vanessa's keen "social commentary."

At a table for the Harvard Business Club: "Those are the banker boys, and we call *those* their Crackberries!" Vanessa said, pointing out the young men in suits and their pet BlackBerries.

At the Harvard International Club, where girls dressed in colorful hijab danced to exotic Middle Eastern music: "Don't sign up—you might as well be signing your name to the No Fly List."

"Vanessa, isn't that a little—"

"No, seriously, they fax the sign-up sheet straight to the CIA!"

Across the way at Women in Business, after Vanessa had grabbed a cupcake from a metallic tin on the table: "See how they're positioned directly across from the Harvard Business Club? Yeah, this club's not real. It's a front for a covert dating service," she decided, watching the girls in pink lipstick and heels recline in their lawn chairs.

Callie laughed. "Seriously," she agreed, noting that three of them wore bikini tops. "Do you think they know the difference between the NASDAQ and a strawberry daquiri?"

"Oooh—good one," said Vanessa.

They passed booths for Intramural/Club Teams ("High school athletes from small towns who weren't good enough to get recruited, even by the Ivy League," Vanessa explained), the *Harvard Lampoon* ("Imagine fifty Woody Allens together in a room!"), and the *Advocate*, a literary magazine, where emaciated men were loitering around in tiny shirts and jeans tighter than Vanessa's J Brands. ("Give it up, Callie," Vanessa instructed, misinterpreting her roommate's interest in the magazine as interest in its members. "They're much more likely to be into their own deep, existential pain—or each other.")

Off in the distance Callie spotted Gregory standing near a table advertising the Harvard squash team, smoking a cigarette like it was the only antidote to an otherwise excruciating boredom.

Who does that? Callie wondered irritably. Serious athletes don't smoke!

She looked around, searching, perhaps, for the coach who was letting him get away with it. Instead she found someone else: "Foxy McFoxerson," standing right next to Gregory and smiling while he encouraged others to sign up.

They made quite a pair, and Callie took an involuntary step toward them. Vanessa grabbed her arm and started whispering fervently in her ear.

Apparently Callie wasn't the only one interested in racket sports.

"Gregory Brentworth Bolton is the sexiest man alive," Vanessa gushed. "Did you see him carrying his boxes the other day? *Shirtless*? Wow. I love him. I know I say that about everyone, but in this case I mean it. I seriously, seriously love him." Vanessa blew a long sigh through pursed lips.

"He's definitely cute," Callie admitted, "but he seems like such an asshole."

"Yeah . . . a *sexy* asshole." Apparently in Vanessa's mind this was an additional attribute. "Our dads used to work together at Goldman Sachs, but Gregory and I never actually had a chance to meet. And now he's living next door—it's destiny, don't you think?"

"Uh—sure." Callie nodded, wondering why she was suddenly feeling so irritated.

"It gets even better," Vanessa continued, beaming with delight. "I Googled *all* of our neighbors, and it looks like Oke-Chihuahua, or however you say it, is some sort of Nigerian royalty. I couldn't find anything on the other two, but maybe they'll surprise us!"

Speaking of "the other two," Callie noticed Matt standing to their left at a table decorated with a huge, impressive banner: THE HARVARD CRIMSON.

"Ick, school paper," Vanessa muttered, but Callie was barely listening. At the table immediately adjacent, a sign—glossy black with white lettering—caught her eye: FIFTEEN MINUTES MAGAZINE. A large group of freshmen clustered in front of the table, overseen by a girl with alabaster skin and thick, chestnut curls. She smiled, glowing like the sun: the center of the universe as they orbited around her.

Vanessa was quick to supply some further information: "That's Alexis Thorndike," she whispered in a deferential tone tinged with what sounded strangely like fear. "She's a junior, grew up in Greenwich, Connecticut, and is a board member of every club or organization that you could possibly imagine. She is also five feet seven inches tall, hates seafood, and refuses to sleep on anything less than five hundred thread count sheets."

"How do you know all this?" Callie asked, whispering, too, in spite of herself.

"Facebook. Now, listen carefully: if she likes you, the doors to Harvard's social scene will open with welcoming arms, but if you get on her bad side . . ." Vanessa's eyes widened as if the thought were too unbearable to be spoken aloud. Callie wanted to laugh, but as she gazed at Alexis, she couldn't help but feel strange stirrings of apprehension and awe.

"Let's sign up," she urged, rushing to join the line.

"What? But I hate writing—I suck at it!" Vanessa protested, trailing behind her nevertheless.

"That may be"—Callie shrugged—"but you never know until you try." (Translation: *I'm too afraid to sign up alone.*)

"You know what?" said Vanessa, starting to nod. "This could be an excellent opportunity to meet some new people." (Translation: *I accept you as my interim friend on the way to bigger and better things.*)

The girls exchanged a saccharine smile as they stood waiting to add their names to the list.

Ten minutes later Callie and Vanessa were following a mob of people headed toward Annenberg, their freshmen dining hall. After standing in line forever and enduring a series of awkward introductions, finally they stepped inside.

The dining hall was huge: it could easily seat over a thousand people. High ceilings and stained glass windows gave the impression that they were entering a great British-style hall. Callie recognized no one.

Vanessa excused herself and headed over to the counter where they kept the vegetarian options—her self-proclaimed "diet strategy" of the week. ("But I *do* care about the animals, too. When I was twelve my pet bunny and I were really very close.")

Suddenly alone, Callie grabbed a tray and filled it with lumpy, colorless food. Not for the first time in the past several days, she missed her mother. Especially her cooking.

Returning to the seating area, she scanned the room, searching for Vanessa. She was surprised to see that, just like in high school, all the football guys were sitting together flinging food at one another with their forks and completely unaware that they were being imitated by the theater people seated nearby.

To her right she spied Matt with some students she assumed had also signed up for *The Harvard Crimson*. A few tables farther off, Mimi, looking miserable, sat surrounded by other internationals. Straight ahead, Callie spotted Gregory with some of the other kids who came from New York City. Several girls sat nearby, leaning over and interrupting one another to attract his attention. They must be who Vanessa had referred to as the "Jewish American Queens," or JAQs (because Jewish American *Princesses* go to *Princeton*, Vanessa had explained). Callie stared for a moment, taking in their patterned wool skirts, matching blazers, and pearls.

Are they for real with those outfits? she wondered incredulously. After all, it was one thing to enjoy *Gossip Girl* (ironically, of course) but quite another to emulate it in the dining hall.

Callie was making her way toward an empty table when she noticed Vanessa on the fringe of this group of her prep school peers. They seemed to be ignoring her. In fact, it looked as if Vanessa was about to fall off the end of the table.

Suddenly she glanced in Callie's direction. Callie smiled and began walking forward, raising her hand in a wave. Vanessa looked straight at her and then, to Callie's surprise, rotated in her seat: her back facing Callie as if she hadn't seen her. Except that Callie was certain she had.

What a bitch!

Quickly Callie glanced at Matt's group again, but there was nowhere to sit. Making her way across the room, she chose a table near the wall, as far away from the traitor as possible.

In a moment she was joined by Dana, whom she hadn't even noticed lurking behind her. Grateful for the company, Callie tried to smile. Unfortunately the gesture was lost on Dana, whose head was bowed in prayer.

Dana might be strange, Callie thought as Dana began to eat in silence, but she was not obtuse. Callie knew they shouldn't have ditched her before the Activities Fair.

Callie sighed. How would she ever manage to fit in at Harvard when she couldn't even figure out where to sit in the dining hall?

"So . . . sign up for any cool activities?" Callie ventured.

"Bible Study."

"Oh . . . neat . . . Anything else?"

"The Harvard Republican Club."

Oh, well. Callie bolted down the rest of her lunch, anxious to return to her room so she could be alone and friendless in private, just a phone call away from Jessica or even her mom, since Evan still didn't seem to be picking up. Standing, she made her way toward the line of people bussing their trays. Dana pulled a book from her bag and started to read.

Next time I'll remember to bring a book, Callie thought as the line inched forward. That way I won't look like such a ginormous loser—

Something hit her from behind. She started to fall, tripping over the tiny freshman boy who had catapulted out of nowhere.

Her tray soared into the air and landed with a thunderous clatter, dishes breaking and food flying everywhere. Her hands flew to her skirt as she hit the ground, praying that she wasn't about to flash the entire freshman class.

Oh no oh no oh NO, she breathed miserably, closing her eyes. Opening them, she found a thousand other pairs staring back at her.

Damn.

The room had gone completely silent. Then slowly somebody began to clap.

In a whisper that echoed all the way from the stained glass windows to the ceiling and back to the floor, Gregory, still clapping, leaned into the center of his table and said:

"Now *that* is embarrassing."

His entire table burst out laughing, and the applause swelled throughout the room. Some people started to whistle and catcall. Four hundred hands were whipping four hundred smart phones from purses and pockets, ready to etch the event in virtual stone, live-blogging from here to eternity. . . .

Status Update via Facebook: Some blond girl just wiped out in Annenberg!

Update via Twitter: Witnessing most embarrassing moment of the decade . . . hilarious

Update via Twitter via Facebook: Glad that wasn't me

SMS to Twitter: Epic fall in the frosh D-hall—food everywhere

BlackBerry to Twitter via Facebook: Bet somebody's glad she wore underwear today . . .

"Who *is* she anyway?" the girl next to Gregory asked as the noise died down.

"Just some girl from California. I think she lives with Mimi," another replied.

"California, hmm . . . I should have guessed. Honey, if you insist on wearing flip-flops, at *least* spring for a decent pedicure."

There was another excruciating surge of laughter. "Poor Mimi, no wonder she's already depressed. . . ." Vanessa's laughter was the loudest of them all.

Uber-bitch!

Callie barely noticed the hands that were grabbing her and helping her to her feet.

"Come on," Matt said, putting an arm around her shoulders and leading her toward the door. She tried to thank him, but instead she could only nod, resisting the urge to sprint the rest of the way home.

THREE

Worse Than a Phone Call; Not as Bad as a Post-it . . . Better Than a Text Message?

From: **Callie Andrews**
To: **Jessica Marie Stanley**
Subject: FWD: We need to talk

Un . . . fucking . . . believable . . .

———— Forwarded message ————

> From: **Evan Davies**
> To: **Callie Andrews**
> Subject: We need to talk
>
> Hey babe,
>
> How's Harvard going so far? UCLA kicks major ass. Anyway, sorry I keep missing your calls. I guess you've probably figured out by now that I've been very busy. . . . We have soccer practice 4 hours a day, it's insane. And prelaw is turning out to be a lot harder than I thought, but I think I'll survive because one of the brothers told me that they keep all the old midterms in a file cabinet at the house. Pretty sick, right?
>
> Anyway, what I'm really trying to say is it's not you, it's me. You're great.
>
> Take care of yourself,
>
> Evan

From: **Callie Andrews**
To: **Evan Davies**
Subject: Re: We need to talk

What? I'm confused. . . . Are you breaking up with me??

From: **Evan Davies**
To: **Callie Andrews**
Subject: Re: We need to talk

Oh crap, Cal. I'm no good at this. . . . I'm sorry. I don't know what else to say. I hope you don't hate me.
Evan

From: **Jessica Marie Stanley**
To: **Callie Andrews**
Subject: Re: FWD: We need to talk

Whhaaaaaat . . . the FUCK?!!? Is he HIGH? Is this the same Evan "Together-Forever" Davies of the infamous Five Year Plan??? Clearly he has been body-snatched by alien invaders. In class right now; can't escape without stepping over 800 toes but will get out pronto—wait for my call.
xxx Jess

Sent via BlackBerry by AT&T

"Callie?" a voice called from the hall, followed by a knock on the door. "Callie—you have to get out of bed. We have to go to—"

There was a pause, followed by muffled whispering.

"Maybe we should just let her sleep?"

"I don't know . . . she's been in there for two days."

Vanessa knocked again, Mimi lingering uncertainly at her heels. "I'm going in there," Vanessa said decisively.

Callie groaned and pulled the blankets over her head.

"Callie?" Vanessa asked. "We were wondering if you want to come to the dining hall? For dinner? And then afterward there's the First Chance Dance. . . ."

Callie groaned again. "Leave me alone. I just want to sleep."

"All right, well, you heard the girl: she wants to sleep," said Mimi, backing away.

"Don't be ridiculous," Vanessa snapped, stepping forward and yanking the covers off of Callie's bed.

"Hey!" Callie yelled, sitting up.

"That's more like it," said Vanessa. "Now look alive because dinner's in ten minutes."

Callie's eyes traveled from Vanessa—hands on her hips, a stern expression on her face—to Mimi, who was hovering uncomfortably near the door.

"Look, guys, I appreciate your concern, but I really just want to be left a—"

"Nonsense." Vanessa cut her off. "We'd ask you what's wrong, but the walls are so thin that everybody already knows. Basically, I don't care if this Evan character looks like Jude Law or if his farts are magical. . . . He sounds like an asshole, and *nobody* is worth two full days of moping."

"Yes, and you look absolutely terrible—like shit," added Mimi, trying to get into the spirit of things.

Vanessa glared. "Mimi, that's not exactly . . ."

Callie began to laugh. And cry. "I just can't believe I wasted two years of my life. . . . And in an *e-mail* . . . I mean, really?"

The silence that followed was unbroken save for the operatic sounds of Dana singing gospel on the way from the bathroom to her bedroom.

"Back home," Mimi said thoughtfully, "we have this saying. 'If the horse throws you off . . . buy a new one.'"

"Sage advice." Vanessa laughed. "'There are other fish in the sea.'"

"That cannot be right," said Mimi, shaking her head. "It is: 'go fishing in another sea—'"

"I'll be okay," Callie cut in, hiccupping and wiping her eyes. "You guys are right—and anyway, I'm starving. Just give me ten minutes."

"Thank god," said Vanessa.

Fifteen minutes later they joined Dana at a table in Annenberg. It was nearly eight o'clock, so the dining hall was emptier than usual.

"Hi. How are you . . . all doing?" Dana asked, glancing at Callie and then averting her eyes.

"I'm all right," Callie answered, trying to smile. "I'm just glad it's only us girls—"

"Is this seat taken?" Gregory asked Mimi, sitting without waiting for an answer.

"Evening, ladies," said Matt, grinning and taking the seat next to Gregory.

"Whoa . . . who died?" Gregory asked as they were joined by his other two roommates.

"Nobody died," said Dana primly.

"Hi, Gregory; hi, Matt. And you are . . . ?" Vanessa asked, turning to the other two as if she hadn't already conducted her own private investigation via Google and Facebook.

"I'm Adam," said the small pale boy on Matt's left. "And this is Okecha—uhm—Okuchu—uhm— Hey, man, how do you pronounce it again?"

"Just call me 'OK,'" the large Nigerian said in his beautiful British accent. "That's what everybody calls me at home."

"Okay, OK, your word is my command," sang Vanessa.

"Nobody's ever made that pun before, clever—well done, you . . ." he said absentmindedly as his eyes locked on Mimi. Clearing his throat, he nudged Gregory.

"Pardon me," said Gregory. "This is Mimi; that's Vanessa"—Vanessa beamed—"and her name is . . . Casey."

"Callie," Callie snapped.

"Right. Callie. And you are . . . ?" Gregory looked at Dana.

"It's Dana, isn't it?" Adam asked. Dana nodded. "I thought I recognized you from Bible Study," he said, smiling.

Dana didn't say a word, but she had suddenly turned very pink.

"So Blondie, where are you from?" OK asked Callie, tearing his eyes away from Mimi.

"Westwood, California? It's part of LA."

"LA as in Hollywood?" OK began. "And you ended up all the way out here at Harvard, eh? Just like—"

"Seriously?" Callie interrupted, dropping her spoon with a clatter. "You really want to go there? Yes, we've all seen the movie, and yes, we all know that blondes are supposed to be dumb, and yes, it *is* a shocking phenomenon that I have blond hair and I got into Harvard. . . . Go ahead, say it. I know you're dying to, so just get it out there. . . ."

OK glanced helplessly from Gregory to Matt. "Just like that girl Elizabeth? Who lives on the floor above us? She's from LA, too." He stopped abruptly, looking a little scared.

"Oh," said Callie softly. "Oh, uhm . . ." The urge to cry had returned in full force.

Matt began to laugh. "I'm guessing people make a lot of *Legally Blonde* jokes around you, huh?"

Callie nodded, relieved as the others joined in his laughter, save for Mimi, OK, and Dana, who hadn't the faintest clue what was so funny.

"So, going to the dance tonight?" Gregory asked, changing the subject and looking, for some reason, at Callie.

"I don't think—"

"Yes, she is," Mimi said firmly.

Vanessa chose this moment to lean in and stage-whisper, "She's a little upset. Her boyfriend—or should we say ex-boyfriend—Evan, just dumped her. In an *e-mail*."

Matt's eyes lit up like a kid's on Christmas morning: "That sucks. . . ."

"Yeah, sorry—rotten luck," added OK.

Mimi shrugged. "I have something that might make you feel better," she murmured, slipping a flask from her purse. And then before anyone could stop her: "One for you, one for you," she said, spiking Callie and Vanessa's drinks, "one for you, whoops—two for me, and one for—"

Dana's eyes expanded to the size of saucers. She slammed her hand over her cup.

"Relax, it's just water," said Mimi.

Callie sipped her drink. More like water . . . and *vodka*.

Vanessa made a face. "I mean, it *could* be worse," she said. "At least it's not as bad as a Post-it note. Remember that episode of *Sex and the City*? Now *that* was brutal. 'I'm sorry, I can't,' stuck right on Carrie's computer screen!"

Callie frowned. News flash, Vanessa: Carrie isn't real. Fictional characters don't feel pain.

"Well, whoever that Evan guy is, he's an idiot," said Gregory suddenly.

What? Was Satan's minion actually saying something nice for a—

"Who comes to college with a girlfriend in the first place? Total buzzkill," he finished, drinking straight from Mimi's flask.

"Thanks for that, Gregory, thanks a lot." Callie retorted. "Or wait—I'm sorry, was it Geoffrey?"

Gregory grinned.

"So . . . I take it you don't have a girlfriend?" Vanessa asked.

"Wouldn't dream of it," he answered, his eyes never leaving Callie's face.

"I don't either!" Matt blurted suddenly. Everyone stared. "Have a girlfriend, I mean . . . I don't have a girlfriend either. Not that I wouldn't dream of it. . . . I would. I mean, I do. . . . I mean . . ."

Dana, for the first time all evening, was nodding her head approvingly. "While I don't think that it's any of our business," she began, eyeing the rest of the table, "I think that's very sensible of you, Gregory. If I were you, Callie, I would view this . . . situation . . . as a positive development. College is *not* the appropriate time for a boyfriend, especially not a long-distance one. Why, just think of all the extra time you'll have to focus on your studies!"

"I couldn't agree more," said Adam (and Dana's smile suddenly seemed a little frozen). "People our age tend to become far too preoccupied with relationships when they should really be concentrating on school and extracurriculars and figuring out who they want to be when they grow up instead of chasing the opposite—"

"*Hell*-o, five o'clock." Gregory whistled suddenly, nudging OK, who followed his gaze to where a cute blond girl in a short skirt was bending over to pick up her napkin.

"Nice enough," OK agreed. "But nothing compared to present company," he added, smiling at Mimi. Mimi yawned.

"Looks like she's coming over here," Matt said as the girl approached their table.

"Hi!" said Gregory. "I'm Gregory Bolton. How can I be of service to you?"

"Gregory . . . ?" she asked, furrowing her brow.

"Yes?" he said, smiling in a way that even Callie had to admit was totally swoon-worthy.

"Why didn't you call me back last night," she said, lowering her voice. It was an accusation, not a question.

"Oh! Oh, right," he said, attempting—and failing—to mask his confusion. "Sorry . . . uh . . ."

"Elizabeth," she hissed.

"Elizabeth!" OK cried. "Elizabeth who lives upstairs! Elizabeth is also from LA," he said smugly, turning to Callie, exonerated.

Callie tried to smile sympathetically at Elizabeth, who stood there seething. After all, if she didn't already know better, it could have been her standing there in Elizabeth's shoes, even though, supposedly, she wasn't Gregory's *type.* . . . Hey—wait a minute! With her light blond hair and athletic build Elizabeth could have been mistaken for her sister. Really not your type?! she thought, glaring at Gregory.

"Well, I'm glad to see that *somebody* remembers my name," Elizabeth said, giving Gregory a hard look. "God! I should have known better. . . ."

"According to Alexis Thorndike, dormcest is never a good idea," Vanessa offered.

The girl glared at the entire table and then stalked off, muttering.

"Whoopsie daisy," said Mimi. It was unclear whether this was in response to Gregory's run-in, or the fact that she had just accidentally tipped the remaining contents of the flask into her orange juice.

"I think it's time for us to go get ready for the dance," said Vanessa.

Mimi drained her glass in one gulp. "Lez-go!" she said, standing dizzily. Promptly she fell back in her seat.

Dana, to everyone's shock, giggled.

Mimi looked at Callie, held up her flask, pointed at Dana, and put a finger to her lips.

It was shaping up to be a very long night. . . .

Lady Gaga blared out of the speakers at the First Chance Dance, telling the students that if they "just danced it's gonna be okay, spin that record, babe, and it's gonna be okay . . ."

"She's singing about ME!" OK screamed, gyrating in some crazy blend of break dancing and ballroom.

"Huh?" Mimi yelled back.

"I love this song!" Vanessa shouted at Gregory.

"Yeah, me too," he agreed, looking at Callie.

One tequila, two tequila, three tequila, four . . .

Somebody was asking Callie to dance. It was Gregory. No, it was Matt . . . Matt-Gregory was telling her she looked pretty. . . .

"Thank you!" Callie screamed at Vanessa as she handed her another drink.

"Where *are* we?" somebody yelled.

"Lowell House."

"No, this is the quad!"

"What? This isn't the First Chance Dance?" Dana cried, sounding panicked.

"No, this is the *Last* Chance Dance!"

"What?"

"Last chance to party before classes start!"

One tequila, two tequila, three tequila, four . . . five tequila, six tequila, seven tequila, more . . .

Matt-Gregory was dancing with someone else now, but Gregory-Matt was still dancing with Callie. . . .

OK looked upset that Mimi wasn't more impressed by his ballroom skills. "Did I mention that I'm a prince? I'M A PRINCE!" he yelled.

"'Purple Rain'!" Mimi shouted as she started dancing with someone else. . . .

"Look at Matt making the moves on Callie!" cried Vanessa.

"Wanna dance?" a random boy that nobody knew asked Dana.

"No! I want to go *home*!"

"But where *are* we?"

Five tequila, six tequila, seven tequila, more . . . eight tequila, nine tequila, ten tequila . . .

FLOOR.

Callie awoke the next morning with a raging hangover. Parched and sore, she rolled out of bed and stumbled into the common room, hoping to find water, extra strength Tylenol and—

Dana perched on the edge of the couch, sitting next to . . .

"Matt?" asked Callie, rubbing her eyes and wishing the room would cut it out with the spinning and sit still for a minute. "What are you—"

"Matt," Dana said loudly, "spent last night *on our couch* because Gregory needed their double for . . . certain . . . unspeakable improprieties."

Matt grinned. "Officially sexiled."

"Great, good to know," said Callie. "Hope he has better luck remembering her name this time," she muttered as Dana handed her a cup of coffee.

"Thanks," she added, noticing a cardboard tray with three more cups in it and realizing that Dana must have gotten up early to get them all coffee.

Suddenly Vanessa's door opened, and a guy strolled out of her room, grinning. His expression had *senior* written all over it.

"Hi," he said, looking at Callie in a way that made her wish she were wearing a bra under her tank top, and sweats instead of shorts. "I'm Je—"

"Jeremy was just leaving," Vanessa said icily, emerging from her bedroom in a satin robe.

"Uh, actually, it's Jeffrey."

"Whatever. Bye now!"

"I'd better get going, too," said Matt. The room's estrogen count had just reached critical levels. "Thanks for the coffee, Dana."

Callie perched on the windowsill and Vanessa settled onto the couch. As Dana approached her with a cup of coffee, she exclaimed, "Seniors! I cannot *believe* how sleazy they are. . . . Just because you want to make out and cuddle doesn't mean that you also want to have sex!"

Dana's hand froze in midair.

"All they want is sex, sex, sex!" Vanessa continued wickedly, right in Dana's ear.

"Say sex again, Vanessa, I don't think we heard you the first eight times," said Callie, gripping her head in her hands.

"What?" asked Vanessa. "It's not like I *did* it or anything. I was just saying that se—"

"No more!" Callie yelled, wincing at the volume of her own voice. "Uhhh . . . my head, my head . . ."

"Hey!" said Vanessa, changing the subject. "I wonder if Mimi's up yet. Last night I saw her dancing with—"

The door to Mimi's room opened with an audible creak, and she slipped out wearing a wrinkly man's shirt, her hair wild with secrets from the night before. She took a few wobbly steps and then tripped over Vanessa's high heels, which were lying abandoned in the middle of the floor.

"Whoopsie daisy!" Mimi cried, giggling insanely.

The door opened a little wider, and Charlie the Prefect tiptoed out from behind her.

"WHOOPSIE DAISY, indeed!" Vanessa squealed. Nodding, she gave Mimi an exaggerated thumbs-up.

Mimi imitated the gesture with a confused look on her face. Then, pointing at Charlie, she offered, "It's okay to have some fun . . . just not *too* much fun."

The girls save Dana, who was looking mortified, burst into hysterics. Callie was laughing so hard that she fell off the windowsill, and Vanessa dropped her coffee.

Naturally, this only made them laugh harder.

Charlie, his face beet red, raced out of the room, mumbling "Er . . . see you girls next week; take care."

"Wow," said Callie, starting to calm down. "Somehow I do not think that was part of his job description."

"So tell us," Vanessa demanded, "does he give good advice?"

"Excellent," said Mimi. Dana, who had been heading toward the spill with paper towels in hand, stood transfixed—trying, perhaps, to work out if "advice" meant what she thought it did.

A phone started ringing from somewhere in Callie's bedroom. "I'll be right back," she said.

"Not so fast, missy!" Vanessa cried. "What was Matt doing here this morning? A little rebound action, perhaps?

"No . . . no rebound action for me."

"Uh-huh, sure," Vanessa said.

But Callie wasn't listening. Making her way toward her room, she wondered if Evan, having finally come to his senses, was calling to ask her back. Two days ago the answer probably would have been yes, but now she was looking forward to saying no. Or maybe she would write him an e-mail.

Sinking onto her bed, she flipped open her phone, smiling at the name on the caller ID.

"Yes, Evan?" she asked in her best Make-it-quick-'cause-I-really-don't-have-time-for-you voice.

She was quiet for a moment.

"Well, it must be *really* important if it necessitated an actual *phone call.* What happened? Is your computer broken, or did you realize that—"

Abruptly she stopped talking. A minute passed, then two, and then her hands started to tremble. Blankly she stared at the wall, the color draining from her face.

"How . . . how is that possible?" she whispered. "Why—*why the hell*—WHY would you DO THAT?"

A pause. "What do you mean 'what I didn't know couldn't hurt me?'

"You're SORRY?" she roared, leaping off her bed. "When—how—why?" she sputtered. She paused, trying to breathe. "When," she finally decided. "*When* did this happen?"

Silence for a moment, then: "SENIOR WEEK? But who . . ." Eyes widening, she sank back onto her bed. "Who else knows?" she whispered.

She sat still, listening, her free hand clenching and unclenching the soft covers on her bed.

"You have to fix this," she finally muttered.

"No, that's not good enough. You have to take care of it *right now.*"

Her breaths were coming in short, quick gasps. She tried to breathe deeply, ignoring the sound of more futile apologies that were leaking out of her phone. It was no use. Leaning over, she stuck her head between her knees. "I have to go. . . ." she whispered, clicking End Call. Her phone slipped out of her hands and fell onto the floor. Head still hanging upside down, she stared at the phone out of the corner of her eye.

Numbly she reached for it. Then she stood. Walking over to her dresser, she opened the top drawer and shoved the phone as far back as possible behind her oldest, holiest socks. Like from there it could no longer hurt her. Ridiculous, since the damage had already been done.

Returning to her bed, she thought of confiding in someone: Jessica or even her mom. . . . But it was too awful to put into words. Closing her eyes, she tried to think of a three-digit number to factor into primes. But the numbers wouldn't come. Her mind kept clouding over with horrible images until eventually, no matter how tightly she squeezed her eyelids, the tears began to flow.

FOUR

SHOPPING PERIOD

"It's Not about the *Classes*: It's about the *Clothes!*"

Dearest Froshlings:

Welcome to "Shopping Period": the trial week when you can "shop" for classes before committing to the four that will comprise your first academic semester.

Shopping Period isn't just about picking your classes. It's the prime time to go shopping for members of the opposite sex. The jeans you decide to wear and the genes you decide to propagate are both choices that I'll leave up to you. What you need to know from me is . . .

how to pick your classes

1. **expository writing 20:** Mandatory. Regardless of skill, you will get a B+.

2. **something useful:** Social Analysis 10a and 10b; Introduction to Micro and Macro Economics. Sad but true: money makes the world go round. As much as we hate to admit it given our "disillusionment" with materialism, there's a reason why Economics is the most popular concentration at Harvard and Celtic Languages and Literatures is not.

(Average increase in earning potential with a BA in Economics: +$150,000/year
Average increase in earning potential with a BA in the Humanities: -$10,000/year)

The math is very, very simple, even if you are an English major.

3. something big: The biggest classes at Harvard are the mandatory General Education courses. People grumble and moan, demanding to know how "Forbidden Romance in Modern China" is going to help in their career as a quantum physicist. Instead of moping, think of attending these classes as going to market on the day a new shipment has just arrived: so many interesting people of different colors and concentrations to look at and choose from, so many fascinating things to do in class other than listening to the teacher.

Here's a list by category of some of the campus faves:

a. **foreign cultures:** The Cuban Revolution–because Fidel Castro and Che Guevara make communism look sexy

b. **historical studies:** Modern European Intellectual History–so you can learn to use terms like *existentialism* and *deconstructionism* properly in a sentence then use them often to make other people feel intellectually inferior

c. **literature & arts:** Poems, Poets, Poetry–get in touch with your beatnik side, or the beatnik guy who sits behind you, and learn to woo with lyricism

d. **moral reasoning:** Justice–doing "the right thing," Harvard style

e. **quantitative reasoning:** The Magic of Numbers–because math really can be magical (and this class is magically easy)

f. science: Life Sciences 1a–future Doctor alert, *Hello!* (Or if the closest you've ever come to going premed involves watching *Grey's Anatomy*, your safest bet is probably Dinosaurs or Cosmic Connections.)

g. social analysis: Food and Culture–snacks provided: enough said.

4. something fun: For many of you the definition of fun is "binary regressions and multivariable calculus." For the rest of us fun is better defined as "easy, engaging, and enjoyable." I recommend Positive Psychology, where homework assignments include hugging at least seven people a day, or Human Sexuality, in which you can earn an A by writing a paper about an "unusual sexual experience."

Best wishes as always,
Alexis Thorndike, Advice Columnist
Fifteen Minutes Magazine
Harvard University's Authority on Campus Life since 1873

Matt stared at Callie, watching her tug at her hair. She had *The Q Guide* in one hand and the *Courses of Instruction* in the other, which she would read with deep concentration for a moment before pausing to scribble some notes.

"Thanks so much for coming over, Matt," she said, glancing up and smiling while he tried to look like he'd been concentrating on his class hunt.

"I've just been freaking out about this whole class thing!" she exclaimed, painfully aware that she had much bigger things to be freaking out about . . . much, much bigger.

"I have *no idea* what I want to study," she continued, determined to stay calm and pretend that everything was fine. As long as Evan keeps his word, nobody at Harvard will ever find out.

"Worst of all, I'm the only one who hasn't figured it out yet! Vanessa and Dana already declared their majors and Mimi's just going to 'go with the flow' and 'try not to flunk out'!"

Hearing her name, Dana looked up from the *Introduction to Neuroscience* textbook she'd been poring over. The three of them were seated around the coffee table in the common room. Mimi was in her bedroom—probably taking a nap—and Vanessa, who subscribed to a far more literal interpretation of the term *Shopping Period*, had gone to Newbury Street to peruse the high-end, designer merchandise.

"It's not about the *classes*, Cal," she'd explained patiently. "It's about the *clothes*!" Still, Callie had elected to stay home. While it was fine for Vanessa, future art history major, to spend the day shopping, Callie had only enrolled in one class—Harvard's mandatory writing seminar—and still had three more to choose.

Flipping through the art history section, Callie wondered what people learned in classes like Buddhist Art in One Cave, Casts, Construction and Commemoration, or a mysterious-sounding course called simply The Thing. To Callie, these titles sounded fascinating and exotic, infinitely exciting—especially compared to high school. But, oddly enough, when she and Vanessa had been flipping through the guide the night before, Vanessa hadn't even *looked* at the list. Instead, she couldn't tear herself away from the psychology section, reading out class descriptions until Callie finally interrupted and asked, "Why don't you just do psych?"

"Mmm." Vanessa had shrugged, tearing her eyes away from the description of Developmental Psychopathology. "It's just not for me."

"Why not?" Callie said. "You seem excited about some of those classes. . . ."

"Well, my mom and I already decided on History of Art and Architecture, so . . ." Vanessa looked completely miserable. The conversation had ended there.

"So, Dana, I take it you're doing neuroscience?" Matt asked, smiling at Dana, who was still reading her textbook intently.

"Neurobiology, premed," she replied, looking up quickly. She gave Matt a rare smile: the kind she reserved for men she found surprisingly bearable. This category included his roommate Adam, who, in her opinion, was aptly named after God's original creation.

True, they hadn't exchanged more than a few complete sentences (what can one possibly say to a boy one finds exceptionally bearable?), but he had smiled while he held the door to C 24 for her after walking her home from church last Sunday morning. If only she hadn't frowned and walked away when he'd said hello in the hall yesterday afternoon.

Dana returned to her book. At the moment studying was priority. In addition to Introduction to Neuroscience she was also taking Life Sciences 1a, Physics 15, and Math 55—the leviathan of math classes that inspired more suicides than Black Tuesday back in '29. She'd picked these classes ahead of time, purchased the textbooks in advance, and studied throughout the summer, determined not to fall behind before things even got started.

Out of the corner of her eye Dana noticed the way that Matt was looking at Callie and frowned. According to Maxwell's law of attraction, the prettier you are, the dumber you're supposed to be. Yet there was Callie, a direct, unfair violation to the fundamental order of the universe. (Dana also fully understood Maxwell's *real* paper about gravitational forces, "On a Paradox in the Theory of Attraction—something in which she took pride.)

Shaking her head, Dana returned to her reading once more. Learning about a neuron's action potential was the only *action* she needed to get during college, thank you very much.

"So, Matt," said Callie, "what do you think you're going to take?"

"Uhm . . . I'm still not really sure. . . ." he began, though Callie thought he had picked all four of his classes yesterday. Squinting, he tried to read her list of potential courses from upside down.

"I was considering Social Analysis 10. Even though it's a full year, that stuff should be pretty useful. You know, economy stuff."

"Social Analysis . . ." she said, looking down. "That's right at the top of my list! We should take it together. It'd be so nice to have a friend in class."

Matt frowned when she said the word *friend*. "Sure, and, you know, maybe one day after class we could go grab dinner. . . ." he began, his insides starting to vibrate at the very thought—

Actually it was his cell phone, ringing in his pocket.

"Hello?"

"Matty!" his mom's voice boomed into his ear. "Matty, are you there? I haven't heard from you in three days—I was starting to worry!"

Blushing, Matt jabbed at the volume button on his cell phone. *"It's my mom,"* he mouthed at Callie, making his way to the other side of the room.

"Yeah, Mom, yeah . . . No, Mom, I'm *fine*, honest. . . . Yes, nothing to worry about . . . The dance?" he asked, shooting a sidelong glance at Callie. "It was all right. . . . No, nothing too crazy, just some binge drinking and bad decisions . . . NO, Mom, *no*, I was just *kidding*. . . ."

He was silent for a while before he began again: "Mom, it's great talking to you, but I really have to go. . . . I'm busy right now trying to pick my classes. No, Mom, I just really gotta go now. . . . *Yes*, I promise to call you tomorrow. . . . *Every day* . . . All right . . . What? No, I didn't get your care package. . . . Well, yes, I *got* it. I just haven't opened it yet. . . . Now? Really? Okay, okay, I have it in my bag. . . . Yeah . . . Thanks. . . . Bye . . . Love you, too. . . ."

Exhausted, he hung up, sinking back onto the futon with a sigh. "My mom, she worries. . . ." he said, reaching into his backpack and pulling out a small brown package. "She wanted to make sure I opened this; it's probably something perishable like homemade cookies. . . ."

His face plummeted like a skydiver without a parachute as he opened the box to find not cookies but an array of colorful, assorted condoms. TROJAN, EXTRA LARGE, LUBRICATED, STUDDED, ULTRA THIN, SPERMICIDAL, SHEEPSKIN—

He slammed the lid back down but not before Callie saw and started to giggle uncontrollably. Oblivious and exasperated, Dana grabbed her book and stalked off to her bedroom.

"*Wow*," Callie teased, unable to resist, "your mom must have a lot of . . . *confidence* in your . . . abilities."

"Yeah," Matt muttered. "I mean no!" he cried as Callie tried to grab one of the condoms and he noticed the EXTRA LARGE label displayed prominently on the front. "I mean, no I don't mean no. I just meant—"

"I should go finish this up. . . ." he said, standing and waving some papers vaguely. He began backing out of the room.

"Okay," Callie said, still laughing. She reached for her *Courses of Instruction*. "Thanks so much for coming over; it was seriously helpful."

She smiled in a way that would have made his face turn bright red if he hadn't already been blushing at full capacity. "Listen," he blurted in a final, desperate attempt, "let me know what you decide about Ec 10. It's at two P.M. on Tuesdays and Thursdays, so we could, like, do a lunch date before or something. . . ."

"Yeah! Sounds great," Callie replied, but she had already picked up *The Q Guide* and started skimming through its pages.

Matt opened the door to the hallway, and the room swelled with the sound of high-pitched giggles. Callie's head snapped back up just in time to see Gregory escorting yet another "BU Bottle Blonde" (nickname courtesy of Vanessa) toward his room.

Bending over her book, Callie tried to pretend she wasn't watching as Gregory paused, staring down into Matt's care package. His face lit up. He dipped his hand into the box and removed a fistful of condoms.

"Please tell Mrs. Robinson I said thank you." He chuckled. As he held the door open for the girl, he turned toward Callie and, unmistakably, he winked.

Callie accidentally tore a page in *The Q Guide* as she flipped it violently, the sound of squeals and shrieks fading as the door to C 24 swung shut.

A minute later Vanessa burst into the common room, her arms laden with shopping bags. Callie kept her head down, hoping that Vanessa would take the hint.

"Are you *still* agonizing over your classes, Cal? Seriously? It's freshman year, it doesn't even count! Now is the time to be experimental, to focus on the more important things in life."

Callie made a point of turning the pages of *The Q Guide* as obviously as possible, skipping over Ethnic and European Studies to examine Government.

"Anyway, you can stop worrying because I already picked your classes for you. We're taking Justice: Mondays and Wednesdays at one."

"What?" said Callie sharply. "What field is that even in?"

"Moral Reasoning, meaning it'll count no matter what you end up studying. Plus, it's way famous! I heard that sometimes fifteen hundred people enroll and they have to hold a lottery to see who gets in! And the professor, Michael Sandal, is like this crazy Communist who inspired that character Mr. Burns from *The Simpsons*!"

"You mean Michael San*del*, the Communitarian?" Callie corrected her. "He *is* kind of famous . . . and I bet the course is good if that many people show up to take it. . . ."

Vanessa let her bags, and her jaw, sink dramatically toward the floor. "Honestly, Cal, I cannot *believe* you sometimes! Who *cares* whether or not the class is good; it's all about the environment, the people, and the vibe."

"What?" mumbled Callie. She picked up her day planner and verified that Mondays and Wednesdays at one o'clock were free.

"Haven't you realized that we have yet to go on a single date?" asked Vanessa. "Our romantic involvements thus far have been limited to getting dumped—that was you—random hookups, sleazy seniors, and don't even get me started on Mimi's nightly sexcapades. It's completely unacceptable."

Callie was silent.

"Anyway, what I've finally realized is this: we've been looking in all the wrong places: seniors, upperclassmen . . . it's never going to work. We have to tap the untapped resources, discover the uncut diamonds in the rough. . . . We have to find us . . ."

She paused dramatically.

"A freshman."

Callie rolled her eyes.

"Stop—I know what you're thinking!" Vanessa continued. "Two weeks ago I was all for 'upperclassmen only,' too, but today I realized something. I was doing a little research"—and by research, she meant Facebook stalking—"and do you remember that guy I hooked up with the other night? Jeffrey?"

"I think it was Jeremy."

"Whatever. I found out today that he has a girlfriend. She's a senior, too, but get this: she is *busted*. And not just too-ugly-to-make-the-cheerleading-squad ugly, or got-cut-from-the-first-round-of-*America's-Next-Top Model* ugly, but, like, ugly-you-look-deformed ugly."

Callie giggled, finally setting *The Q Guide* aside.

"So I'm thinking, 'What gives?' He's like, *super* hot, and his girlfriend looks like Marilyn Manson. Why stick with crotchety old Manson when you could have a youthful Monroe?"

Callie thought that a "youthful Monroe" was a little generous for Vanessa, but she waited, intrigued nevertheless.

"That's when it hits me. Shovel-face over here must have started dating what's-his-name during their freshman year, four years ago, before he realized he was hot! Before he even *was* hot. You have to catch them when they're young and still at the bottom of the food chain, before they can appreciate their own potential, and then you raise them to adore you, to rely on you, to need you. Get it? It's like a . . . it's like a . . . fish farm! That's it! Project Fish Farm. Don't you see? Justice is the ideal pond."

Callie laughed as she pictured Vanessa going to class with an enormous net and lassoing a bunch of poor, pimpled, unsuspecting freshman boys and dragging them kicking and screaming to a giant pool of water surrounded by a tall, wired fence. *Fish Farm: a boot camp for future husbands of the certifiably insane.* Watching it would be better than watching reality TV.

"Okay, you win," Callie capitulated. "But if I take Justice with you, will you take Ec 10 with me?"

"Investment strategies and future venture capitalists? Now you're talking sense!"

Callie shook her head and pulled out her study card, adding *Justice* underneath *Ec 10* and *Expos.*

"Great!" she cried, starting to relax. "Three down, only one more to go! Now listen to a description of this English class called the Nineteenth-Century Novel—"

Callie stopped midsentence as OK barged into the common room, panting. His face shone with sweat. Frantically he wheeled around and bolted the lock on the door.

"Well," said Vanessa loudly, "I'm glad you could finally make it to our open house event. Would you like a special tour of the premises?"

OK gave her a blank stare, apparently impervious to sarcasm. "Do you—" He paused. "Please pardon the imposition, but do you mind if I stay here for just a moment?"

Callie and Vanessa exchanged a look. "Why?" asked Callie. "Is something wro—?"

Loud clumping noises suddenly filled the room. It sounded like a stampede of wild animals had broken loose outside in the hall.

"Oh, bollocks! Bloody hell!" OK cried, jumping up and darting across the room to stare out the peephole. He shrieked and then came scampering back. "I'm screwed! Absolutely, *royally, screwed . . .*"

"Well, if you're actually royalty like they say, I don't suppose there's any other way. . . ." Vanessa paused, listening to the voices that were coming from the hall.

"Where is he?"

"Which one's his room"

OK moaned and closed his eyes. "Hide me!" he pleaded.

"First, tell us what's going on," Vanessa instructed.

"I—well," OK began, "I'm trying to give some people the slip."

"*Which* people?" asked Callie.

"I'd rather not say."

"Fine," said Vanessa, standing and heading toward the door. "Then we'll just have to go outside and see for oursel—"

"No!" cried OK, racing to block the door. Eyes wide, he looked from Vanessa to Callie. "It's the paparazzi," he whispered finally.

"The paparazzi!" cried Vanessa, glancing in the mirror to check her hair.

"Yes, the so-called 'journalists' who report the news back home and in London."

"Oh." Vanessa's face fell.

"Here?" asked Callie. "But why . . . ?"

"They believe I'm involved in some sort of scandal," said OK. "But I haven't actually got anything to do with it!"

"What sort of a scandal?" Vanessa demanded.

"Vanessa, clearly it's private!" cried Callie.

"Not anymore!" Vanessa exclaimed.

OK sighed. "I suppose I owe you ladies an explanation. It's about my girlfriend—my *ex*-girlfriend, actually—who is rather famous, or should I say *in*famous, back in Britain. We haven't spoken since summer, but apparently she just eloped with some techno music singer and the tabloids . . . the tabloids . . . ," he trailed off with a groan.

Vanessa's lips parted in disbelief: "Are you telling me that your ex-girlfriend is *Sissy* from *Sissy and the Space Cadets*? She's like Miley Cyrus's British soul sister, only with less *Disney* and more pole dancing!"

"So you've heard of her," OK answered, nodding glumly. "Our relationship was terrific fun for a while, but in the end Father was right: she's a bit too wild, even for me—always getting tattooed in the wrong place and photographed at the wrong time. . . . Anyhow, when it came time to end things she asked if I wouldn't mind keeping up appearances for a while to spare her from the additional press. . . .

"Then, next thing I know, she's in Germany hosting an international music festival and promoting her new album alongside some bugger called Franz or Hans—"

"Hans?" Vanessa interrupted. "Don't you mean Hansel Eberhardt, the 'Techno Prince of Europe'?"

OK frowned. "He's not actually a *real* prince, you know."

"Yes," said Vanessa, "but he does *really* know how to wear a pair of tight, white pants!"

"It must have been so hard on her," Callie interjected. "First getting dumped and then having to deal with all the gossip and attention . . ."

"Hard on *her*?" OK asked, staring at Callie. "*She's* the one who tipped off the papers in the first place! Probably married the poor bloke just for a bit of extra attention. Wanted proper revenge, didn't she? Well, she's gotten it all right; that's for certain. Won't leave me bloody well alone—"

There was a pounding at the door. Everyone froze.

But then Mimi's voice grew audible from the hall: "For the love of— LET ME IN! Who bolted the door?"

OK moaned and made a beeline for the bathroom.

As Vanessa opened the door, Callie caught a glimpse of several reporters crowding around on the other side of the hall.

"Oh mon dieu, *girls*," cried Mimi, waving a copy of *Tatler* as she slipped into the room. "Have you seen this article? 'The Secret Heartache of an African Prince,'" she began. "'Okechuwuku Zeyna, one of Nigeria's brightest stars, was recently devastated by the news that longtime girlfriend—or so he thought—Sissy Seraphina had been married to Sexy Hansel frontman Hansel Eberhardt, in Berlin the previous weekend. Her new album, *Two Princes*, is set to drop this month. Sources say that Okechuwuku, a first-year at Harvard University, was overheard vowing to duel his usurper in a fight to the—'"

"Mimi he's—" Callie began.

"Here," Mimi finished as OK emerged from the bathroom.

Vanessa giggled and tossed her hair. Turning toward Callie, she silently mouthed, "*Candidate!*"

Project Fish Farm had begun.

FIVE

BiG FiSH

"PROCRASTINATION IS LIKE MASTURBATION: IT'S FUN FOR A WHILE, BUT IN THE END, YOU'RE ONLY SCREWING YOURSELF."

—ANONYMOUS

https://www.BoredatHarvard.net//BoredatLamont

User106608: Soo bored, and so freaking horny. Anyone up for a rendezvous in Pusey stacks?

User231709: Gay or straight?

User106608: Gay, obvi

User231709: Meet outside fifth floor bathrooms in five minutes . . .

User519410: Anyone have notes for LS1A today? Accidentally slept in.

User726311: Sure, what's your e-mail?

User836708: Party at the Spee tonight! Hot sweaty Eurotrash, ++ass&cocaine

User957309: You're not even in the Spee, you stupid fag

User725409: Just saw Lexi and Clint fighting on the steps AGAIN—anyone know what their status is?

User836708: Not sure but he's one sexy slice of man candy; praying he'll do us all a favor and come out of the closet already . . .

User892712: Ha-ha, fat chance.

User462710: I hear she's a bitch.

User592807: Alexis Thorndike is the BEST dressed person on campus. Wouldn't miss her weekly column for the world!

User948711: Anyone see a copy of *Tatler* this week?

User038711: Are you talking about the Sissy Seraphina thing? I think that guy lives in my dorm.

User982611: I <3 Sexy Hansel!!! Hansel Eberhardt is HOTT!

User746209: Gawker picked up the story too. First Danica Bennington and now this . . .

User652412: Gawker search: Marine Aurélie Clément—you won't be sorry.

User836708: *This* is Marine speaking and I'm here to tell you to shut your silly American faces or I will bust out of rehab and steal cocaine from a stripper in Ibiza—again!!

User528407: You people are pathetic. Don't you have anything better to do than gossip shamelessly about other peoples' lives?

User652412: Don't *you* have anything better to do, you fucking hypocrite?

User746209: Hear, hear!

Sanders Theatre is a stately, cavernous arena located in the western wing of Memorial Hall. The stage in the middle of the main room is surrounded by a mahogany semicircle of balconies and pews, adorned on either side by statues of famous colonial Americans dating back to the early nineteenth century. Refracted light shines in muted, colorful hues from the stained glass window above the balcony, illuminating the Latin inscriptions engraved on the wall above the stage.

This is the place where orators like Winston Churchill, Theodore Roosevelt, and Martin Luther King Jr. delivered speeches to change a nation; where some of the world's most renowned musicians have traveled from afar to grace the stage; where eminent academic and literary figures have gathered to share their knowledge and insight with the younger generations.

This is also the place where students in the later stages of adolescence go to gawk, flirt, sleep, whisper, twitter, poke, surf the web, and even—on occasion—to learn.

Welcome to Justice with Professor Michael J. Sandel, the Anne T. and Robert M. Bass Professor of Government at Harvard University, Mondays and Wednesdays at one P.M. Section times TBA; open to Freshmen–Seniors.

Callie wiggled uncomfortably in her seat, trying not to wrinkle the brand-new, never-been-worn Marc Jacobs sundress that Vanessa had insisted she borrow for their first day of class. Because they had arrived with less than two minutes to spare—Vanessa's fault, in Callie's opinion, for forcing her to change; Callie's fault, in Vanessa's opinion, for her naive failure to cooperate—they were sitting all the way up in the balcony, right behind—to Callie's horror; to Vanessa's delight—a large group of JAQs (Jewish American Queens), PSPs (Prep School Princesses), and WASPs (predatory, flying, stinging insects).

The PSPs were instantly recognizable in their miniskirts and frilly blouses or variants of The Uniform: that classic, East Coast private school look that consists of designer jeans, polo shirts, and pearls. Every movement sounded like money.

Vanessa, her blue headband harmonizing with her Ralph Lauren polo and navy Longchamp shoulder bag, was a perfect clone.

"Hi!" she cried, addressing the girls in a tone that made Callie cringe. "What's up, guys?"

Some of them merely turned, the charms on their timeless, silver Tiffany bracelets clinking, and faced forward once more, but a few greeted Vanessa by name and asked how she was doing. Callie couldn't remember any specific faces from The Dining Hall Debacle of the Decade (or so it was being called on Twitter) and wondered if any of them could recognize her.

Sure enough, the girl seated directly in front of Vanessa frowned as her gaze traveled from Callie's plain shoulder bag down to the "ten-dollar, bargain-bin flats" that Vanessa had tried, and failed, to talk her out of wearing.

"I like your dress," the girl said suddenly. It didn't sound like a compliment. Callie was trying to decide whether or not to say thank you when the girl added: "I'm Anne. What's your name?"

"Callie. Callie Andrews."

"And I'm her roommate, Vanessa Von Vorhees!" Vanessa chimed in, pinching Callie on the thigh in a way that clearly said *I told you so* about the dress.

Seriously? thought Callie. She found it hard to believe that people actually cared about this stuff. Why should it matter what she wore to class—or, for that matter, ever?

"Freshmen, right?" said Anne with an appraiser's eye.

"Right," said Callie.

"By the way," Vanessa added as Anne started to turn back around, "I absolutely adore *your* dress! Who's it by?"

As Anne replied, Callie's eyes began to wander around the room.

Most of the other first-years were clustered in the front rows closest to the stage. Callie spotted Mimi sitting next to OK among a crowd of people who looked distinctly foreign. OK had edged as close to Mimi as possible. Any closer and he'd be sitting on her lap.

Glancing to her left, Callie was startled to find Gregory staring back at her. Before she could look away, he gave a deceptively friendly wave and then mouthed: "*I caught you!*"

He was surrounded by a seersucker-and-loafer-wearing entourage whose attire indicated that if your pastel-colored polo featured an alligator or a man on horseback, you were welcome to join their Gentlemen's Club. It would have looked much more fitting if they were holding mint juleps instead of MacBooks, betting on horses rather than waiting for class to begin.

Turning around quickly before Gregory could fathom new ways to embarrass her, she caught sight of a bunch of people in the very back of the balcony wearing gray sweatpants and sweatshirts featuring the Harvard Department of Athletics logo. What would have happened if she hadn't busted up her knee? Would she be cracking jokes with the athletes instead of hovering on the outskirts of the prep school crowd, faking it miserably in Marc Jacobs?

Down on the stage a man who did bear a striking resemblance to *The Simpsons* character Mr. Burns began tapping the microphone and clearing his throat.

Vanessa pulled her MacBook out of her purse. "Time to start taking notes!"

Surprised, Callie followed Vanessa's example and removed her laptop from her bag. Quickly she logged into her e-mail while Professor Sandel discussed the logistical aspects of class. There were no new updates from Evan. Suddenly, a chat box materialized:

Vanessa: look at my computer screen!

Callie looked. Vanessa had navigated to the Facebook profile for Anne Goldberg, class of 2012. As Callie squinted at the photo, recognition dawned: this was the same girl who had complimented her dress and was currently seated directly in front of them. That's not creepy . . . no, not at all.

Vanessa: i knew it! she's anne GOLDBERG, she went to Deerfield. she's in the pudding!

Callie: the pudding? what's the pudding?

Vanessa: you've never heard of the PUDDING? really Cal what would you do without me? will explain after class. what a find!

Callie watched Vanessa tab back over to Facebook and click the Add as Friend button on Anne Goldberg's profile. Callie saw "The Pudding" listed as one of Anne's activities.

What could it be? she wondered, annoyed that Vanessa wouldn't tell her. A Jell-O appreciation society?

It was just like Vanessa to dangle information without offering an explanation. Callie decided that ignoring her would be the best punishment. She deliberately closed the Gchat box into which Vanessa was typing "check out those hotties to our right i think i recognize the one sitting next to grego—" and opened Microsoft Word, tuning in to Professor Sandel, who was patiently explaining to a horrified-looking first-year that the John Locke he was referring to was not a character on the popular ABC TV show *Lost*.

As Sandel settled into his lecture, Callie's fingers flew across her keyboard, eager to record every word:

"Five people are tied to a train track," he postulated, "and the train is coming full speed ahead. You can't do anything to untie them, but you do have the option to pull a lever that will divert the train onto a different track. There is only one person tied to this alternative track. What do you think is the 'right' thing to do?"

"Pull the lever!" someone shouted from the third row.

"Why?" Sandel asked with a crafty smile.

"Because it's better for one person to die than five."

"Ahh . . . how utilitarian of you. But now let me ask you this. Instead of standing near a lever that can switch the direction of the train, you are standing on a bridge above the tracks. There is a very *large* lady standing next to you on the bridge, and you can choose to push her down onto the tracks, which will also stop the train and save five peoples' lives. Do you do it?"

This time the speaker hesitated. One of the boys sitting near Gregory piped up: "Yeah! Push her off!"

Sandel laughed. "But wouldn't you feel guilty about pushing her? Doesn't that intuitively seem more 'wrong' than simply pulling a lever?"

"No, she's fat," the boy muttered so only the balcony could hear.

"What was that?" asked Sandel.

"I said: No, it shouldn't matter if you *feel* worse about pushing her off than you would about pulling the lever, because saving five people's lives is still the right thing to do."

"So, what you're telling me is that the right thing to do is to always sacrifice the one person in order to save the five?"

"Yes," said the boy confidently, smiling at his peers.

"And this larger woman . . . what if she were your mother instead?" Sandel finished triumphantly. The grin faded from the boy's face.

Turns out, there *is* such a thing as a highbrow "yo mama" joke.

"That's what I thought," said Sandel. "Community often trumps utility. Now if you would all turn to page nine of Bentham's *Principles of Morals and Legislation . . .*"

There was a rustle of pages as people—upperclassmen, mostly—began searching for their texts. Callie turned to Vanessa, intending to ask if she had known they were supposed to buy the books ahead of time. Vanessa was still typing furiously, but her notes had nothing to do with Professor Sandel's lecture.

Instead Vanessa was working on an Excel spreadsheet:

Project Fish Farm.xls

Fish	Home Pond	High School	Family	Harvard Pond	Orientation
Gregory Bolton	Manhattan	Collegiate	Goldman	NYC/Prep	Straight
OK Zeyna	Nigeria	British Int'l	Royalty!	International	Straight
Logan Samson	Manhattan	Collegiate	Lehman ☹	NYC/Prep	Metro?
Adrian Carlyle	DC	Georgetown Day	Carlyle (obvi)	NYC/Prep	Straight
James Hoffmeyer	Manhattan	Collegiate	Hoffmeyer Realty	NYC/Prep	Straight

Callie watched in awe as Vanessa would look up, glance around the room, identify a freshman *fish* of interest, and then locate her newest target on Facebook. She would scan his profile, examine his list of friends, take notes on her spreadsheet, and then finally click the Add as Friends button if he satisfied her criteria.

Once again it was difficult to decide if Vanessa was insanely funny or simply insane. With effort Callie tore her eyes away from Vanessa's computer screen and tried to focus on her own, but it was considerably harder to concentrate on the lecture now that she knew what Vanessa was doing. She wondered if the list were in order: had Vanessa put Gregory in the number one spot on purpose, or was that simply a coincidence?

She glanced over in his direction and found him, once again, staring back at her.

Is he a mind reader? Quickly she bowed her head low over her laptop, willing herself to focus. . . .

Callie's shoulders slumped with relief when a chiming clock announced the end of the hour: class had been very interesting but not entirely because of the lecture. She stood to leave, tugging anxiously at her borrowed dress. The plan: return to her room as soon as possible and change before the dress gets wrinkled or ruined.

Vanessa, however, had a different agenda. "Come on, Cal, we have to go to Lamont Library—time to do some work!"

"Lamont?" asked Callie. "Why would we go to a library on the first day of class? He didn't even assign any homework!"

"Not *home*work, silly. Project Fish Farm. I overheard some people saying that *everybody* hangs out at Lamont—or rather, *Club* Lamont."

"Everybody hangs out at the *library*?"

"It *is* Harvard," Vanessa replied.

The steps of Lamont were swarming with students taking advantage of the weather while it was still warm, smoking, sipping iced lattes, or standing on the grass under the oak trees and chatting. Mimi, OK, and Gregory were already there, entangled in a circle of sunglasses and smoke. Mimi's voice came drifting above the crowd, asking to bum a cigarette; Callie watched as three overeager boys scrambled to oblige. OK emerged victorious, sliding the cigarette smoothly between her lips, but then not so smoothly burning his fingertips in his haste to offer her a light.

Just as they were approaching the group, Gregory threw his head back in laughter at somebody's joke. The smile lit up his entire face. Callie froze, her feet having temporarily forgotten how to make forward motion.

"Hi, guys!" said Vanessa. "Gregory, OK, Adrian, Logan . . . Mimi."

"*Salut, ça va?*" said Mimi. "Did you guys enjoy the class?"

"Cassie here looked like she was absolutely riveted," said Gregory before either Callie or Vanessa could answer. "She just couldn't *take her eyes off* of the professor. Could you?"

"It's CALLIE," said Callie, the feeling flooding back into her toes.

"Oh, you know Callie, she *loves* class; it was so nerdtastic the way she kept taking notes all during the lecture," Vanessa began blabbering. She was still talking when Callie grabbed her arm and yanked her inside the library.

"Hey! Just because he can't remember *your* name," Vanessa snapped as they swiped their IDs and headed past the security guard and into the lobby, "doesn't mean you have to get all *huffy* about it!" They passed a circulation desk on their left and, behind a set of double glass doors on the right, a bustling café. Vanessa's ceaseless yammering continued as they walked down a large aisle with books, tables, and study alcoves. ". . . because, you know, he and I, we have this *connection* that simply cannot be denied—"

Vanessa stopped talking abruptly as a hundred heads looked up in unison.

They had accidentally wandered straight into the main reading room. For a moment all eyes were on them.

"*Sorry,*" Vanessa mouthed, gripping Callie's hand. Tiptoeing, they backed out of the room. Those who had looked up lost interest quickly—returning to their iTunes, instant messenger, or the intrigues of anonymous gossip sites; whispering, poking, poker tournaments, high-stakes games of footsie, and/or fabricated romances built on furtive, or lingering, glances. In short, every activity possible with one exception: studying.

Still gripping Callie's hand, Vanessa dragged her back toward the set of double glass doors that were flanked by the sign LAMONT CAFÉ. Here, students could order a cappuccino and the daily dish of gossip for two dollars and fifty cents. Talking permitted—but Inside Voices, please.

At the moment every table was occupied save one. Vanessa slung her shoulder bag across it, marking their territory. "Sit," she ordered, and Callie obeyed, taking the chair by the window with an excellent view of both the café and the grassy area outside the library in front of the stairs. Through the glass she could see Mimi and OK hanging out but no sign of—

"I'll be right back," said Vanessa.

"Mmm," Callie murmured, leaning back in her chair as far as she could without tipping over. Still no visual on Gregory. Not that she cared.

Turning, she saw Vanessa in line at the counter, waiting to order a drink. Two tables to her right, Callie recognized Anne Goldberg and several other girls she'd seen in Justice. However, all eyes at the table were focused not toward Anne but on the striking brunette seated directly to her left.

Alexis Thorndike.

What is it about her? Callie wondered, leaning forward to get a better look. Brown curls were held aloft from Alexis's face by a delicate headband, pale, thin wrists visible from beneath the tapered sleeves of a navy blue blazer layered atop a fluttery white blouse.

Callie glanced down at her own outfit. The colors of her dress suddenly seemed too bright; creases were forming at the tops of her thighs, and she could feel the fabric sticking slightly to the chair beneath her. She looked back at Alexis who, raising her eyes at the exact same moment, caught Callie staring.

Callie flushed and turned toward the window. Reaching down, she fiddled with it for a moment until finally it opened. The breeze that floated in had a calming effect.

"Callie?"

Turning, she found herself face-to-face with Bryan Jacobs, who had been two years ahead of her in high school and had briefly dated Jessica during their sophomore year.

"Bryan!" she cried, leaping up and giving him a hug.

"I *thought* that was you!" he said, taking the seat across from her as she sat down. "I'd recognize that hair anywhere. How have you been?"

"I've been good," she said. "Still trying to get the hang of things, but otherwise . . ."

Callie trailed off as Vanessa returned to the table, balancing two enormous lattes, one on top of the other, in one hand and a blueberry muffin in the other.

"Could you move?" she asked Bryan. "You're in my s— Oh." She stopped, registering his appearance for the first time.

"I'm so sorry," he said, standing immediately—which revealed his substantial height—and holding out the chair. "Please, have a seat."

"Oh—no—that's okay, you can have it," Vanessa gushed, oblivious to the lattes, which were teetering dangerously.

"Nonsense," said Bryan with a smile. "I'll go grab another one."

In a moment he was back, pulling a chair up to the table. "Bryan," Callie began, "this is my roommate—"

"Vanessa," Vanessa interjected, holding out her hand.

"It's a pleasure to meet you, Vanessa," he replied, returning her appreciative stare. "Wow, I can't believe they paired the two of you together: you must live in the cutest room on campus!"

Vanessa glowed, absentmindedly twirling a finger through her hair.

"So, Cal, how's Evan doing?" he asked, turning to Callie. "I haven't talked to him in a while."

"We broke up."

"Really? That's too bad. What happened?"

"I'd *much* rather hear more about *you*," Vanessa said quickly, winking at Callie and sliding one of the lattes toward her across the table. Callie smiled gratefully. "What year are you, and what do you like to do for fun? I'm guessing water polo—or swimming," Vanessa continued, her eyes resting on his broad shoulders and arms.

Bryan chuckled. "Good guess," he said. "I played water polo and soccer in high school. That's how I know this one," he added, nodding at Callie.

Callie sipped her drink, trying not to think about Evan as Bryan and Vanessa fell into an animated conversation. Soon she found her eyes wandering back toward the table two to her right. Alexis had disappeared, but Anne was still there. She was looking—no, make that *glaring*—at Callie. In shock, Callie glanced over both shoulders just to be sure. In the meantime Anne stood and began walking toward them.

"Hey, Bryan," she said warmly when she arrived. "We still on for lunch?"

"Sure thing," he said, tearing his eyes away from Vanessa, whose fingers had paused mid-twirl. "Just catching up with an old friend from high school. Have you met Callie?" he asked.

"High school," said Anne, smiling suddenly. "Of course—that makes sense. And yes, I do know Callie. Nice to see you again!"

Callie looked at Anne in surprise and noticed the way she was glaring—not at Callie but, rather, at Vanessa.

"Ready?" asked Anne, turning to Bryan before Vanessa had a chance to speak.

"Yes," Bryan said, standing. "Well, it was great to see you, Callie, and lovely to meet you, Vanessa. You ladies should come to the party we're having at the Fly Club this Friday. The theme is 'calypso.' It's gonna be awesome."

Anne frowned.

Callie was about to ask what "calypso" meant or what "club" he was talking about, but Vanessa cut her off:

"Fantastic! We'll be there."

"Can't wait!" said Anne, giving Bryan a *look*. Turning, she walked away, Bryan following closely at her heels.

"What's 'calypso'?" Callie asked when they were out of earshot.

"Only the best thing that ever happened to us," Vanessa said dramatically. "We've hit the mother lode!"

"What?" asked Callie. "Why can't you just tell me what it is? Why don't you ever explain—"

"Shhh!" hissed Vanessa, looking cautiously around the room as if they were CIA operatives rather than teenage girls. Callie decided that if Special Agent Von Vorhees mentioned High-Priority-Top-Secret-Operation-Find-Fish one more time, she was going to punch her in the nose (job).

"We mustn't be overheard. . . ."

Callie clenched her fists—

"But I promise an explanation is forthcoming. . . . For now all you need to know is that it involves mixing, mingling, and maybe more with the hottest, classiest boys on campus."

"So it's a party, then—"

"Oooh, I see Brittney over by the computers!" Vanessa shrieked, standing. "I absolutely must say hello. BRB!"

TYT: take your time, Callie thought irritably as Vanessa rushed over to some girl she must know from prep school. Sipping her latte, Callie gazed out the window searching for . . . *uhm* . . . No One in Particular. . . .

Instead she noticed Alexis standing at the foot of the steps. She appeared to be in the middle of a heated conversation with the tall boy whose back was facing Callie. Though Callie couldn't see his face, she could tell—even from a distance—that Alexis was livid.

"Over?" Callie heard her cry. She tried to shrink away from the window. "How many times have you said that in the past few weeks?"

"This time is different," Callie heard him say. She was dying to see his face, but she kept her eyes trained toward the table. "This time I mean it."

"Don't you walk away from me," Alexis said, her voice dangerously calm as the boy started to turn. "Nobody walks away from me."

Risking a peek, Callie saw Alexis standing there silent, swaying slightly.

The boy, whoever he was, had gone.

SIX

"Are You on the List?"

Peons:

You've moved in, you've survived orientation, and you've even picked your classes. By now you're probably wondering, What do people do around here for fun?

While 80 percent of the student body admits to never leaving their rooms except for meals, class, and trips to the library, the remaining 20 percent actually knows how to have a truly amazing time.

who are they?

Mostly sons and daughters of New York Socialites and Investment Bankers, of LA Barbie Moms and Pro Football Players, of OPEC Oil Kings and European Royalty–in addition to a handful of individuals with "obscure parentage" who are cool in their own right.

where can you find them?

Every Thursday, Friday, and Saturday night *by invitation ONLY* at our beloved "secret societies": the Harvard Final Clubs.

Back in 1791 the first Final Club was founded. Members gathered around a roast pig dinner and established their motto, "*Dum vivimus vivamus*" ("While we live, let's live"). Now there are eight All-Male Final Clubs, each established over a century ago and headquartered in beautiful brick mansions located conveniently throughout Harvard Square. (Combined net property value: ~$17,000,000.)

Every year each club extends membership to an elite set of roughly twenty men from the sophomore class, upholding the beloved mantras of exclusivity, secrecy, affluence, and elitism that set the tone back in 1791.

Freshman boys: Sorry, but you'll have to wait your turn within the hierarchy. By the time you're a sophomore, you might have a chance at membership; by the time you're a senior, you might have a chance with a freshman girl!

Freshman girls: Congratulations. Your novelty and naivete will be sufficient to secure you an invitation to the best parties on campus. Be careful, though, when an invitation to a party becomes an invitation to "check out the upstairs." Sadly, there really is no such thing as a free lunch (with an upperclassman boy).

Sometimes here at Harvard it can feel like everybody who's anybody is in a Final Club; and even out in the real world the alumni rosters are so full of surnames like Roosevelt and Kennedy, that it's easy to start suspecting that every male graduate who is rich or powerful or famous must have been a member (even if he later tries to deny it for political reasons).

So, what about the majority of students for whom membership will never be anything other than an unattainable dream? How is it the other half–excuse me, other 80 percent–lives?

"Exclusive," "elitist," "classist," "sexist," "hetero-normative," "racist," and "just plain dumb" are all words that have been used in an onslaught of critiques against these private institutions–and not just by individuals whose quest for membership proved futile.

Critics are especially keen to point out that the only two all-female Final Clubs–the Bee, est. 1991, and the Isis, est. 2000–do not enjoy the luxury of owning their own houses but are instead forced to rent space from their male counterparts.

Ladies, you have a choice: you can struggle for liberation in the tragically phallocentric universe that is Harvard society or you can give in to the system and embrace a series of parties that you'll never forget, starring music, dancing, drinking, drugs, glamour, costumes, and sex. . . . You can stay home in protest or do whatever suits you behind closed doors (as long as you do your best to keep track of your underwear). Frosh Femmes looking for a fairy-tale ending ought to remember that it was a glass slipper Cinderella left behind and not a Victoria's Secret thong.

Alexis Thorndike, Advice Columnist
Fifteen Minutes Magazine
Harvard University's Authority on Campus Life since 1873

"I finally figured out your secret!" Vanessa cried, turning away from her makeup mirror and fixing her eyes on Callie.

Callie, who had been allowing Mimi to curl her hair, stood up so quickly that the curling iron burned her scalp. Mimi cursed loudly and leaped back. Callie's heart began to thump in her chest. She swallowed. "You did?"

"Yes, I did. I can't believe you've been holding out on us: we're your roommates, after all," Vanessa said.

Mimi looked at Vanessa expectantly.

"What . . . how . . ." said Callie, her cheeks turning pale. Had Vanessa overheard her on the phone with Evan? Was it possible that somehow, someone at Harvard had found out?

"Not so fast. I want to hear you say it," said Vanessa, brandishing a tube of lipstick like a dagger.

"I, uh, don't know, what, uhm . . ." Callie stammered, feeling like her heart was about to fall out of her chest and into her ankles.

"*You* . . ." began Vanessa menacingly, advancing toward Callie, "are in LOVE . . . with a certain *boy* . . . from across the hall!"

"What?" cried Callie. Mimi sighed through pursed lips and turned back to the mirror, clamping an eyelash curler over her eye.

"It explains so much," said Vanessa, outlining her lips in red. "I'm just amazed that it took me this long to figure it out!" She chuckled, blotting the lipstick with a tissue.

Callie couldn't help but smile. Her secret was still safe—at least it was for now.

"Well, I wouldn't go so far as to call it a *crush*," she started to explain. "Especially because he's such a—"

"Nerd?" finished Vanessa. "I know."

"Right . . ." said Callie absentmindedly. Such a huge jerk. Nerd? Wait, what?

"I mean, I would totally be embarrassed to admit it, too," Vanessa continued. "If *I* were hopelessly in love with a big, tall, geeky—"

"Matt?" interjected Mimi, eyeing Callie's reflection in the mirror as she dabbed bronzer on each cheek. "You are having a love connection with . . . Matt?"

"Matt? Wait, what? No, I—"

"Admit it! Admit it—I command you!" Vanessa screamed. Running over to Callie, she began to tickle her incessantly.

"Stop!" cried Callie, laughing uncontrollably. Her eyes began to fill with tears.

"Confess!" Mimi cried, rushing over to join the assault. "Confess or we will torture you *jusqu'á la mort*!"

"Callie and Matt-y sitting in a tree," Vanessa sang, "K-I-S-S-I-N-G! First comes love—"

"Stop!" yelled Callie, falling on the floor with laughter.

Vanessa continued louder and louder: "THEN comes marriage, THEN comes the BABY IN THE BABY CARRIAGE!"

Mimi and Vanessa collapsed on top of Callie, laughing hysterically.

"What's so funny?" Dana asked, emerging from her room. She

had let her long brown hair hang loose and wore a black dress—conservative, by most standards, but daring for Dana, as it showed a far more liberal amount of ankle than usual.

"Dana!" cried Callie as the other two stood wordlessly and turned back to their mirrors. "You look nice! What are you up to tonight?" Silently she prayed that Dana already had plans. Bryan's invitation to Calypso, their first Final Club party, didn't seem like it could be extended infinitely—not to mention that Vanessa would kill her—but if Dana weren't busy, Callie knew that she just wouldn't have the heart to exclude her.

"I have a date!" said Dana, and then, as if frightened by her own bold use of the word, she amended: "Well, not a date, just a . . . trip to BerryLine. Mainly to review some common structural isomers and check the answers to our first problem set. . . ."

"And get some frozen yogurt?" Callie added gently.

"Yes," said Dana, returning Callie's smile. "Yes. Anyway, I have to go. Adam's probably waiting—"

"Adam?" asked Vanessa, wheeling around. "You mean that tiny shrimp who lives across the hall?"

"Vanessa," Callie warned. "He seems really nice, Dana. You guys will have a great time!"

"Thanks," Dana said awkwardly. Then she slipped out into the hall.

"OHMYGOD!" Vanessa laughed as the door was still only halfway closed. "If the elephant and the field mouse decide to get married, they might have a shot at making normal-sized babies!"

Who's calling *who* an elephant? Callie was just about to say as much out loud when she caught herself, watching Vanessa walk up to the full-length mirror and begin neurotically pinching her sides. (This week, Vanessa was only eating white foods of all the things: "If it's colorful, it has dye in it, which means it's not organic.")

"Shit! It's already nine forty! Let's get dressed!" Callie said, grabbing Vanessa and steering her toward her room.

In honor of the theme "calypso," the girls had all purchased different colors of the same low-cut, sleeveless nylon dress. Mimi, decked out in silver, was her usual supermodel self. Vanessa, who had opted for bronze to bring out her highlights, was appearing a little bustier than usual but looked fantastic nevertheless. Together they had decided that Callie would wear the gold. After weaving fake flowers around their necks and in their hair, the look was complete.

"*Whew-eee*," Vanessa whistled. "Your friend Bryan was right: we *are* the cutest room on campus! What a charming, intelligent young man. I like him."

Callie laughed. "To Bryan," she toasted, accepting the bottle of tequila that Vanessa had just handed her. She took a swig and then passed it to Mimi.

"Callie, are you *sure* you don't want to borrow a pair of heels?" Vanessa asked.

"Yes!" Callie said, smiling at the flip-flops on her feet. "Whoa, Mimi—slow down!" she added, realizing that Mimi had been hitting the bottle for a full five seconds with no sign of stopping.

"Yeah," said Vanessa. "Unless you like spending your summers with Lohan and Spears."

"What?" said Callie.

"Nothing! Nothing . . ." said Vanessa.

"It is all right." Mimi laughed. "I believe Vanessa is referring to my summer at the facility in Switzerland. And no, I did not see Lindsay there, but we were not encouraged to socialize with our neighbors."

She didn't look like she was kidding. Callie's mouth fell open. "Wait . . . So you were like . . . an *alcoholic* or something?"

"More like I was bored at *boring* school," Mimi said. She took the bottle from Callie and threw back another shot. Mischievously she grinned. "Alcohol was never really my primary problem . . ."

The girls were chattering nonstop as they bustled out of the room and down the stairs, across the Yard and toward the Fly Club for Gentlemen, as those "gentlemen" liked to call themselves. Mimi knew the way and had in fact been asked to the party independently of Bryan's invitation because she'd hooked up with a member last Wednesday: a football player from a place called something like Mini-soda whose name she couldn't remember—that is, if she had ever even asked for it in the first place. (Don't hold it against her: if you'd locked lips with one prefect, one football player, one graduate student, one Justice teaching fellow (*whoopsie*), and one visiting professor (*double whoopsie*), you might not remember all of them either!)

Perhaps this was what her professor from Drugs and the Brain had meant when he referred to swapping "one addiction for another."

A group of older girls walked by and muttered the word *freshmen* in the same tone of voice Mimi sometimes uttered *Americans* or *Oprah*.

"Why didn't we think to wear jackets?" Callie moaned.

First Law of Thermo-identify-namics: you can always tell a freshman girl by (the absence of) her clothing.

"Oh, screw 'em," exclaimed Vanessa. "They're just jealous cause they're a couple years closer to the three Bs: that's Botox, Boob jobs, and Being-left—for a freshman!"

A few minutes later they arrived in front of a beautiful brick mansion that looked more like a private home than a secret society. Elegant white columns flanked the club's front door, nostalgic and imperious. The building itself seemed to belong to a time of tailcoats and white gloves—except for the booming hip-hop music that was presently blaring from the upstairs windows.

A bouncer was working the back door. Callie froze.

"Names?" he asked, clipboard in hand, face expressionless.

"Mimi, Callie, and I'm Vanessa."

"You ladies have ID?"

Crap! thought Callie. Who knew you had to be twenty-one to get into a college party?

She watched as Mimi and Vanessa flashed their Harvard College ID cards. Miraculously, the bouncer looked at the IDs, looked at her roommates, looked at the list, and then made a little check with his pen before stepping aside to welcome them in.

So *that's* what they meant by "Invitation Only." Nobody cared how old you were; all that mattered was whether or not your name was on The List! Smiling, Callie handed him her ID card.

"Have a nice night, Ms. Andrews," he said.

"Thanks!" she cried, hurrying to join her friends.

"Callie, you're such a dork—" Vanessa started to say, but her voice was promptly drowned out by the blast of music and noise that greeted them at the top of the stairs.

This was no high school party.

There were three elaborate bars attended by elderly bartenders in identical "island" attire: one whose sole job seemed to consist of working the margarita machine and ensuring that the constant supply of slushy "girlie" drinks never ran dry. Cocktail waitresses wearing grass skirts and coconut bras were wandering around offering the guests trays of pineapple, papaya, and piña coladas.

A live band strummed ukuleles lazily, singly softly in a foreign tongue that made Callie think of white sand, clear blue water, palm trees, and hot sun. Perhaps she was imagining because she'd learned online that Calypso was an island nymph in Greek mythology, but the air seemed to smell like ambrosia.

Couples were twirling across the dance floor: shirtless guys in nothing but swimming trunks danced with girls in short, colorful dresses while other couples lounged in beach chairs arranged along the wall. The dance floor had been decorated with fake flowers, inflatable animals, and palm trees. Blow-up monkeys and flamingos whooshed past, propelled by the dancers as the band struck up a faster number and people really began to move. . . . Welcome to Calypso. . . .

Vanessa materialized out of nowhere with three drinks in hand. "Sex on the Beach!" she said loudly over the music, thrusting a cup at Callie.

"What?" asked Callie, staring down at what looked like a piña colada.

"SEX-ON-THE-BEACH!" Vanessa cried again, pointing. And Callie suddenly understood: in the corner of the room, atop a mound of imported sand, a half-naked couple looked—and may well have been—in the middle of the act.

Next to them on the "beach" a giant kiddy pool was filled with not water but a disturbingly bright blue-colored liquid and hundreds of neon straws.

"Mini-soda!" Mimi screamed to a confused boy who'd just approached her. "No?" said Mimi, frowning. "Brent? Brad? Chadwick?"

"Tyson," he said, forgiving her on the spot and steering her onto the dance floor.

"She loses her English when she drinks—can't understand a word she's saying!" Vanessa yelled at Callie.

Callie wasn't listening. Instead she was staring at a tall, shirtless boy with sexy-shaggy brown hair who had just brushed up against her arm on his way to the dance floor. Pausing, he looked back: he was strangely familiar, yet unrecognizable in the dark.

Her eyes widened as she sipped her drink. She wanted to follow him out onto the dance floor, but such a bold move would first require a little liquid courage. . . .

Four piña coladas later she was in the midst of violating the one rule she'd made at the beginning of the party: *Do not drink from the neon straws in the kiddy pool.* Now she could not for the life of her remember why. Was it because little kids usually peed in kiddy pools? There weren't any kids at this party! Plus, she was so thirsty and the water was so blue. . . .

The band had been replaced by a DJ, the lights had been dimmed, and the guests were now dancing wildly in a frenzied crowd. Vanessa, usually the encourager, had suddenly turned enforcer.

"Come on, Cal," she urged, "that's probably not the best idea. . . ."

"Shmanessa!" cried Callie, her eyes blurry and unfocused. "Vanurssa . . . I luvvrrve you. . . . He-he. You have such pretty faces!"

"That's great, Callie. I love you, too, but maybe we should go sit down for a second?"

"*I* love you, too, Callie!" said a nearby boy, sliding into the conversation. "Would you like another drink, sweetheart?"

"Thanks but no thanks," said Vanessa, stepping in between Callie and Trouble with a capital T. "Why don't you go crawl back into the Dumpster where you came from?"

Shrugging, he walked away. With a smile Vanessa turned back to Callie.

She was gone.

"Oh, shit," Vanessa muttered, shaking her head.

"I thought maybe you'd be a little more excited to see me?" asked a voice on her right.

"Bryan!" cried Vanessa. "It's great to see you! It's just, I lost Callie and I'm worried about her because I think she's had too much to drink. . . ."

"I'm sure she's fine," Bryan replied, laughing a little. "It's always the normal-seeming ones who turn out to have a real wild and crazy side—"

"Well, wild and crazy or not, I still need to find her," Vanessa said. Smiling apologetically and refusing Bryan's offer to help her search, she made her way toward the restrooms.

Inside the bathroom a girl was getting sick—but thankfully, she wasn't Callie. Next Vanessa checked the coatroom and discovered, to her chagrin, the same couple who'd been together earlier on the "beach."

"Sorry!" cried Vanessa as she hurried away. "Now where would I be if I were Callie. . . ." she muttered under her breath, really starting to worry as she made her way back into the room adjacent to the dance floor: a lounge filled with swirling cigar smoke and massive leather couches. There she spotted Mimi in tight embrace with yet *another* boy. Or maybe this was the same one from Wednesday. It was hard to keep track.

"Mimi!" said Vanessa gingerly. "Uhm . . . sorry to interrupt, but have you seen Callie anywhere?"

"Là-bas," said Mimi, pointing to a darkened corner. And sure enough, there was Callie: sprawled across a couch on the other side of the room.

But she was not alone. Attached to her lips was a boy: a sketchy, random, probably older, and, all right, fine, yes, incredibly handsome boy.

"I think we should go save her," Vanessa said, turning to Mimi. "She's completely wasted."

"All right," Mimi answered, looking at her companion like he was a rerun of an old TV show that she could catch again any time she pleased.

"Wait!" he cried, downcast and sullen. "I didn't even get your name! Maybe you could give me your number so I could call you sometime?"

"Je suis désolée, mais je ne parle pas l'anglais," Mimi answered with a cold little shrug. *"Au revoir."*

They made their way across the room until they were hovering over Callie and her newfound friend, whom Vanessa would later dub "Sketchy McKisserson." In the dim light Vanessa thought she could discern a handsome, eligible, and oddly familiar face under all that long, shaggy brown hair. She hesitated for a moment, worried that she might accidentally be "cock-blocking" her roommate in the Jane Austen sense of the term: that is, inadvertently preventing a socially fortuitous match. Then again, even if this guy weren't a sleazy bastard, Callie was still way too drunk to be making out with anybody.

"Sorry, buddy," said Vanessa, grabbing Callie and dragging her up off the couch. "It's way past her bedtime."

"Wait!" he said, standing. "Let me walk you guys home."

Vanessa paused, squinting through the darkness at his face as if she was trying to place where she had seen him before.

"I am thinking we can take it from here," Mimi said, stepping in and wrapping an arm around Callie's waist.

"Bye!" cried Callie, tripping on herself as her roommates

supported her between them. "You're a kood gisser. . . . Ahg! I mean, a good kisser. . . . I like you!"

"Thanks," said Mimi, to whom Callie's comment had accidentally been addressed. "Let us get you home, *ma chérie*," she added, patting her on the head.

As her roommates were escorting her toward the door, Callie snatched up an inflatable monkey and tucked it safely under her arm.

"Soo-vuh-near!" she cried, showing it to Vanessa.

"Yeah, you picked a good one, you little klepto," Vanessa said. "Now let's get that little monkey home—he must be pretty tired. I bet he's going to feel sort of sick tomorrow after playing in the kiddy pool."

Between the two of them, they managed to escort an extremely wobbly, incoherent Callie back to Wigglesworth. They followed her into her bedroom to make sure she made it safely, and Mimi watched as Vanessa slid Callie's flip-flops off her feet, guided her into bed, and pulled the comforter up around her chin like a patient, loving mother.

"That was quite decent of you, taking care of her tonight," Mimi whispered.

"What?" said Vanessa. "Oh, it was nothing—"

"Nessa?" Callie asked blearily through half-closed eyes. "Nessa . . . I kissed a boy!"

"Yes you did, you bad girl." Vanessa laughed. "Now go to sleep!"

"Very, verrrry bad." Callie yawned. "If only I could remember his . . ."

Where am I? Callie woke with a start. She lifted her eyelids, which felt heavy like dumbbells, and recognizing her bedspread, allowed them to shut once more.

Where are my clothes! she wondered, lids jolting open again. With enormous effort she threw off the bedspread: gold dress—*check*, no strange bedfellows—*check*.

Slowly she began to piece together her fractured memories from the night before. There had been something involving a monkey, a swimming pool, and a pool table. No, that couldn't be right. . . .

The hazy image of shaggy brown hair swam into focus: hair that fell irresistibly across a pair of light green eyes, obscuring a face without a name. . . .

Yes, there had definitely been a boy: a boy who had cornered her, whispering that he'd noticed her from the moment she'd arrived and had been trying to think of how to approach her all night. He'd looked at her in a way that made her feel, for the first time in a long time, like she was the only girl in the world. . . .

Then again, maybe the entire episode had only been a dream. That bit about the monkey certainly didn't make sense.

Suddenly she noticed her clock: 3:00 P.M.

Ugghh . . . I'm completely worthless! Too lazy to take off her dress, she pulled on some tattered gray sweatpants and lumbered into the common room.

"*Yeeeep!*" she cried, throwing her hands over her eyes. The sudden glare of light streaming in from the windows was deadly.

Mimi, Vanessa, and Dana were all waiting for her on the couch.

Mimi held a glass of water and some Advil; Vanessa, a steaming cup of coffee. Both were smiling tolerantly. Dana was frowning, but her *I-told-you-so* expression of disapproval was softened by the bagel and cream cheese she held in her outstretched hand.

"You guys are the best." Callie moaned. She plopped down on the armchair and reached for the Advil.

"We know!" sang Vanessa cheerfully. Her eyes glinting, she added: "Guess who kissed a *boy* last night?"

Dana clapped her hands over her face in horror. "How did you *know*? Oh, I swear I didn't mean to do it; it just happened. . . . It was—it was an accident!"

Callie, Vanessa, and Mimi were silent for a moment; then they burst into hysterical, delirious laughter.

"Wow, I guess *I'm* the only one who *didn't* get busy last night." Vanessa laughed.

"*What?*" said Callie, completely bemused.

"Oh, Callie, please," said Mimi. "Do not be coy with us, darling."

"Yeah," Vanessa chimed in. "I'd believe it if you couldn't remember his name, but there's no way you can't remember his tongue!"

"Oh dear," said Callie, frowning as the memories returned. "Was it really that bad?"

"*Bad?*" said Vanessa. "Sweetie—no! It's about time!"

Vanessa and Mimi exchanged a knowing look, and Callie wondered for a moment if they were messing with her, when she suddenly spotted an inflatable monkey sitting serenely in the corner of the common room. . . .

SEVEN

COMPiNG

CAN YOU KEEP UP?

From: **Alexis Thorndike**
To: **[FM Signup List]**

Dear Recipient:
You are receiving this e-mail because you signed up for more information about *FM* magazine at the Freshmen Activities Fair. For those of you who thought that signing up was the equivalent of joining our organization: sorry, but guess again! Welcome to a little process here on campus that we like to call "COMP." Think of it as an audition that involves writing a series of practice pieces, including articles, surveys, op-eds, and anything else that we can dream up for you to do.

From the *Lampoon* to the *Advocate*, Harvard has many clubs and societies that cater to every imaginable interest of the student body, but let me be the first to say that we are thrilled you have chosen *FM*! The magazine is a sister organization of *The Harvard Crimson*, our daily newspaper founded back in 1873. (But in contrast to the *Crimson*, we actually get to have some fun!)

Before the fun starts, however, you do have to survive a semester of COMP. Unfortunately, not everyone will make it on to the magazine; but if you do, it is well worth the work! I know it can seem tough: after all, you strived so hard to get to Harvard and now you find yourself facing a seemingly endless application or initiation process, whether it's for a club, a secret society, an extracurricular activity, or even an upper-division seminar. All I can say is: hang in there. This is Harvard, after all, not high school!

So please come and join me, Alexis Thorndike, your COMP director on this Friday afternoon, October 1, at 3 P.M. on the second floor of the *Crimson* headquarters for an additional information session and to kick off the start of this semester's COMP!

Looking forward to seeing all of you there,
Alexis Thorndike

As September faded into October, the days grew shorter and colder. Chilly winds blew leaves crisply about the Yard, and students arrived for their classes pink-cheeked and red-nosed, bundled in hats and scarves.

Though unused to the weather, Callie had managed over the past few weeks to acclimate to her new environment, gradually falling into a comfortable routine.

After breakfasting at eight thirty, she would read during her time before class. Morning lessons lasted anywhere from one to three hours, then off to lunch with Matt, Vanessa, or Mimi, if you could find her. Following lunch were the afternoon classes; then she would head to Lamont and spend four hours completing the work she could have done in two if she'd chosen a less social venue.

Dinner in Annenberg often stretched across several hours as students rotated around the room speed-dating style. Following dinner the hours between eight and twelve were reserved for reading, which she preferred to do in her bedroom or on the common room couch.

On any given evening around eleven thirty you could almost always find all four roommates scattered about the common room: Dana color-coding her Life Sciences notes and looking up, furious, every time Vanessa sighed dramatically (which was often) or tried to initiate a conversation about which boy she liked best that week (oftener still—though obviously nobody compared to her "one, true love," aka Gregory); Mimi, whose eyes always seemed half-closed, was usually sleeping in the armchair instead of working.

Callie's focus generally lasted until around midnight, when she would throw down her book—awakening Mimi with a start—and demand to hear interesting stories from the day. Vanessa would then declare that she was hungry (she made a point of never dieting at night because that would be, like, neurotic). If the refrigerator was empty, they would order pizza or sketchy Chinese food from The Kong: restaurant by day, dance club by night.

Uninvited but always welcome, the three girls (Dana preferred to stay behind and study) would often troop across the hall with their snacks to exploit Matt and Gregory's comfy leather couch and the miraculous wonders of TiVo. Mimi was finding that she had a strange affinity for violent American video games, and OK, to no great surprise, was still suffering from a not-so-strange affinity for Mimi.

All in all, life was good, and lately Callie was finishing her reading earlier than usual, sometimes even reading ahead. At the beginning of the year she'd been anxious about balancing school and extracurriculars (or, more like her dad had been anxious, reminding her that the three most important things were "academics, academics, and academics"). But now, with COMP right around the corner, she was settled, confident, and eager to begin.

Thus, on Friday the first of October, after running into each other at Hemenway Gymnasium, Callie and Matt were heading across the Yard back to Wigglesworth, discussing *The Harvard Crimson*'s

COMP information session that they would be attending at three o'clock. Matt was planning to check out the daily newspaper's editorial board; whereas Callie still had her heart set on *Fifteen Minutes* magazine. She had grown addicted to the magazine in recent weeks—especially the advice columns and blogs—and couldn't wait to meet Alexis officially.

Now Callie was listening to Matt as he outlined the other major organizations on campus—trying her best not to shiver as the autumn wind brushed past her legs, which were bare save for her running shorts. Matt's older brother—former member of the *Harvard Lampoon*—had apparently "popped a blood vessel" when Matt told him he was thinking about COMPing the *Crimson*.

"Why?" asked Callie, laughing as they walked down the steps past Widener Library on the way to their dorm.

"Well," Matt began, "the *Crimson* and the *Lampoon* have been bitter rivals since forever ago, when the *Crimson* staff stole the *Lampoon*'s mascot from their castle and presented it as a gift to the government of the Soviet Union. The Lampoon retaliated by stealing the president of the *Crimson*'s chair and giving it as a ceremonial gift to the prime minister of Iceland. Apparently nowadays the *Crimson* keeps the president's chair chained to the wall. I can't wait to see if it's true!"

"Wait a second: did you say that the *Lampoon* has a *castle*?"

"Yeah, haven't you noticed that big purple and yellow building right across the street from Lowell House? It's pretty hard to miss—I mean, it's a castle, and when the weather is nice, the members are always sitting outside playing music and throwing things at unsuspecting pedestrians. My brother says that inside there are tons of secret passageways and relics from the famous pranks they've pulled over the years."

"So, can anyone who wants to just go inside?" Callie asked, ready to tear off in the direction of the castle immediately.

"Unfortunately, no," Matt answered, shaking his head. "Nobody is allowed inside except for members, and you can't even get into their parties as the guest of a member until your senior year. Same thing goes with the *Crimson*. You have to go through several intense rounds of writing practice newspaper articles—or humor pieces, in the case of the *Lampoon*—and then they judge you on how journalistic you are, or how funny you are, or the strength of your artwork or ability to solicit ads for the business board. . . . You get the idea."

"Right," said Callie, nodding. "And once we finish COMP, we're in?"

"Well," said Matt, "sometimes it's not that easy; otherwise everyone would do it. Joining is considered a rite of passage, and some organizations make people COMP for a year and a half before letting them in, just to mess with them or test their commitment."

"A *year and a half*?"

"Yeah, it's pretty brutal," said Matt, opening the door to his room and holding it for Callie. She stepped inside.

"Wow," she sighed, making herself comfortable on the leather couch. "I really hope we both make it before our sophomore year."

A dreamy expression passed across Matt's face as he savored the way she had said "our" before "sophomore year."

"Especially since by sophomore year," she was saying, rousing Matt from his trance, "we might be busy punching Final Clubs. Which one do you think you'll join?"

"I don't think I'll be joining any of them," he answered, his expression turning serious. "I'm just not okay—"

"What?" someone yelled from one of the bedrooms.

"Oh! Not talking to you buddy, sorry!" Matt yelled back.

"Bloody hell, not again. . . ."

Matt chuckled. "No matter how hard we try, that just keeps happening. Anyway, as I was saying, I'm just not *comfortable* with the fact that the male clubs don't allow women to join and that they only let girls inside the building based on the shortness of their skirts."

"Hey! That's not *entirely* true," Callie cried. "There are a few all-female clubs, and plenty of women get invited to the parties because they are *friends* with members, regardless of skirt length."

"That may be," said Matt, making a visible effort to keep the jealousy out of his voice, "but I still wouldn't want a woman I cared about to go to some of those parties, and Callie"—this was the moment of truth—"I care about *you.*"

Suddenly the door flew open and Gregory strolled into the room.

"Am I interrupting something?" he asked, throwing his backpack onto the couch so that it almost hit Callie, landing next to her with a loud thunk.

"Not at all!" she cried, leaping to her feet. "I was just on my way out, actually. Have to do some reading for the Nineteenth-Century Novel before the meeting."

"Jane Austen?" said Gregory. "She's my favorite. Everybody likes *Pride and Prejudice*, but I've always felt that *Persuasion* is vastly underrated."

"Oh, *please*," Callie muttered, rolling her eyes—as if *he* even knew how to read. "So, I'll pick you up at two forty-five?" she asked Matt.

"Oh . . . you're taking him out on a date? Isn't that sweet," said Gregory.

"It's a meeting, not a date," she said through gritted teeth. She pulled the door shut behind her.

Matt let his face fall into his hands. "You know what, Gregory?"

"What?"

"Sometimes you really *suck*."

Gregory grinned. "Thanks."

Callie had been reading for barely five minutes when Mimi walked into the common room looking jittery and frazzled.

"Cigarettes," she muttered, "need some cigarettes . . . No, no, you already had two packs today. . . . Coffee? *Oui* . . . need some coffee . . ."

"Mimi?"

"Callie, darling, I was just looking for you—I need some coffee—cannot concentrate at all—want to come with? My treat?"

"Uhm . . ." Getting coffee was probably the last thing that

Callie felt like doing, but something in Mimi's expression made her pause.

"All right," she agreed, putting down her book.

A cold blast of wind assaulted them as they stepped onto the street, and Callie pulled the collar of her thin fleece closer around her neck, cursing the New England weather and cursing Mimi—then cursing herself for not changing out of her skimpy gym clothes. And she'd just been getting to the good part of the book, too: in, wouldn't you know it, *Pride and Prejudice*. She'd already read it about a thousand times, but it was still classic, still a masterpiece. But *Persuasion*? It's totally sophomoric. Underrated, my ass . . .

To make matters worse, the line at Peet's Coffee was dauntingly long. What she wouldn't give to be back in the fictional realm of the drawing room at Netherfield Park instead of here in the real world with Mimi. Sighing, Callie tried to think of an excuse to leave. . . .

"Yeah, I was really confused when I got an invitation to their first punch event," a boy in front of her was saying, adjusting the red scarf around his neck. Even as a Fashion Ignoramus, Callie could still see that with his violently orange hair and copious freckles, this was a very poor choice of accessory.

"I mean, I don't know *anybody* in the PC, I'm not a legacy, I don't wear tuxedos to class, I don't sing in an a cappella group, and I'm not ridiculously rich. But I decided that I ought to check it out anyway—"

"Oh no—don't tell me that you actually went!" his friend

exclaimed, a bucktoothed boy who was unfortunately short and stubby looking.

"I did," said freckle-face, looking down at his hands. "And the members were just as confused as you are about why I was invited. . . ."

"Was it . . . ?" his friend asked in a hushed voice.

"*Lampoon*?" said freckles. "Yeah. They sent about twenty fake invitations to various sophomores, and then the members had to deal with explaining to us why we weren't supposed to be there. They were pretty nice about it, for the most part, but I did overhear someone comment about 'who shows up to this sort of event wearing a band uniform.'"

"What? You wore your *band uniform*? What were you *thinking*?"

"I don't know, I don't know. I had to go straight from practice and . . ."

Their voices faded away as they picked up their drinks and headed toward the door.

Numbly, Callie allowed Mimi to order for her. As of yet, nobody had stolen her homework or refused to compare answers on a problem set, so she had all but forgotten how ruthless her fellow classmates were rumored to be.

It was tragic how much acting and looking the part played a role. But if that's what it takes to succeed, she thought, reaching for her coffee, then that's what I'll have to do. . . . She could hear Vanessa's voice agreeing enthusiastically in her head, reminding her that people can't *see* talent or passion when they first meet you—they can see only how you present yourself. *"I'm not asking you to change your personality, Cal. I'm just asking you to change your clothes!"*

And change them she would, Callie decided, glancing down at her sweaty gym gear. There was still time before the meeting.

Quickly she turned to find Mimi—but before she even knew what was happening, she had spilled the contents of her Nonfat, sugar-free, Venti Vanilla Latte all over the sweater of a boy who had been standing behind her.

Holy crap, not now! She closed her eyes. Opening them, he was still standing there, his telltale camel-colored cashmere practically screaming Burberry. There was no way she could afford to replace it.

Mimi to the rescue! Conjuring some napkins out of nowhere, she patted the boy's sweater, saying "*Oh, mon dieu*, Clint, *je suis désolé*. I am such a terrific klutz that I bumped into Callie and kaput—the fault belongs to me."

All the irritation Callie had felt for Mimi in the past twenty minutes vanished instantaneously. Glancing at her roommate thankfully, she added: "I'm so sorry, too! I didn't even see you standing there! Maybe you could give me your sweater and I could have it dry-cleaned for you?"

A strange expression passed through his gray-green eyes before he said slowly, "Well, that would be a bit awkward, wouldn't it? If I just pulled my sweater off right here and then walked home half naked?"

And that's when Callie, who was trying to figure out if she

was supposed to laugh, really looked at him.

Her stomach dropped. He was the same upperclassman who'd escorted her and Vanessa to the Activities Fair, the same boy whom she had the vague sensation of seeing again somewhere else. . . .

But today it was as if she were finally seeing him for the first time. He was at least a head taller than her, with an athletic build and a huge smile that stretched across his face, causing those adorable crinkles to form around the corners of his eyes. His short, light brown hair was windswept at the moment, and she caught herself actively resisting the urge to reach up and run her fingers through it.

Looks aside, it takes a pretty damn cool guy to stay calm when a stranger has just spilled a boiling venti-sized vat of vanilla-something all over his expensive sweater.

In fact, she thought, drifting further and further into dreamland, I wouldn't mind if you took that sweater off right now and—

Once again: Mimi to the rescue! "Callie, this is Clint. Clint, you remember—"

"I'm Callie," she blurted. "It's a pleasure to meet you—I mean, officially."

Clint smiled: the same odd, indecipherable expression in his eyes. He stared hard at Callie for a full three seconds in a way that made her tug nervously at her running shorts, wondering if perhaps he didn't remember her from the day of the Activities Fair.

"Okay," he said after a pause. "Nice to meet you, too—*officially*. And don't worry about the sweater," he added with a glimmer in his eyes. "It was a gift from my ex-girlfriend, so I was planning to burn it anyway."

e, x: there were no two letters in all of English or mathematics that were more beautiful.

Back inside her room, Callie threw open her dresser drawers and pulled out a pair of Seven jeans that Vanessa had given her because they were "getting too small."

"Actually, they never really fit me in the first place," Vanessa had confided as she forced Callie to accept them. "I was trying to subscribe to the whole buy-a-really-expensive pair-of-jeans-that-are-one-size-too-small-as-an-incentive-to-lose-weight strategy, but it obviously didn't work out. . . . Take them, seriously, or they'll go to waste."

Her clock read 2:53. Shit, she thought, rifling through her shirts. Quickly she chose a white Ralph Lauren sweater that was also on loan from Vanessa, who enjoyed playing "Fairy Godmother" to Callie: her own personal Cinderella doll.

In a final moment of inspiration Callie reached for the nonprescription reading glasses that Jessica had given her right before their college interviews so that she would look "well, less blond." Glancing in the mirror, Callie decided that she seemed very fashionably journalistic indeed. Perfect. If only Clint could see her now . . .

Skipping down the stairs as fast as possible, she crossed the Yard and made her way toward the *Crimson* headquarters. A sign on the front door pointed her to the *FM* information session.

She was a few minutes late, but fortunately the meeting had yet to begin. She smiled as Vanessa waved at her from the back of the room, where she'd been saving a seat.

As Callie settled into her chair, a girl standing at the front of the room began to speak—a girl whom Callie quickly recognized.

Alexis Thorndike.

"Hello, everyone, and welcome to the first official COMP meeting for *Fifteen Minutes* magazine. As most of you already know, I'm Alexis Vivienne Thorndike, and I will be your COMP director over the following months. Most people call me 'Lexi,' but to you guys, I am God."

A few people started to laugh.

But they shut up very quickly.

"In the future," she added, addressing no one in particular, "please try to be on time."

Callie felt herself go pink. I was only two minutes late, she thought, feeling bad about it nevertheless.

Vanessa leaned over, her expression grave: "Remember what I said about not getting on her bad side, Cal," she hissed. "Make no mistake: she will destroy you."

Callie swallowed.

"Don't stress about it too much, though," Vanessa offered consolingly. "Word on the street is she's been a complete bitch ever since Clint Weber dumped her a few weeks ago, so I wouldn't necessarily take her hostility personally."

Callie nodded, removing her glasses—which were starting to hurt her eyes—so that she could get a better look at her COMP director.

Alexis was not too tall and not too skinny, but perfectly proportioned and immaculately dressed. A thin headband with a tiny side bow rested delicately across silky brown hair that fell in beautiful ringlets all the way down to the middle of her back. Everything about her glowed: feminine, spotless, and white, from her dainty Milly blouse to her soft, fair skin and a smile where full lips parted to reveal small even teeth. Standing at the front of the room, she looked radiant, almost angelic: as if she could do no wrong, as if she could accomplish anything.

Clint Weber, Callie etched in the corner of her notebook, biting her lip as she wondered . . . could this be the same Clint she'd bumped into—literally—earlier?

"Clint Weber—could you Facebook him?" she asked Vanessa. After spending several weeks together, her roommate's creepy stalker habits were starting to rub off.

"Sure," Vanessa murmured, reaching into her Fendi tote and pulling out her beloved iPhone.

Callie continued to watch Alexis—Lexi—with fascination. What was it about her that made it impossible to avert your eyes?

Maybe it's the way she looks so confident up there in front of the room . . .

"Every week you'll be asked to submit five pieces to the editors for review," Lexi explained in a sweet, clear voice, flashing a smile at the eager freshmen and nodding to the dedicated sophomores who hadn't made the cut last spring but had come back, determined, for round two.

Or the way she dresses, like, perfectly . . .

"The editors will return your pieces with their written feedback and a list of your assignments for the following week," she continued. "Then, on the last Saturday in October, you will submit a portfolio with ten samples of what you consider to be your best work." As she spoke, Lexi began to walk, strolling up and down the aisles.

Or it could be the way her long, thick curls bounce when she moves. . . . Callie thought, admiring Lexi's grace as she stepped lightly—like a dancer—in her Chanel flats. They were a pearly shade of ivory, with two interlocking golden Cs above the toe.

"After we've had a chance to review your first portfolios, only half of you will be asked to continue. You'll have a few weeks to prepare a collection of new pieces for your second portfolio, which you will submit before we leave for Thanksgiving break. Only a fraction of you will remain in the running for the third and final round. Then we, the editors, will make our last cuts and you—if you survive this long—will find out if you made it after winter break."

Callie suddenly noticed somebody standing in the frame of the doorway, watching her.

It was Matt.

Shit! She had completely forgotten to pick him up before the meeting. *"I'M SORRY!"* she mouthed. Matt frowned and then vanished down the hall.

"Dammit I need a newer version of this phone!" Vanessa muttered. "The internet is so freaking slow. . . . Download, dammit!"

Vanessa's eyes were glued to her phone so intently that she didn't notice Lexi, who was now—Callie registered with dismay—less than fifteen feet away.

Callie nudged Vanessa, who remained fixated on her phone as Lexi, still speaking fluidly, moved closer and closer, until she was so close that Callie could see the whites of her big brown eyes.

In a final act of desperation Callie elbowed Vanessa *hard*—so hard, in fact, that her phone flew out of her hands and landed facedown on the floor with a heart-stopping clatter.

Lexi stooped to retrieve it. "Here you go," she said, smiling sweetly as she extended the phone toward Callie.

Bitchy? thought Callie, relief sweeping over her. What was V talking about? She seems perfectly nice to me—

"What the . . ." Lexi muttered, the smile melting off her face. Her hand had frozen in midair, clutching Vanessa's phone. All three of them could now see the image that had just finished downloading onto the screen.

His hair had been much shorter in person than it appeared in his profile picture, but still there could be no mistake: Clint the Coffee Victim and Clint Weber were one and the same.

Vanessa gasped.

As if the siren song had ceased, they caught a glimpse of the beautiful, blue-blooded Lexi transforming into something terrible and strange. It didn't last longer than a heartbeat, but Callie was certain that Lexi had given her a look of death.

As the phone slipped through Lexi's fingers and crashed onto the hardwood floor, it split in two with a sound that ricocheted around the room. The screen turned a Do-Not-Resuscitate shade of black.

"Oh, my bad!" said Lexi. "I'm very, *very* sorry about that." And the Oscar goes to—

"From now on, though," she continued as she faced back toward the front of the room, "let's all try to do a better job of paying attention while I'm speaking."

For a moment Callie and Vanessa sat silent, watching Lexi walk away.

"Callie," Vanessa whispered in a tone you'd use at a wake. "Why didn't you tell me that the person you hooked up with at Calypso was Clint Weber?"

"What!" Callie spat back.

"*Clint Weber*! Sketchy McKisserson? Foxy McFoxerson? They-are-all-the-*same PERSON*!"

Realization dawned like lightning: that light brown hair ruffling in the breeze at the Activities Fair, the same brown hair that had obscured a pair of light green eyes as he leaned in to kiss her on the couch, the same green eyes that had stared at her with such a strange look in the coffee shop, the look that had been, finally, recognizable in the photo on Vanessa's phone . . .

Suddenly Callie's own phone vibrated from somewhere deep in the bottom of her book bag.

Oh god, not now . . . she prayed, digging frantically. Fortunately, it had only vibrated once, meaning: 1 new text message.

She didn't recognize the number.

She flipped open her phone. Vanessa leaned in to look over her shoulder.

I can't believe you didn't recognize me from the other night—I didn't realize my haircut was THAT drastic. I enjoyed being assaulted by you today. Let's do it again sometime!

—Clint

"Callie," Vanessa whispered mournfully. "You're done for."

EIGHT

PUNCH

WEDNESDAY, OCTOBER 13

8:15 P.M.

2 GARDEN STREET

COCKTAIL ATTIRE

THE HASTY PUDDING SOCIAL CLUB, EST. 1770

After a week and a half of covert text messaging Callie had finally agreed to meet up with Clint for a "secret" rendezvous: secret in her mind because she had no intention of telling her roommates and secret on his end because he'd refused to reveal where they were going. She'd received instructions via text an hour earlier to meet him in front of the John Harvard statue at 11:45 P.M. . . . which was precisely thirty minutes from now.

So, while Mimi, Dana, and Vanessa were lounging around taking advantage of their Sunday as a day of rest, she was stuck in her bedroom hurrying to finish a sample story for *FM*, a bit of "investigative journalism" Lexi had ordained involving freshman necklines and hemlines: *"Are they statistically lower and shorter than those of the female upperclassmen?"* And: *"Do we take this as an indicator of greater promiscuous sexual activity or merely as a result of low self-esteem?"*

Seriously? Was this even a real assignment? Callie wasn't fluent in her COMP director's particular dialect of prep school sarcasm, so it was impossible to tell. Blowing a frustrated gust of air through her lips, she turned back to her computer screen, wondering how many rewrites it would take until she finally managed to impress Lexi enough so that she would stop thinking of Callie as the girl who doodled her ex-boyfriend's name on her notebook and iPhone-stalked him during important meetings. . . .

Sometimes freshmen make clueless mistakes when it comes to their ~~love lives~~ clothing choices, she typed. *But please don't hate ~~me~~ them. After all, sometimes a cute ~~boy~~ skirt is too tempting to resist. . . .*

Out in the common room Vanessa was practically drooling as she watched Dana sink her teeth into an enormous slice of pizza. Vanessa didn't need a scale to tell her to avoid eating pizza (diet strategy of the week: fasting for Ramadan—"No, I'm actually *very* spiritual"), but due to her demanding schedule, Dana was stress-eating enough to feed a family of four. Forget the fabled Freshman Fifteen: she was riding a nonstop ticket to the Freshman Twenty-five.

Mimi yawned and poked Vanessa in the side.

"Vanessa!" she cried, waving her hand in front of her roommate's face in order to break the pizza-induced trance. "Vanessa, tell me a humorous story. I am so-oh bored. . . ."

Vanessa hesitated, but then her eyes lit up.

"Oooh, okay, I know! So, yesterday I'm sitting in Lamont Café with a bunch of my old girl friends from school. Well, we're bored, so we decide to play this game called 'Fuck-Chuck-Marry'—you know the game, right?"

Mimi shrugged, and Dana, cringing visibly at the word *fuck*, tried to bury her nose in her laptop.

"Oh, that's right: foreigner, *hello*! Well, anyway, it's pretty simple. I'd name three guys . . . say, OK, Gregory, and Matt, and then you would have to say which one you want to fuck—"

Dana cringed again.

"—which one you want to chuck—off a cliff, that is—and which one you want to marry."

"All right," said Mimi, nodding. "So, let me see . . . I choose Matt for my husband because he is so nice—"

"Ew, *no*," Vanessa cut in, shaking her head. "That was just an example so you could understand the necessary background for the story. So"—she began raising her voice as Mimi scowled—"we're sitting there in Lamont Café playing Fuck-Chuck-Marry and somebody proposes three highly influential politicians who shall remain nameless—"

"Who?" Mimi demanded.

"That's classified information, Mimi, though I'm sure you could guess if you put your mind to it. . . ."

Mimi shrugged again. Dana shifted uncomfortably in her chair.

"So anyway," Vanessa continued, "this girl throws those names out, and *everybody* at the table goes silent—except for me, who starts debating very *loudly* which one I'd like to fuck, who I'd like to chuck, and who, by process of elimination, I'd have to marry. . . . As this is happening, I can't figure out why everyone is staring at me looking nervous and one girl is motioning at me to stop talking, but I keep going, and I'm right in the middle of contemplating the merits of fucking one of them—"

"I thought you said you were a *virgin*?" Mimi interrupted.

"Oh, for christsake Mimi, it's a *game*! Now would you *please* let me finish?"

"Let me guess," Dana piped up suddenly, looking extremely irritated. "One of their daughters was sitting right behind you?"

"How did you—" Vanessa began, looking dumbfounded, as if she'd forgotten that Dana knew how to speak.

"Every 'highly influential politician' has a daughter at Harvard. That's old news. Frankly, I think it's *rude* and indecent to be talking about you-know-what in a *library*."

"What's rude—*talking* about fucking in the library?" Vanessa asked. "What about all the people who are actually *fucking* in the library? It's probably happening right now in Widener as we speak. I hear 'Medieval Weaponry' is a real prime location to—"

"I can't hear you!" Dana screamed, throwing her hands over her ears. "I-can't-hear-you-I'm-not-listening-I-don't-hear-you-LALALALALALALA—"

"Hey, guys!" Callie called, stepping out of her room and making her way toward the front door.

"Where are *you* going?" Mimi asked, sounding accusatory—or maybe that was just Callie's imagination.

"Library," she said, reaching for the doorknob.

"On a Sunday?" Mimi raised one eyebrow. "We never go to the library on Sundays. . . ."

"You look pretty dressed up—even for Lamont," Vanessa said, eyeing her suspiciously.

Callie shrugged.

"Hold on, I'll come with you," said Dana, taking her hands off her ears and standing.

"No—uh—sorry—I have a . . . study group."

Dana frowned, as in, *If there were really a study group, I would have known about it.*

"Study group for *what*?" Vanessa wheedled.

"For economics, okay? I promised I'd meet Matt! And hey, since when do I have to tell you guys everything?" she added as the three of them stared.

Then Vanessa started to nod in a very understanding, very *annoying* way. "She's meeting *Matt*. To *study* . . ." she explained to the other two as if everything suddenly made sense.

"Oooh," said Mimi. "So *that is* why you are all dressed up."

"Dressing up—for the *library*?" Dana erupted out of nowhere. "Study *dates*—in the library? Doing you-know-what—IN THE *LIBRARY?* . . . What is WRONG with you people?" she cried, gripping her head in her hands. "I'm going to study. Actually *study*. IN MY ROOM," she added, slamming her door. Vanessa and Mimi started laughing uncontrollably.

"Yes . . . and *I'm* going to study in the *library*," Callie said, stepping out the door.

"*Sure* you are." Vanessa gasped for breath.

"Have fun!" Mimi called.

It was cold waiting outside in front of the John Harvard statue, but nonetheless Callie was glad she had opted for tights and a skirt instead of jeans. She shivered as the wind blew past, mussing up her hair, which she had arranged with more care and attention than usual. Her hands flew to her head to smooth it out.

A set of soft-gloved hands suddenly covered her eyes.

"Guess who?"

"Clint!" she shrieked, leaping around. "Erm—uh—hey," she stammered in a much lower, more casual and—hopefully—cooler tone.

"Hi." He smiled, stepping forward to give her a hug.

His sweater was the softest, warmest, fuzziest thing in the world. It smelled like cinnamon and autumn leaves. She didn't want to let go.

Clint chuckled. "Are you cold or something?"

"Wha— *Oh*—yes, freezing!" she said, realizing that she had in fact held on a bit too long.

"Here," said Clint, unwinding a maroon cashmere scarf from around his neck and draping it across her shoulders. "Allow me."

She stood still, averting her eyes so as not to stare while he knotted the scarf at her neck.

"How's that?" he asked.

"Much better."

"You sure? We could stop for coffee or a hot chocolate on our way. . . ."

"Coffee?" she echoed vaguely, glancing at his sweater. "We'd better not risk it."

Clint laughed. "Good point. Shall we, then?" he asked, offering his arm.

She accepted it and they began to walk. "So, where are you taking me?" she asked.

"If I told you that, it would ruin the surprise!"

Instead of heading toward Harvard Square they were moving deeper and deeper into campus. They finally stopped in front of the Science Center. Clint stepped forward to get the door—and she was surprised to see that it wasn't locked, even though it was almost midnight.

"Oh, I get it! You need help with your homework," she teased. "It's all right—no need to be embarrassed, asking a freshman. . . ."

"Hush, you," he admonished, taking her hand.

Wandering through the building, they made their way toward the elevator bank in the back. A night watchman guarded the entrance.

"Evening, Clint," he said with a tip of his hat.

"Hiya, Miles, how ya doing?" Clint asked.

"Can't complain," Miles answered. "Good night for lookin' at the stars, eh?" he added, winking at Callie.

Reaching into his wallet, Clint retrieved a small card with his picture in the corner, and the words *Astronomy Club*: *MEMBER* written across the top.

Astronomy Club?

Miles glanced at the card, nodded, and waved them through.

"So!" Callie said once they were inside the elevator. "You must be what they refer to as a closet nerd?"

"Hey, don't knock it till you try it."

The elevator stopped on the very top floor.

"Penthouse, mademoiselle," he said, keeping one arm pressed against the elevator doors and ushering her into the hall.

There was a door at the end of the hallway. It unlocked with a click as Clint ran his card across the scanner, the door popping open to reveal a tiny, circular staircase winding up.

At the top Callie found herself inside a dome-shaped room. The walls were completely black except for a few colorful posters of planets and pictures of the galaxy. In the center a huge cylindrical case—big enough to fit at least three people inside—extended from the floor all the way to the ceiling.

"What is this place?" Callie asked, examining what looked like a supercomputer resting on one of the desks along the wall.

"A well-kept secret," Clint replied. "Open only to graduate astrophysics students and members of the Astronomy Club."

"How many members are there in the Astronomy Club?"

"Well, our numbers have fluctuated over the years, and we had to start denying applications due to the club's popularity," Clint said, laughing. "But . . . as of right now, you're looking at it."

"You're the only one? That's the lamest thing I've ever heard!" she cried, meaning exactly the opposite.

"Yep." He grinned. "Now check this out. . . ." He pushed a button on one of the desks and the black walls suddenly started to slide open, revealing the midnight sky.

He pushed another button and the cylindrical case in the middle of the room began rotating slowly. A ladder descended from the ceiling, leading up to a platform placed directly underneath an enormous telescope.

"After you," he said.

When Callie reached the top, she was level with the telescope: advantageously situated in front of an observation deck with seating designed for two. Their own personal love seat.

Clint joined her and started fiddling with the telescope. Pulling it closer, he aimed it toward the gap in the ceiling, focusing the lens.

"Go ahead, have a look," he said.

She could see lots of stars and a big reddish mass that looked like it might be a planet. "It's beautiful," she said, turning and offering the telescope to Clint.

He pulled it toward him and pressed his eye to the glass.

"What's that big red, blobish thing?" she asked.

"Blobish thing?" He laughed, leaning back. "Mars. Though personally I think 'big red blobish thing' is far more descriptive. Perhaps we should write in, ask them to change it?"

"Sure," she agreed. "I never cared much for '*Mars*,' anyhow."

"Oh yeah? What's your favorite planet?"

"Uh . . . Earth? Obviously?" She laughed. "You?"

"Pluto. Without a doubt."

"But Pluto's not even a planet!"

"Stop!" Clint said, pretending to look scandalized. "I don't think I can date a girl who doesn't appreciate the awesomeness of Pluto. We were robbed."

"So—this is a date."

"Maybe. Now I'm not sure," said Clint, wrapping his arm around her shoulders.

"Well, what about the stars?" she asked, glancing back through the telescope. "Can you tell me anything about the stars?"

"Uhm . . . okay. Now let's see. . . . That one up there is Orion's . . . Shoe. And see a little to the left: that's Cassandra. And that funny *blobish thing* on her right is a purse: Cassandra's Purse. It's one of the most famous constellations in the, uh, aurora borealis."

Callie stared at him, incredulous.

"And what about that one?" she demanded.

"Which one? Oh, that one's easy—that's the Little Brown Dog."

"The Little *Brown* Dog? Why is the dog brown?"

"Because during the big bang, the, uh, gaseous chemicals that were released in that constellation family had a distinct brownish color—"

"You're making this up, aren't you?"

"Of course," he said, laughing as she whacked him on the arm. "To tell you the truth, my specialty is the planets, not the constellations. . . . Mostly I just like coming up here and looking out the telescope," he continued. "It's the only place on campus where I feel alone . . . away from it all."

Turning, he looked at her. "You probably haven't been around long enough to realize, but people tend to get too wrapped up in the whole Harvard thing. I really do love it here, but sometimes a guy just needs a break."

Oh, if only he knew how much his words were resonating, even though it hadn't even been two months . . .

She thought about all of the outfits that Vanessa had forced her to borrow, all of the times she'd felt embarrassed in front of people like Gregory without knowing why, the way all of the kids who grew up in New York or went to private school seemed to speak their own secret language . . . and she thought she knew exactly what Clint was talking about.

"So, if this is your special place where you come to be alone, why'd you bring me?" she asked.

"Because," he answered, turning to look at her, "*you* are not a Harvard girl. Or at least not a typical one from some East Coast prep school who's too privileged to notice that she's studying at the greatest institution in the world and thinks the only thing that matters is her social life. What's the point of having advantages if you're not going to take advantage of them?

"Anyway, there's no way a girl who runs around coffee shops in her gym clothes—spilling on innocent victims, might I add—and wears flip-flops to a party is going to take two and a half hours to get ready."

"So, what you're saying is you brought me here because I'm a messy, sloppy klutz?"

"Exactly. And I mean that in a good way. Don't ever change."

Callie smiled. It was quite possibly the nicest compliment anyone had ever given her.

Now was the point in the date where he was probably going to try to kiss her. Any moment now it was going to happen, and she was ready for it; she was waiting. In fact, she was dying for it to happen . . . and it would . . . any minute now. . . .

Hell, it wasn't like it was their first time—what was he waiting for?

Ah, there we go. . . . the lean-in . . . the hair tuck . . . the cheek brush . . . the long look . . . any moment now it was going to—

Beep, beep, beep. Clint's phone vibrated angrily in his pocket. Flipping it open, he frowned.

"I'll call he—them back later," he muttered, pushing the button to Ignore. "Sorry," he added, sticking the phone back in his pocket.

"No worries," Callie answered. Tentatively she moved her hand so it was resting above his knee—

Abruptly Clint stood.

"Hey, we'd better get going! It must be *way* past your bedtime, freshman." He was smiling, but he was already halfway down the ladder.

What the fuck? WTF?!?@#?$#?@???

The walk home was relatively silent save for the sound of the leaves crunching under her feet. Crushed—kind of like her expectations for the evening. When they reached the door to her entryway, he turned to face her. He leaned in. Her pulse quickened, but with a hug and a promise to call, he was gone.

FTW?!?@#?$#?@???

She was not in a good mood by the time she reached the top of the stairs. In fact, so preoccupied was she by thoughts of her date—well, really, the end of her date (if you could call it a "date") because the rest of it had been *perfect*—hadn't it, *hadn't it?*—that she almost didn't notice the two white envelopes sticking halfway out from under the door.

Stooping, she snatched them up. In ornate calligraphy they were addressed to:

Vanessa Von Vorhees
Wigglesworth C 24

and:

Marine Aurélie Clément
Wigglesworth C 24

"Mimi! Vanessa!" she yelled as she walked into the common room. "You've got mail!"

"Oooh, I wonder if this is what I think it is," Vanessa said, her eyes lighting up. Even Mimi looked excited as she tore hers open, which was unusual given her equilibrium state of spiritual ennui.

"Oh my god!" cried Vanessa, reading her letter and then hugging Mimi ecstatically. "We're going to punch together! Oh, I knew it! I so knew it!"

"Who are you going to punch?" Callie asked as her roommates began to scream and jump up and down.

As casually as possible, she sidled back over to the front door, scanning the ground. Glancing over her shoulder, she opened the door and double-checked the hallway. It was empty.

Wandering back into the room, she sank onto the couch. She felt invisible, a blip on the social radar that was fading away fast. Soon she would be just as obsolete as VCRs, bell-bottoms, and landlines. . . .

Mimi was the first to notice.

"Oh!" she said, giving Vanessa a meaningful look. "These are just some punch invitations for the Pudding . . . no big deal. . . ."

"No big deal?" cried Vanessa. "Of course it's a *big* deal! This is the Hasty Pudding Social Club we're talking about here: getting in is the first step to punching the Isis or the Bee, and from now on we'll be invited to all the Final Club parties!"

"The Pudding?" asked Callie, vaguely remembering something.

"It's the only social club on campus that's coed and admits freshmen," Mimi explained, trying to look sympathetic. "It is really not that cool."

"Not that cool?" Vanessa was oblivious. "Are you forgetting about

the clubhouse? And all the upperclassmen *boys* who are also members? What about all the lunches and dinners and parties?"

"Yes, there are those, too," Mimi said, giving Vanessa another significant look as Callie sank deeper and deeper into the couch. "But members can bring guests whenever they want so . . ."

At the word *guests* a lightbulb suddenly switched on in Vanessa's head.

"Oh, Callie," she said in a voice that, instead of cheering Callie up, made her feel ten times worse.

"Dana did not receive one either?" Mimi offered.

Make that twenty times worse. No, more like a hundred. Billion. Squared.

"Where is Dana, anyway?" Callie asked, noticing that the door to her room was open.

"She said she was going to Adam's to study, and by god, I think she meant it literally," Vanessa said, smiling at her own little joke.

Oh, right, of course. Even Dana had a boyfriend to keep her company; whereas Callie had no one: no boyfriend, no invitations, no friends. . . .

"Callie," Vanessa said, sitting down next to her on the couch. "Callie, just say the word and I—we," she added, glancing at Mimi, who nodded her assent, "won't go." Vanessa swallowed hard, watching Callie as if she'd just bet her entire life savings on Red and was watching the roulette wheel spin slowly toward Black.

"No, of course you guys have to go. It's no big deal. . . . You guys can, like, invite me as a guest sometimes or something. . . ."

"Certainly—*if* we get in, that is," Mimi said. "You never know, do you? I have probably accidentally kissed so many other people's lovers by now that there is no telling what could happen."

"Oh, Mimi!" Vanessa snapped, reverting back to her old self. "Of *course* we're going to get *in*! I mean, you're *you*, and I went to high school with half of the members. . . ."

"Don't worry, Cal," she said. "Once we're in, we'll do everything we can for you during the spring punch season."

"*Oui*," agreed Mimi. "*If* we get in, we should have no trouble punching you next semester. As long as you do not do anything to piss off a member and get yourself blackballed, it should be fine—"

She stopped talking abruptly at the look on Vanessa's face.

"Oh god . . ." said Vanessa, "I completely forgot that Lexi's in the Pudding and . . ." She stared hopelessly at Callie.

" . . . and I made out with her ex once," Callie finished. Once and only once.

"Well, you did not *know* he was her ex when you did it!" Mimi said. She started to giggle. "I cannot *believe* that you did not remember him that day you spilled your drink all over his sweater! I thought you were *acting*, and I was just trying to play along—"

Ugghhh . . . Clint was the *last* thing she wanted to talk about.

Now Vanessa was laughing, too. Still giggling, Mimi looked at her expectantly. Callie tried to force a smile. It wouldn't come. Instead, all she could think about was the price of a plane ticket back to California: one-way, please. If only she could turn back the clock, go back to high school where girls went out of their way to be friends with her and guys were always pulling crazy stunts to attract her attention, even when she was with Evan . . . Evan . . . If she actually owned a time machine, she would arrange to make an additional stop on her way to the Globe Theatre to watch Shakespeare performed in the Elizabethan era, and instead of saying yes when Evan first asked her out, she would punch him in the face.

Maybe wanting a new boyfriend was a dumb idea after all. Maybe all men were assholes, prone to evil behaviors and evil things.

Speaking of evil, at that instant the front door flew open and Gregory, followed by OK, strolled in wearing matching grins, identical white envelopes in hand.

Gregory noticed Callie and a look of sympathy—sarcastic, no doubt—stole across his face. "Surely you must have been invited, Callie?" he asked, adopting a tone of mock kindness and pretending to be disappointed.

"Have to get back to my research," she muttered, standing up and heading toward her bedroom. Well, at least he'd called her Callie. Without *really* meaning to she slammed the door behind her.

Sinking into her desk chair, she stared blankly at her computer screen: *Hemlines and Necklines: It's a Personal Choice.*

This was all Lexi's fault. . . . Lexi knew that Callie was after her boyfriend (well, congratulations—no real worries there), and she had made it her mission to socially annihilate her.

Slamming her computer shut, Callie stood up and walked over to her bed. Plopping down, she grabbed *The House of Mirth*, her new favorite book from English class, and began flipping angrily through the pages.

> It is less mortifying to believe one's self unpopular than insignificant, and vanity prefers to assume that indifference is a latent form of unfriendliness.

Yeah . . . it was much more likely that everybody just forgot about her. Regardless, Lexi was still a b—utthead. A *butthead* with great hair, perfect skin, clothes straight out of *Vogue*, and the only boy Callie found interesting at Harvard locked down on speed dial #1. Well, maybe not the *only* boy, but *he* didn't count. . . .

Just then she thought she heard a light tapping on her door.

"What do y— *Oh*!" she cried, leaping off her bed. *The House of Mirth* tumbled to the floor.

"Hey," said Gregory, bending to pick it up. Then he closed the door behind him.

Her breath caught in her chest. She took a step backward, bumping into her desk.

"What's up?" she asked, taking the book and trying to breathe normally. For the first time she noticed exactly how tiny her bedroom was—the bed, currently unmade, the most prominent thing in the room.

"I just came in to see . . ." He paused, watching her shove Edith Wharton back onto the shelf. "You arrange your books by genre and . . . publication date?"

"No, actually by genre and the title's rank on my list of favorites. I mean, it's not like a *written* list—well, okay, there *is* a copy on my computer. . . ."

Why—WHY—had she confessed this aloud? And to him? And why was she still talking?

"That's so—" he began.

"Dorky? I know."

"I was going to say *cute*. . . ."

Cute? Sarcasm, maybe?

"And dorky, yes."

Sarcasm, definitely.

"So you like Feynman?" he asked, pulling a book from the popular science section.

She opened her mouth intending to lecture him about touching other people's things, but instead she said, "Yeah. *Surely You're Joking* is one of my favorites. Mine and my dad's. We must have read it out loud together like a billion times."

Gregory smiled in a funny sort of way as he thumbed through the pages. "That must have been nice."

"What, you and your parents never read together?"

Gregory shrugged. "The only thing my dad ever reads are the stock reports in the *Wall Street Journal*, and my step-mom . . . Well, let's just say I'm not even sure she knows how. That's probably why she flunked kindergarten."

Callie laughed. "Ah, Step-mom . . . Thank goodness we haven't gotten there yet. Though, with my dad, he's more likely to pledge eternal love to Euclid or Pythagoras than remarry a twenty-five-year-old. . . ." Was this it? Were they finally having a real conversation? "How old were you when—"

"I should get going," he said abruptly, returning the book to its position on the shelf.

"Why did you even come here in the first place?" she asked, not really expecting an answer, not really bothering to keep the edge out of her voice.

"Oh," he said. For the first time since she'd known him, he looked caught off-guard. "I just came in to ask if you were . . . uh, if I could have a copy of your Justice notes? I missed class on Thursday, and I'd ask OK, but he's kind of an idiot, and I know how thorough you are. . . ."

Why was he asking for her notes at the same time that he made fun of her for being a good student! Or wait, no: was that supposed to be a compliment? Or—

"So could you just e-mail them to me? I really have to run."

"Uh . . . sure," she said.

"Thanks. It's gbolton@fas. Well . . . see ya," he said, slipping through the door.

Shaking her head, Callie sat down at her desk. She logged into her e-mail. There was a new message waiting for her:

From:	**Evan Davies**
To:	**Callie Andrews**
Subject:	Update

Hey Cal,
I tried explaining that it was just some stupid high school dare and that nobody was ever meant to see it other than the graduating seniors on the soccer team. But my big brother just won't listen to me. He said that we need the points in order to secure a win in the scavenger hunt we're doing for initiation. I'm trying to make him see reason, but if he doesn't I promise I'll take care of it one way or another. Please call if you need anything. I am so sorry about all this. Really, I am.
Evan

Numbly she picked up her cell phone and dialed Jessica's number. Jessica answered on the third ring.

"Callie! I haven't heard from you in over a week! Where the hell have you been, girl?" Her voice sounded so warm and sunny that Callie immediately burst into tears.

"Callie—what's wrong?" Callie had never cried in high school—not even when her parents announced their decision to divorce. But now, ever since she'd started at Harvard, it seemed like she was on the verge of tears almost every time that she called.

"Jess, do you remember when Evan and I got keys to the soccer team locker rooms—right after we both made captain?"

"Yes . . . ?"

"And do you remember when I told you how we used to sometimes have—uhm—*Captains' Practice*?"

"Yes, but what does that have to do with—"

"Apparently he told some people, too. Ted, Jerry, a couple of seniors on the team—only they didn't believe him, and so they told him to *prove it*. . . ."

It felt good to finally confess.

NINE

Sealed With a Kiss

From: **Theresa Frederickson**

To: **Callie Andrews**

Subject: Where are you??

Callie sweetie,
Where are you? Are you OK? Is this the right e-mail address? Neither your father nor I have heard from you in over six days now. . . . Is everything all right? Are you sick? Are your classes too hard? Do you have enough warm clothing? Do you want to come home? Nobody will think any less of you if you decided you needed a break from school and wanted to take a year off. Maybe you're not getting enough sleep. Are you getting enough sleep? I knew I should have been stricter about bedtimes.

Sweetie, you can tell me: is this about Evan? Because if this is about Evan, I have to say that I never liked him, not one bit, and you are much, much better off without him. And take it from me; I've had my share of dealing with incompetent men—no disrespect to your father. He seems to think I should "relax" and "leave you alone." "She's probably just busy!" he says. Well, respectfully, I disagree. Do you know he actually had the audacity to call me a "spaz"? Me? A spaz? I don't even know what that means!

Callie Isabelle Frederickson Andrews, you call me the moment you read this e-mail, do you hear?

I love you.
Mom

From: **Thomas Andrews**
To: **Callie Andrews**
Subject: Please call your mom

Dear Cal-bear,
Please call your mother. When she doesn't hear from you in over a week, she starts calling me at work, asking if I think we should phone the police or book a flight to Cambridge. Did I mention that by "calling," I mean calling every hour?

When you can, send us an e-mail and let us know how you're doing.

Love,
"Yer old man"

From: **Callie Andrews**
To: **Thomas Andrews**
Subject: RE: Please call your mom

Hi Daddy,
Please tell Mom that I AM ALIVE.

And I'm sorry that I haven't written in so long. Harvard is fine, classes are fine—I especially like a course I'm taking called the Nineteenth-Century Novel.

Everything's fine, really; it's just that things are so different on the East Coast that sometimes I feel like I don't belong here. A bunch of roommates got invited to a party and I didn't. . . . I know it's such a stupid thing to be upset about, but I am. I'll live, though. More time to focus on my math homework for economics, right?

Love you too,
Cal-bear

P.S. When I taught you the meaning of the word *spaz* I expected you to keep it private! She really is, though, isn't she? Do you still have friends at the med school? Maybe they can write her a prescription for Xanax.

From:	**Thomas Andrews**
To:	**Callie Andrews**
Subject:	Please call your mom

Glad to hear you're alive; that's great news. Will pass it on, along with prescription meds, to your mother. Oh, she'll love that. I'm sorry I can't offer you more advice on your social life (though if you have any questions about linear algebra, I'm your guy). Just remember what Feynman said: "What do you care what other people think?" That, and if you decide to become an English major, I'll disown you.
—Dad

"Just one kiss . . ." said Gregory, his tone softening suddenly.

"You can't be serious. . . ." she trailed off, forgetting herself and falling into his eyes like Alice tumbling down the rabbit hole: deep down into an abyss that was a maddening shade of blue. . . .

"Hey! I never noticed before," he said, leaning down, "but your eyes are green." He raised his hand, perhaps to brush the hair from her face, and as if he were a hypnotist, her eyelids began to feel heavy. His hand compelled her forward, up closer and closer until her eyes started to close and—

Wait a minute, wait a minute: REWIND.

Callie awoke from a nap with a start on Wednesday evening overcome by the strange sensation that there was something she should be excited about, only she couldn't remember what.

Then it dawned on her: tonight was the Pudding Punch event, and *she* had no reason to feel excited because she had not been invited.

She had, however, listened to both of her roommates talk about it incessantly over the previous few days. Vanessa had been especially bad, running out to get waxed, plucked, trimmed, exfoliated, manicured, moisturized, highlighted, and styled—all in preparation for the *momentous* event.

There was a knock on her door. Callie threw the covers over her head, pretending to be asleep. It was no use. Vanessa flipped on the light and said, "Callie, I know you're awake. Come on, get up! You can't sleep forever. Plus I need your advice on something."

Callie poked only the top third of her head out from beneath the sheets, giving Vanessa a look that clearly said: *What do you want?*

Vanessa was holding two red dresses, one in each hand. "I need you to tell me which one I should wear. *Mimi* seems to think—"

"I can hear you!!" Mimi yelled from the common room.

"—that they look exactly the same! Which one do you like better?"

Callie gazed at Vanessa in disbelief. The dresses were virtually identical.

"The one on the left," she muttered, throwing her head back onto her pillow.

"See?" Vanessa cried as she rushed back into the common room. "I *told* you there is a difference between a red strapless Carolina Herrera dress and a jacquard bustier dress by Dior—they're not even in the same genre!"

Callie almost wanted to giggle. Mimi's reaction had to be priceless.

Sighing, she rolled out of bed and trudged into the common room.

"*Eeiggah!*" Vanessa shrieked, visibly recoiling at the sight of her. Glancing in the mirror, Callie couldn't blame her: she was wearing her oversized gray sweatpants and a tattered long-sleeve shirt, while her hair—which she hadn't washed in three days—stuck out in crazy angles from her head. She didn't care.

She greeted Mimi and then headed toward the cabinet above the refrigerator. Her stomach rumbled angrily. She pulled out a bag of popcorn—extra butter, extra salt—and flung it into the microwave.

While the popcorn exploded in loud, satisfying pops, she glanced over at Mimi. She looked stunning: modeling a dark blue Dolce & Gabbana cocktail dress for Vanessa. Vanessa nodded her approval before slipping into her own gorgeous gown that clung to her curves and made her look dangerously voluptuous.

The clock on the wall read 7:15. There was still an hour left before the event: a cocktail party held at the Pudding's clubhouse on Garden Street. Clearly, Mimi and Vanessa were testing out their outfits early because they were *so excited about the party.* . . .

She pulled her popcorn out of the microwave and tore it open. Those dresses—just two of the dozens both Mimi and Vanessa had in their closets—couldn't have been worth less than three thousand dollars each. How many starving kids in Africa could you feed for that amount? Callie thought bitterly, shoveling handfuls of popcorn into her mouth. The butter was making her fingers greasy, so she wiped them on her shirt. I bet if I were Vanessa, she thought poisonously, I'd be wiping my hands on that dress—wouldn't matter at all, would it, when you can just buy another one?

She wanted to keep thinking self-righteously about Africa, but her mind wouldn't stay focused. . . . She was poor, too, in a different way, and at least *they* didn't have to worry about losing all their friends to the Pudding, never finding a boyfriend, and trying to make it onto some stupid magazine.

Her self-hatred mounted as she continued crunching her

popcorn. She was watching Vanessa whirl and twirl—a reddish blur in front of the full-length mirror—when she thought she heard someone moving around outside in the hall.

With another sigh she pulled herself up off the couch and, popcorn in hand, started toward the door.

Her heart froze. A small white envelope slid across the floor. She sprinted the last few steps and flung the door open, yelling "Hey—wait!" as the boy who had left the invitation raced toward the stairs.

"Clint?"

Clint stopped dead in his tracks. Turning around, he held out both his palms: "Guilty as charged."

Callie was suddenly aware of the popcorn bag she held clenched in her fist and realized, with horror, how she must look.

Instead of continuing down the hallway like he was supposed to, Clint was making his way back. She did her best to shrink into the doorframe, trying to recall the last time that she had brushed her teeth.

He bent and picked up the invitation, which was addressed in the same ornate handwriting that had been scrawled across Mimi's and Vanessa's envelopes.

Callie Andrews
Wigglesworth C24

"Listen," he said, handing her the invitation as the color mounted in her cheeks. "Do you think we could keep this between you and me? All of the invites were technically supposed to go out on Sunday, but there was no way I was going to let the coolest freshman on campus go uninvited."

Then he smiled his incredible eye-crinkling grin, and for a moment Callie forgot everything. Clint wanted her. He had gone out of his way to invite her. And now, there he was: standing on her doorstep and looking at her in a way that made it hard to remember she hadn't showered in days or that her hair was sticking out from her head like pipe cleaners.

"Thank you so much," she said, trying to speak softly so that he wouldn't get a whiff of her breath. She paused. "You know, about the other night . . . You left so quickly, I wasn't sure if you wanted to see me again."

"No, it's not like that," he said. "Sometimes things are just complicated when they should be easy. . . . But this morning I realized that it really should be as simple as I like you and maybe you like me, so I invite you to a party and then you say yes?"

"Yes—but . . . ," she said, pausing again. "About the *other* other night . . . I don't usually drink that much—"

"Stop!" he cried, laughing. "Just say you'll come."

"I'll come."

"Good!" He smiled. "In that case, I'll see you in an hour!"

Her heart still pounding, Callie bounced back into the common room, flinging the popcorn bag into a nearby trash can.

"You guys!" she cried. "Guys—I'm coming, too!"

"What?" said Mimi, emerging from her room wearing only her

underwear and smiling wider than she had smiled all year. "How?"

"I just got the invite. You wouldn't believe who— There must have been some sort of mix-up," she said with a shrug.

"Or *maybe*," said Vanessa, running out of the bathroom, "I was able to work my magic and get you onto the list!" She squealed and clapped her hands. "I didn't want to tell you in case it didn't work, but I spoke with a girl I know from the Hamptons who is also on the board and I just happened to mention your name. . . .

"Still," she added, paving the road to hell with good intentions, "I wouldn't get your hopes up. From what I hear, it's very hard to get in if you're an addition to the original Punch list."

Callie wasn't going to let anything spoil the moment. She didn't care if she made it to the second event—rumored to be a luncheon at the clubhouse followed by a final cocktail party—she was just so happy to be invited . . . and to be invited by Clint.

After taking the fastest shower of her entire life, she ran into her room and pulled out the fanciest thing she owned. It was the black minidress with a silver sequin top that she had worn to her high school graduation party, and even though it had been heavily discounted, it still made her look like a million bucks—or so she hoped.

She brushed her hair until it shone like platinum, then dabbed on light makeup and fastened some cheap, silver costume jewelry in her ears and around her neck.

Ready, she stepped into the common room.

"Wow . . . ," Vanessa said, her eyes opening wide. An odd look flickered across her face, almost as if she was—was it possible?—

jealous. Callie blinked, certain she'd imagined it as Vanessa continued: "You look . . ."

"Great," said Mimi. "Really, really great. I am *pink* with envy!"

Vanessa laughed as Callie looked nervously at her dress. "Really? It's not too much?" Callie asked.

"Not at all!" Vanessa cried. "It's just that I don't think either of us is used to seeing you in anything other than a T-shirt and jeans."

"Ha! Yes," agreed Mimi. "You are usually a terrible dresser. *Absolument terrible.*"

"Thanks," said Callie, laughing.

"And those awful flip-flops that you always w—" Vanessa froze midsentence when she noticed the shoes in question on Callie's feet. "Oh my god—no—absolutely not. Be right back . . ."

In a moment, she returned, brandishing a pair of black stilettos.

Callie accepted them gratefully. She put them on. They fit perfectly.

"I'm *so* glad that all three of us are going tonight," Vanessa said. "Nothing could be more fabulous!"

Battling perilous cobblestones, the girls made their way across the Yard hand-in-hand, past Cambridge Commons, and onto Garden Street. A few minutes later Callie found herself staring at the front door of a large Victorian-style house. The three girls squeezed hands and then walked into the Pudding.

It looked less like a mix-and-mingle cocktail party and more like a reunion between old friends. All the members—denoted as such by the color on their name tags—already seemed to know all of the guests—or if they hadn't actually met them in person yet, they had at least memorized their names, family background, and hometown (New York City, nine times out of ten).

Callie had no way of knowing, but the fall semester Punch event was more of a formality than anything else: spots had already been reserved for people from established families and prep schools across the East Coast, with a few places set aside for students of international prominence and fewer still for people from non-eastern states with a lot of electoral votes, like Texas and California. As Vanessa had predicted, nearly every invitee was automatically guaranteed admission. Only a handful of individuals were up for discussion. They were considered to be a group of "dark horses," and Callie was the darkest of them all.

Alexis Thorndike stood out from the center of the crowd, looking immaculate in her navy blue striped Chloe dress cinched at the waist by a wide brown belt. She was ignoring all the admiring looks she was getting. Instead, she had eyes for only one person, and that person was Callie.

Callie glanced to her left and then to her right: casting around desperately for Mimi or Vanessa. Unfortunately, they were both off at opposite ends of the room: Mimi surrounded by a group of upperclassman boys, Vanessa kissing up to the female members of her private school family tree. OK and Gregory weren't there yet, and Clint was nowhere to be found.

She was alone. And her feet hurt. How did anyone ever manage in heels?

Lexi, on the other hand, was surrounded by a gaggle of girls, including Anne Goldberg, to whom she was muttering fiercely, staring daggers all the while.

"Hi, I'm Brittney," a girl to Callie's left said, smiling. Name tag: Red. Member.

"Callie," said Callie, pointing to the blue square on her chest.

"So, Callie, where are you from?"

"I'm from Westwood, California."

"Oh, very cool. Did you go to Harvard-Westlake?"

"No."

"Oh. The Marlborough School?"

"No . . ."

"Brentwood? Archer?"

"West Hollywood High," said Callie, putting her out of her misery.

"Is that . . . is that a *public school*?"

"Last time I checked."

"Oh . . . Oh! Your dad's that producer guy, you know, the one who, like, did all those movies—God, those were hilarious!"

"Uh, no . . . he's a professor at UCLA."

Brittney, nearly out of options, was starting to think exit strategies. "So, uhm, who do you know here?"

"Well, there are my roommates, Vanessa and Mimi, and these two guys who live across the hall, OK and Gregory. . . ."

Oh. She meant members.

"And, uhm, Clint Weber—"

"Clint! Ohmygod, so hot! And so nice," Brittney exclaimed, thankful that she had finally found a common ground. "The thing with Clint is: he's super cute and, like, way smart, but he's almost *too* perfect, like you sort of wonder what must be wrong. . . . But I guess none of that matters because he's *completely* off limits—if you want to live until your senior year," she added, glancing at Alexis.

"Uhm . . . will you excuse me for a minute?" Callie asked.

"Sure," said Brittney, looking relieved.

"Hi, I'm Brittney!" Callie heard her say as Brittney turned to a vaguely familiar blond freshman.

"Elizabeth."

"Elizabeth . . . what a pretty name. Where are you from, Elizabeth?"

"Hancock Park."

"And where did you go to school?"

"The Marlborough School."

"Ohmygod, so you must know . . ."

One foot in front of the other, Callie instructed herself, wobbling in Vanessa's heels as she joined a long line for the bathroom. Like base during a game of tag: as long as she was there, no one would wonder why she wasn't busy socializing.

It was time to face the facts. No matter where she went at Harvard, no matter her accomplishments or achievements, she would never be like Mimi or Vanessa: born into an Old Boys' network in this stupid, exclusive, impossible world that everyone seemed to want to be a part of, *including*, if she was honest with herself, well . . . me.

But she just couldn't picture herself gushing with empty compliments or implying that she had gone to one of LA's elite prep schools and had the money it must have taken to buy the borrowed shoes on her feet. She would have to find her own place, on her own terms. Her dad was right: she shouldn't waste time worrying about what other people thought. The members of the Pudding would either hate her or love her, and if they hated her . . . well, screw 'em.

Oh, but it was so much easier said than done.

She was next in line now, praying that whoever was ahead of her would take a while so she could stay just a little bit longer. . . .

"Toilet's clogged!" a guy called, stepping out of the bathroom. "Can I get a plunger over here?" he yelled at several club members gathered under the archway that led to the main room.

"You'd think that when you're the president you'd no longer get stuck cleaning up other people's shit," he muttered to Callie without really seeing her. Then he noticed her name tag.

"Callie—Callie Andrews, right?"

"Uh . . . yes."

"Tyler Green," he said, holding out his hand. "I hear good things."

"You—you do?"

"Yes." He smiled. Leaning in, he added in a whisper: "Clint's my roommate."

"Oh!"

"He's not here yet, but he should be any minute." Suddenly Tyler seemed to remember where they were. "You don't want to go in there," he said, nodding over his shoulder. "But there's another one upstairs on the left. It's 'members only,' but hey, not for nothing I am the president. PLUNGER! SOMEBODY! NOW!"

Callie smiled weakly. "Uh, nice to meet you. . . ."

"You too. Come find me later when Clint gets here. Remember: upstairs on your left."

She took her time locating the staircase, grateful for the excuse to continue avoiding the event. In a few minutes she'd have to return, but for now she was safe.

Well, not quite.

Gregory emerged from around the corner and stepped down onto the top stair just before she reached it. Stopping, he placed a hand on each banister. She wasn't sure if she had ever been this close to him. There was a tiny scar on the left-hand side of his chin shaped like a miniature crescent moon.

"I didn't know they were going to send a search party," he said. "Or did you finally realize that you just can't live without me—not even for five minutes?"

"I—uhm—you're blocking the way," she said. "Do you mind?"

Instead of moving he just stood there, smiling stupidly. "But 'O, wilt thou leave me so unsatisfied?'"

"What is that? *Romeo and Juliet*?"

"Is it?" He shrugged. "I thought I made it up." He still wasn't moving. "Your line now."

Callie rolled her eyes. "What satisfaction can you—"

"*Canst thou*—"

"—*canst thou* have tonight?"

"A kiss, of course."

She laughed a little in spite of herself. "Only if you move."

They stood for a moment, watching each other.

"Just one kiss . . ." said Gregory, his tone softening suddenly.

"You can't be serious. . . ." she trailed off, forgetting herself and falling into his eyes like Alice tumbling down the rabbit hole: deep down into an abyss that was a maddening shade of blue. . . .

"Hey! I never noticed before," he said, leaning down, "but your eyes are green." He raised his hand, perhaps to brush the hair from her face, and as if he were a hypnotist, her eyelids began to feel heavy. His hand compelled her forward, up closer and closer until her eyes started to close and—

—and he tapped his finger expectantly, once on each cheek.

Callie froze, lips parted in confusion.

"Oh!" said Gregory, his voice aching with amusement. "I forgot that in *California* they don't kiss to say hello! What should we do, then—*dude*—will a high five suffice?" He held up his hand, his eyes alight with triumph.

"*Move*," she breathed, pushing past him. But before she could round the corner, she felt his hand on her shoulder:

"Hey—wait a minute now, I was only kidding," he said without a touch of remorse, his eyes dancing along the lines of her collarbone, down, down across her hips. . . .

"Yeah, *right*," said Callie, her voice trembling. "Look, can't you just leave me alone?"

"I can't, I'm obsessed with you," he said sarcastically. Turning, he walked back down the stairs.

Shaking, she found the bathroom. She slammed the door, locking it behind her. Whirling around to face the mirror, she found a girl the color of a ripe tomato wearing a little black dress staring back at her.

Jamming on the faucet, she wet a towel with cool water and dabbed her face, neck, and arms. Focus, she chided herself. Get a grip! Then she sat down on the edge of the toilet seat and rested her head in her hands: waiting for her heart rate to stabilize. It was a nice bathroom, really . . . no reason she shouldn't stay just a few more minutes . . . or an hour.

Then again, if she spent the entire event locked in the bathroom, *they*—Lexi, Anne, Gregory—would win.

Resolved, she emerged from the bathroom. She walked down the stairs and reentered the main room with her head held high—only to realize: she was alone. Again. What was she supposed to do, walk up to a group of people and interrupt their conversation? And why did every opener she could think of sound like a cheesy pickup line: Is this seat taken? Can I get you a drink? That dress is stunning. . . .

She felt a presumptuous tap on her shoulder.

Didn't I *just* tell him to leave me ALONE? She turned, furious, to really give Gregory a piece of her mind and—

Found Clint. He was grinning from ear to ear, extending a glass of champagne in her direction.

"I didn't realize *you* would be here tonight," he said, his eyes twinkling. "What a pleasant surprise!"

Pleasant indeed. He looked *incredible* in his coat and tie. He smiled. Instantly she relaxed. "You're just all about the surprises, aren't you?" she said.

"I'm not surprised by how beautiful you look tonight."

"Really? I thought you said you liked me messy and dirty?"

"I don't remember using the word *dirty*." He laughed as she started to turn pink. "But there's a time and place for everything."

Callie smiled and sipped her champagne.

"Seriously, though, I'm really glad you could make it. Want to come with me and say hi to some people?"

Clint stayed near Callie for the rest of the night. Placing his hand on the small of her back, he would guide her around the room, introducing her to other members of the Pudding and making sure that her champagne glass was never empty.

Maybe it was the champagne or maybe it was Clint, but Callie felt like a protective shield had been cast around her: any worries or fears were now on Mute. Even Lexi with her jealous stares and angry whispers didn't seem quite so scary anymore.

By the end of the night she was no longer a nameless face. Instead, she had become The Girl Who Clint Weber Couldn't Take His Hands Off Of. It wasn't quite as good as just being Callie Andrews, but it was a start.

"Ready to go?" asked Clint. She nodded slowly as if in a dream.

"C'mon, then . . . I'll walk you home." He held up her coat and helped her into the sleeves. She closed her eyes, allowing him to wrap the jacket around her.

"So you'll let me know about lunch on Tuesday?" Brittney cried, rushing over as they were halfway out the door.

"Sure." Callie smiled. "I'll let you know."

Clint put his arm around her waist as they walked down the steps, and she rested her head on his shoulder. The champagne bubbles had risen from her stomach into her brain, and she couldn't stop giggling as he guided her across the Yard.

When they arrived in front of Wigglesworth's bright green door, Clint turned to face her. He brushed his hand against her cheek, but this time she was determined not to get her hopes up. . . .

Feeling faint, she began rifling through her purse in search of her key card.

She could feel his eyes boring into her, his breath smelling sweetly of champagne. She was searching deeper and deeper within her purse when suddenly, without warning, the thought of Gregory floated into her head. He had been such an *asshole* earlier. He was really nothing compared to Clint. . . . Clint is so per—

Her fingers closed around the edge of something thin and hard.

"Found it!" she cried, brandishing the card victoriously.

"Yes, you did." He smiled, cupping her chin in his hands. And then he found her lips.

TEN

strange interlude

Harvard Dating 101: *What Every Novice Needs to Know*

top ten faux pas
committed by college freshmen

1. When someone asks you if you have "plans for the evening," never just say no: it doesn't make you sound "straightforward," it makes you sound like a loser. Instead, try something along the lines of: "That depends . . . what did you have in mind?"

2. One drink before a date to calm the nerves and loosen the tongue is acceptable; three is sloppy and five means the only date you should be scheduling is one with your sponsor at Alcoholics Anonymous.

3. When embarking on a first date, always make good use of signals and the buddy system: arrange for a friend to call you midmeal and inform you of a potentially dire "family emergency" in the event that the cute guy from your chemistry class doesn't look quite so cute without his lab goggles on or that pretty girl you met in Lamont turns out to be a man-hating Women, Gender & Sexuality major. . . .

4. Never assume that the other person is going to pay. Hello, ladies, this is the twenty-first century here! While personally I'm a bit old-fashioned and allow a man to treat, it is my firm belief that women should always offer–and be prepared–to at least split the bill. If anything, cash and credit cards are always handy in case you need to cab it home once you hear about that pressing "family emergency."

5. Ladies (and Metro-men): Always allocate your wardrobe with care: wearing the same outfit twice in a row was a lot easier back in the day before Facebook became everybody's personal paparazzi.

6. Learn to gauge the intensity of your crushes' feelings based on the type of date he/she has proposed:

a. Study date: probably wants to be "just friends" or they need help with their homework and only asked because you look like a huge nerd

b. Coffee date: testing the waters; alternatively, this person has commitment issues and can't stand to spare more than 15 minutes of their time

c. Lunch date: obviously you're not quite good enough for dinner

d. Dinner date: gettin' pretty serious . . .

e. Dinner and a movie: clichéd but classic–but be cautious that the "movie" doesn't turn into "Hey, why not just watch that movie at my place" because

f. "Wanna come over and watch a movie?"=BOOTY CALL, no exceptions

7. In an era of text messaging, Twitter, GChat, MySpace, and Facebook, the wait-three-days-to-call rule is *so* twentieth century; finding someone you really like at Harvard is rare and calls for immediate action.

8. Never accept a date from a boy/girl that a friend of yours has a serious crush on. Do your best to remember that it's bros before hos and chicks before dicks.

9. It's important to at least give dating at Harvard a try (*ahem* attn: boys who spend most of their nights at BU or BC). There is nothing sweeter in this life than being able to give your children the gift of "double legacy."

10. Don't ever get drunk and hook up with your best friend–it's really not what Plato had in mind.

Happy Hunting,
Alexis Thorndike, Advice Columnist
Fifteen Minutes Magazine
Harvard University's Authority on Campus Life since 1873

Even though it was barely nine o'clock on a Friday morning, the sun was already shining brightly through the dusty windows, casting a glow on the two individuals who were sleeping soundly, side by side. Callie was curled up at an awkward angle, but Matt was stretched out flat on his back. He was smiling.

Bbbbrrrrringgggg! BRrrriinnng! Brrrrinnng!

Callie groaned and rolled over. Her back was aching and her entire body felt sore. She opened one eyelid. There was Matt's face: inches away from her own. Her eyes flew open in horror. *What the hell happened last night?*

"Make it stop. . . ." Matt muttered, groping for her phone.

Looking up: Callie spotted one green desk lamp;

Down: a ratty oriental rug;

Left: stacks of papers scattered across the floor;

Right: empty cans of Red Bull overflowing the trash;

Up again: old newspapers framed and mounted across the walls . . .

The Crimson. Relief swept over her as it all came flooding back: how she and Matt had vowed to pull an all-nighter in order to finish their work for COMP. At some point they must have fallen asleep. . . .

Thank goodness I didn't hook up with him, she thought, well aware that delirium due to sleep deprivation could often lead to bad decisions of which, in the words of Alexis, Plato would not approve. Recently Callie had managed to get back into Matt's good graces, and she didn't need to go messing it all up—though he did look cute in a dorky sort of way with his hair all rumpled and his glasses askew. . . .

His smile seemed forced as he tossed the phone into her lap.

"Score!" she joked as it landed between her thighs.

He smiled ruefully and shook his head, then lay back down, spread-eagled.

"Hello?" Callie said, answering her phone.

"Callie?" Clint's voice crackled over the line.

"Clint! Hi! What's going on?" she asked, straightening up immediately.

"Sorry, did I wake you? I can call back late—"

"No!" Callie cried, jumping from the floor and smoothing her hair as if he could somehow see her through the telephone. "I'm awake, I'm awake, I swear! What's up?"

"Well, again, I'm sorry for calling so early, but I wanted to ask you as soon as possible: do you have any plans for tonight?"

"No, I don't have any plans at all!" Callie cried eagerly—perhaps a little *too* eagerly, because she quickly corrected herself: "Er . . . I mean, nothing *special*."

She began to pace around the tiny office, grinning at Matt, who was still lying disconsolately on the floor.

"Great!" Clint replied. "Then would you like to go to a date event tonight?"

Callie covered the phone's mouthpiece with her hand and did a victory dance. Matt groaned and got to his feet.

"Date event!" Callie squealed.

Matt winced and headed for the door. Callie turned, motioning distractedly that he should stay, but he shook his head and mouthing, "*I'll see you later*," escaped into the hall.

In the meantime Clint was explaining: "Yes, the Bee is having a date event tonight at a club in Boston as part of their third round of Punch."

"The Bee? Doesn't that mean it's going to be a bunch of sophomore girls? I thought freshmen weren't even allowed to go!"

Clint laughed. "Wow, you've only been here for six weeks, but you already know all the rules! Well, according to *my* rules, you are allowed to go, but only if you agree to go as somebody's date."

There was an awkward pause, and his words started to tumble out a little faster: "It's usually a pretty good time. It's a theme party, called the Mad Hatter's Ball, meaning everyone is expected to show up wearing a crazy hat, though there's this one guy who comes every year wearing a chicken suit. . . ." Clint's laugh sounded nervous. Adorably nervous: like he was worried that she might turn him down. (As if anyone in their right mind ever would!)

Speaking faster still, he added: "If you'd feel more comfortable, you can invite Mimi and Vanessa. A couple of my friends still don't have dates and I'm sure they'd be thrilled to take either of your roommates—"

"But *I* would be *your* date, right?" Callie asked.

"Yes!" he exclaimed, sounding relieved. "Yes, fantastic."

"Cool," she said smoothly as a wave of confidence swept over her. "And I *will* bring Mimi and Vanessa—I'm sure they'd love that." (And by "love that" she meant "worship me forever.")

"Great! We'll pick you up tonight in front of Wigglesworth at ten. You just need formal attire and some sort of a hat, the crazier the better."

Callie suddenly thought of something. "Wait—you said it's at a club in Boston? Does that mean we need to have IDs? Because you know . . ." She felt herself starting to blush.

"Relax," he said. "I know you're not twenty-one yet. It'll be taken care of."

"Awesome." Callie yawned, too sleepy to ask for more details. "So, all I need is a dress, a hat, and my roommates, and I'll see you at ten?"

"Right," said Clint. "See you at ten."

Callie was elated. But then, as she gazed at her papers scattered across the floor, the paper cups half filled with stale coffee, and the empty pizza boxes from Pinocchio's overflowing the trash can, her spirits started to sink.

In the corner stood a stack of boxes filled with old *FM* issues from the past ten years that she was supposed to finish archiving before the weekend was up. On the desk she caught sight of a draft of her piece about "Scoping a Campus Character." Lexi's unforgiving red pen had covered it in so many cutting comments that it looked like a wounded soldier bleeding crimson ink.

She sighed. As long as she was in the *FM* offices, forced to write draft after draft of pieces that were never going to appear in the magazine, she felt trapped in Lexi's territory. But it wasn't just limited to the building. Everything worthwhile at Harvard had been annexed under *Queen* Alexis's domain: the *Crimson*, the Pudding, Clint. . . . No matter where she went, she always felt as if she was crossing some invisible boundary.

She needed to get some air. She left the office and headed down the stairs. She should have been thinking about what dress Vanessa might let her borrow and what funky hat she would wear, but instead she couldn't stop obsessing about Lexi.

In the days that followed the Pudding event people who had never noticed her started greeting her in classes or as their paths crossed in Harvard Yard. It seemed her status had gone from "not" to "hot" virtually overnight. Yet nothing about her had changed. She still didn't own the right clothes or purses or shoes. What she did have was the attention of what many of the older girls considered to be the most prized accessory of them all: Clint Weber. She'd refused to look when Vanessa Googled him but could tell from her roommate's expression of silent awe that good looks and Southern charm were not his only assets.

Just last night when she was rushing toward the *Crimson*, a pretty, well-dressed sophomore, clearly an East Coaster, had stopped her in the street to ask where she'd purchased her jeans. Callie had smiled and answered vaguely, "Oh, just some LA boutique off of Rodeo Drive"—a colorful version of the truth, which was, in fact, that she'd owned them longer than she could remember and had no idea where they came from. Frustrated, she wondered why she'd bothered to lie; why she cared what some random girl thought about her stupid jeans.

And then there were the other looks. Maybe she was paranoid

or exhibiting signs of latent schizophrenia and it was all just in her head, but the group of upperclassman girls that sat in front of her in Justice had been awfully cold: shooting her vicious glares during class or ignoring her completely.

Just when she was starting to feel like she was finding her place and even having fun, it was all going to be taken away from her because she had unwittingly crossed the most powerful socialite on campus.

Even with Clint on Callie's side, Lexi would surely find a way to exclude her from the Pudding. Then she'd be left behind while everyone she knew or liked was admitted: Vanessa, Mimi, OK, and Gregory. Gregory . . .

"Gregory!" she blurted in shock as she nearly tripped over him. He was sitting on the front steps of the *Crimson*, accompanied, as always, by a bored expression and a cigarette. He stood up hastily to face her. His hands and cheeks were pink with cold—like he'd been waiting for a while.

"Hey," he said, offering her a smile. A *real* smile.

Callie frowned, wondering what *real*ly funny or embarrassing thing she had done to elicit such a genuine expression. She put her hands on her hips and stared at him expectantly. He just stood there looking back without breaking the silence.

"Are you waiting for someone?" Callie finally asked. "I have a key so I could let you in. . . ."

"No thanks. I'm just enjoying the scenery," he answered, staring straight into her eyes.

"Ohhh-kay," Callie replied slowly, arching her eyebrows.

He did not elaborate.

She turned and started to walk away. He was more unpredictable than the location of a spherical pendulum with a nonlinear restoring force, or which cast member on *The Hills* would become the latest frenemy. It was maddening.

"Hey, Callie!" Gregory called suddenly, sounding—could it be?—embarrassed.

Callie turned and placed her hands on her hips, waiting.

"Are you heading back to the Yard?"

She nodded.

"Want to grab a cup of coffee or something?"

Callie froze, staring at him as he took a final drag of his cigarette before flicking it onto the brick sidewalk and grinding it under his heel. She couldn't detect any irony in his tone, but that didn't necessarily mean he wasn't harboring malicious ulterior motives. Was this a trick—or a truce? An olive branch or another one of his twisted games?

Yes—no—okay—go to hell—sure, why not— She was still wrestling with herself over how to reply when his NYC entourage rounded the corner, rowdy and obnoxious as usual. Out of bed before ten? The universe was truly out of whack.

"Hey, Casanova!" one of them yelled, while another one whistled rakishly. "Whassamatter, buddy? Already run through all the Wellesley blondes?"

"Yeah, man, what's the deal? I thought you preferred outsourcing to BU?"

The corners of Gregory's mouth twitched slightly, but his eyes never left her face. "Ignore them," he said, keeping his voice low. He looked at her, still waiting for an answer.

She stared back. She glanced at his friends and then at Gregory. She was on the verge of accepting when past experience and the preponderance of evidence that proved he was, twelve to zero, an *asshole* made her change her mind.

"Thanks for the offer, but I actually don't have time for coffee right now. I have to get back to my room and—"

"Coffee?" asked Gregory as his groupies arrived within earshot. "Is *that* what they're calling it these days? You don't have to be shy, neighbor. Why not just come out and tell me what you really want?"

His friends broke into appreciative laughter.

"Argh!" Callie rolled her eyes and turned her back on the sounds of whistles and high fives. Why, *why*, did he take a sadistic pleasure in torturing her? She could understand how Vanessa had developed a huge crush on him before school had even started because he was so mind-numbingly . . . *uhm* . . . yeah, mind-numbing, but he was completely insufferable the moment he opened his mouth.

As she arrived at Wigglesworth, she felt a rush of gratitude for Clint. Great guy, great looking, *not* an asshole. Stepping through the door to C 24, she decided to rouse Vanessa first, since it usually required the efforts of two people to wake Mimi from her Ambien-induced coma.

Vanessa was wearing a dainty silk negligee and her furry princess eye mask, but she was snoring louder than a trucker with a sinus infection. Stifling a giggle, Callie perched on the edge of the bed and whispered: "Princesssss . . ."

Vanessa snorted loudly, swatting the air with her hands.

"Vanessa," Callie prodded, her voice breaking with laughter. "Vanessa, wake up, I have some news you might be interested in. . . ."

Vanessa moaned and lifted the mask halfway up her forehead. "What?" she muttered, rubbing her eyes. "Gossip?"

"No." Callie smiled. "Even better. Let's wake Mimi and then I'll tell you."

"*Cal*-lie," said Vanessa irritably, swinging her legs over the side of her bed nevertheless. "Why are you doing this to me? You *know* I require at least nine hours of sleep in order to look my best. . . ."

"Yeah, well, I figured you'd appreciate a twelve-hour warning given the amount of time it takes you to get ready," Callie retorted, pulling Vanessa up off the bed before she could respond.

Together they entered Mimi's room—or as it was known before ten A.M.: the War Zone. This was because in the morning Mimi always looked like she'd survived a war—or an insane night of partying—even if she'd stayed in all evening working on a problem set. Her hair was always plastered wildly across her face, the sheets tangled in a tight little ball or discarded with the comforter on the floor, and more often than not Mimi would be wearing only a T-shirt or only a mysterious pair of boxers left by Joe Question Mark—as if she'd gotten bored halfway through changing into her pajamas.

They crept in cautiously: nervous—and with just cause—that Mimi might have a visitor. (Joe . . . ?)

Thankfully, today Mimi was alone and fully covered. Callie began patting her shoulder, but Vanessa, bitter about being woken so early, dove for the window shade and *yanked*. Bright morning sunshine flooded into the room, and Mimi sat up with a start, crying: "Monkey-fuck-winks and a tub of toothpaste!"

Callie and Vanessa sprang back in horror.

"Have either of you seen Margaret Thatcher?" Mimi muttered, burrowing under her tangled sheets. "She was supposed to meet me here. . . ."

Vanessa's mouth fell open and Callie started to snicker.

Mimi popped her head out from under the sheets, blinked three times, and then innocently asked, "What?"

But before they could answer, she shut her eyes and dove back under the covers.

"Let's try a different strategy," Callie murmured, motioning Vanessa to follow her into the common room. They brewed a strong pot of coffee and poured three cups. Vanessa seized their Costco-sized bottle of Advil, and thus sufficiently armed, they walked back into Mimi's room.

Callie waved the coffee under Mimi's nose like smelling salts until Mimi finally opened her eyes and accepted the steaming mug. She frowned at the Advil in Vanessa's outstretched hand.

"Couldn't get anything stronger, could you? Demerol? Celebrex? Vicodin? Percocet? Morphine? Anything that might mimic my endogenous enkephalins?"

Vanessa looked at Callie questioningly.

"Pharmacology 165: Drugs and the Brain," Callie whispered. Then: "Meems, look, we're sorry to wake you, but you asked me to get you up early so that you could work on your paper and I—"

"Callie supposedly has something to tell us," Vanessa interrupted.

"Yes I do," Callie answered, and then proceeded to explain her morning phone call with Clint.

Vanessa was ecstatic. Mimi seemed ambivalent as usual, but she grinned and said, "Eh . . . what the hell. I shall turn my paper in late. It is supposed to be a 'Nietzschean reading of *The Bacchae*,' for my Contemporary Theater class, so a little Dionysian revelry could technically be considered research."

"Dionysian revelry? Endogenous enkephalins?" Vanessa repeated incredulously.

"You are forgetting that I am a genius, no?" said Mimi, sipping her coffee.

"A genius who is . . . *failing French class*?" asked Callie in disbelief, lifting a handwritten note from Mlle Badeau off of Mimi's desk.

"French!" Vanessa cried. "Why would you even be taking it?"

Mimi shrugged. "I thought it would be an easy A . . . but as it turns out, I keep forgetting to go. Did you know language classes meet *every* day?"

"*C'est stupide*," said Callie.

"*Je sais, je sais* . . ." Mimi answered.

"You two are weird," Vanessa said. "You'd better not embarrass me in front of the Bee girls—after we get into the Pudding, they'll be the ones punching us next year!"

"Yeah," said Callie, agreeing that it might be wise to befriend some older girls—very wise, indeed.

ELEVEN

Mad Hatter's Ball

The Ladies of the Bee Club

cordially invite you & one guest to . . .

Mad Hatter's Ball

Friday, October 22, 2010

Festive Cocktail Attire & your Craziest Hat

Alley Cat Lounge at The Estate Club

10 pm

By Invitation Only

1 Boylston Place, Boston, MA 02116

"Mon dieu, I look like a *prostituée*," Mimi said, studying herself in Vanessa's full-length mirror.

"Well, if that means what I think it does," said Vanessa, "then I'm going to have to say that I agree." She strode over to Mimi and plucked the white nurse's hat off her head. "I'm pretty sure this hat has more fabric than your dress!"

"Hey!" said Mimi, tugging at the bottom of her white, skin-tight garment: one of those "gray area" purchases where you can't tell if it's meant to be a top or a dress.

(Word to the wise: if you can't tell, always, *always*, assume it's a top.)

"You are the one who chose this *stupide* hat for me!" Mimi said. "Are not all nurses slutty in the month of October? What is it you call . . . Hallow's Eve?"

"Yes, but *Halloween* is still a week away," Vanessa explained.

"Eh . . . *Je m'en fiche.*" Pouting, Mimi wrapped a knee-length, crocheted jacket around her body and dropped onto the couch to watch Vanessa make the final adjustments to her Cleopatra-inspired headdress.

"Come out already!" Mimi yelled toward Callie's room. "We want to see your hat!"

"Coming!" was Callie's muffled reply. Soon her feet, in Vanessa's heels, could be heard clicking down the hall as she made her way into the common room.

"*Voila!*" she cried.

Mimi whistled and Vanessa let out an appreciative "whoop!"

Instead of a hat Callie had purchased a short, shiny, pink-haired wig with bangs. To match she wore big hoop earrings and the gorgeous, pink-sequin vintage dress that Vanessa had finally agreed to let her borrow.

"Dammit, see! *This* is why I didn't want to lend it to you!" Vanessa said, pretending to be angry. "Because it looks better on you than it does on me and now . . . I'm sorry, but I'm going to have to kill you."

"We are pink with fear," said Mimi.

"No, Mimi, it's *green* with fear," Vanessa said. "I mean, envy. Whatever. I hate you both."

Callie's phone beeped several times from within her purse. "That must be Clint!" she cried, digging to retrieve it.

"Oh, shit!" Vanessa screamed, running to the mirror and readjusting her headdress for the 897th time. "We're running late again!"

Mimi, bundled in her coat and ready to go, smiled serenely from the couch and gave Callie an exaggerated two thumbs-up. Ever since Callie and Vanessa had taught her about various American gestures like thumbs-up and high five, she had been using them at every opportunity to her great personal amusement.

Callie flipped open her phone and was surprised by a message from Matt.

HEY CAL—BACK AT THE CRIMSON.
JUST WANTED TO LET YOU KNOW
I MOVED ALL OF YOUR COMP
ASSIGNMENTS OFF THE FLOOR.
I WOULD HAVE WAITED FOR YOU
TO COME BACK LATER TONIGHT
AFTER YOUR DATE, BUT I HEARD
LEXI WAS STOPPING BY SO I JUST
DID IT FOR YOU. THEY'RE ON THE
SECOND DESK NEAR THE WINDOW.
HAVE FUN.

Shit! she thought, guilt rushing over her. She'd completely forgotten to clean up the mess.

She opened her phone and started drafting a frantic apology but was interrupted by Vanessa, who grabbed her arm and dragged her from the room. All she was able to manage as they made their way down the stairs was a hasty:

OMG SO SORRY! COMPLETELY
FORGOT—YOU'RE A LIFESAVER.

A BMW X5 pulled up in front of Dexter Gate, and Callie felt for a moment like she was back in Los Angeles, land of the overpriced SUV. Following close behind, a dark blue convertible approached the curb, top up, driven by . . .

"Hello, neighbor." Vanessa whistled through her teeth.

"What the hell?" Callie blurted out as Gregory parked behind Clint's BMW. "Who invited him?"

"Probably an upperclassman Bee girl looking for a hot, sexy, gorgeous . . . date," Vanessa said, her eyes glazing over as if the entire Porsche 911 Carrera (Callie could now make out the front logo) were made of diamonds.

"Compensation car," Jessica's voice whispered in her head. *"The man must have a tiny, tiny penis."*

"SHOTGUN!" Vanessa screamed, diving into the front seat of the Porsche, high-speed-chase style. Gregory smiled his most winning smile and then turned to look at Callie.

But Callie had eyes only for Clint: Clint, who had just rushed around from the driver's seat of his car to open the back door in a touching throwback to gentlemanly chivalry. Clint, who then turned to Callie, removed the top hat that matched his tuxedo, and bowed.

Gregory's mouth appeared to be fighting a war with gravity—and losing. He turned on the radio and started blasting music, leaning toward Vanessa and averting his eyes as Callie and Clint embraced.

Clint kissed Callie lightly, once upon each cheek, before stepping back to introduce Mimi to her date, who had just emerged from the front seat of Clint's car: Fahad Alami, a Saudi Arabian raised in Washington, DC, whose white suit made his dark skin and wide-set brown eyes pop. A dark purple turban sat ironically upon his head.

Mimi gave Fahad a quick once-over, and Callie recognized her tiny frown as a covert seal of approval. Fahad, on the contrary, was gazing openly at Mimi like she was an angel descended from heaven and could only stammer, "I—I noticed you at the Pudding, and it's very, very nice to finally make your acquaintance."

Suddenly a beautiful, exotic-looking girl with long dark hair, red lipstick, and a huge smile popped her head out of the backseat of Clint's car and cried in a Spanish-sounding accent:

"Mimi, darling, is that you?"

"Tatiana!" Mimi exclaimed. "I cannot believe this! When was the last time I saw you? St. Bart's?"

"I believe it was Ibiza, but I forgive you for not remembering as I have a difficult time recalling the events of that evening myself. . . ." Tatiana trailed off, noticing Callie.

"Clint, who is this *gorgeous* girl?" she asked, turning to him expectantly. "Wherever did you find her?"

Callie beamed and introduced herself.

"You *are* gorgeous," Clint whispered in her ear as Mimi climbed into the backseat and Tatiana introduced her to her boyfriend, Alexander. Everybody in the car with the exception of Mimi was a junior, and every seat in the car was . . .

Taken.

"Callie," Clint whispered, "would you mind riding over with my buddy Greg? I'd obviously prefer to take you myself, but there doesn't seem to be any room left and Greg mentioned that you guys are friends, so . . ."

Friends? In what universe did Gregory consider her a friend? Were they friends when he'd made fun of her in Annenberg? When he'd nearly molested her on the staircase at the Pudding? When he pretended to invite her to coffee—excuse me, *sex*—in front of his groupies?

She would have liked, more than anything, to yell, *YES, I MIND!* at the top of her lungs, but Clint was standing there looking so hopelessly apologetic that all she could do was gape and nod. She allowed him to escort her to Gregory's compensation car and hold open the door. Trying to smile instead of sulk, Callie slid into the deep leather of the bucket seats and pulled her seat belt across her lap.

As Clint motioned at Vanessa to roll down her window, Gregory began adjusting the rearview mirror. It shifted and suddenly Callie could see two blue eyes—staring straight at her. She yanked the sequined dress down her legs as far as it could go, shifting uncomfortably in her seat.

Clint leaned into Vanessa's front window and said to Gregory, "You know how to get there, right? And would you mind waiting for James while I run by the gas station so he can follow you in his car?"

"James—Hoffmeyer?" said Gregory, sounding pissed.

"Yeah, you know Hoffmeyer?" Clint replied. "I only met him earlier this week at Pudding Punch but the guy's a riot!"

"Yeah, I knew him back at school. . . . ," Gregory replied slowly.

"Hoffmeyer as in Hoffmeyer Realty?" Vanessa asked, looking at Clint like he was Santa Claus.

"That's right, my dear." Clint beamed down at her. "Only the best for you."

Vanessa turned around in her seat and mouthed to Callie: "*O-M-G: I love him!*"

"So we'll meet you there, Greg?"

"Sure thing."

Callie's phone beeped: 1 NEW TEXT MESSAGE.

It was from Vanessa.

CLINT RULES! JAMES HOFFMEYER!
I'VE BEEN TRYING TO FIGURE OUT
HOW TO MEET HIM FOR WEEKS!
THIS IS A GREAT DAY FOR SPECIAL
OP PFF.

Shaking her head, with a sidelong glance at Gregory, Callie texted back: WHAT ABOUT YOU-KNOW-WHO??

Vanessa's fingers flew, texting her reply. Callie stole another peak at Gregory, but he was simply staring out the window, looking bored—angry, even, no doubt about having to wait.

DIDN'T YOU LEARN ANYTHING
IN EC 10? IT'S CRUCIAL TO
DIVERSIFY YOUR INVESTMENTS!
YOU-KNOW-WHO'S STOCK IS
HIGH-RISK, HIGH-REWARD.
HOFFMEYER = REPUTABLE INDEX
FUND. RELAX!! YOU ALREADY
FOUND YOUR FISH—NOW IT'S
MY TURN! ☺

Callie laughed and shook her head. Suddenly somebody honked loudly, obnoxiously. Callie turned around to look just as Vanessa squealed: "It's him! That's James!"

James honked again. Is that really necessary? Callie wondered, empathizing with Gregory's furious expression reflected in the rearview mirror.

"Let's go!" cried Vanessa, facing forward in her seat again and checking her hair and makeup in the side mirror. "The sooner we arrive, the sooner I get to meet my date!"

"I wouldn't be so eager to date that guy if I were you," Gregory said as he revved up the engine.

"What? Why not?" Vanessa sounded alarmed. But then an enormous smile broke out across her face. "Gregory," she said coyly, "you're not . . . *jealous*, are you?"

Gregory shrugged and pulled out onto the street. But then he shot a furtive glance into the rearview mirror and added darkly: "Maybe I am."

What? thought Callie, folding her arms across her chest. *Gregory jealous over Vanessa? But that's imposs—*

Ignore him! Think about something useful, like economics. Apparently Vanessa was doing a better job of internalizing the material than she was. . . . Maybe *that* was why Gregory liked Va— No, ridiculous! Impossible. Think about something— Oh, just give up. She stayed silent during the rest of the ride to Boston, staring out the window while Vanessa and Gregory chatted—no, *flirted*—the whole way there.

When Gregory finally pulled up in front of The Estate club, Callie darted out of his car. She ran over to Tatiana, Alexander, and Clint, who were taking furtive sips from Mimi's flask.

Clint gave Callie an enormous hug. His breath smelling slightly of Johnnie Walker Blue, he leaned toward her and said, "Sorry about the car ride. From now on I'm not letting you out of my sight!" Wrapping his arm around her waist, he offered her the flask.

Callie felt a wave of warmth coursing through her body that had nothing to do with the whiskey. It was enough to erase the awkward trip over, but still, she smiled when she noticed that

Vanessa had attached herself to James's arm while Gregory was nowhere to be found.

The line to get in to The Estate was a parade of Chloe, Diane Von Furstenberg, D&G, Zac Posen, and more, each spectacular dress adorned with a fancy, funny, or creative hat—crazy hats big and small with fur, leather, lights, sparkles, feathers, and more.

Callie glanced self-consciously at her dress but decided that she had nothing to worry about. Clint had said she looked gorgeous, and his was the only opinion that mattered.

Maybe there's a spot for me in this world after all, she thought as Clint slipped an ID into the palm of her hand. The name on the card read Marianne Smith, and hair color was the only thing she had in common with the girl in the photograph.

"This looks nothing like me!" she whispered.

"Don't worry, *Marianne*," he said, smiling down at her. "They're not *really* carding: some Bee girl will just look at the IDs and check our names off of the guest list. That big bouncer's more for show than anything else." Callie craned her neck to try to get a glimpse of the bouncer, but her vision was blocked by the couples ahead of them.

Clint squeezed her hand. "Seriously, don't stress out about it. I took care of everything."

Mimi, Fahad, Tatiana, and Alexander slid by the bouncer and into the club: a sea of disco lights and crazy hats. James and Vanessa, who were directly in front of Callie, also entered the club with ease.

"Marianne Smith," she said, reaching to hand the bouncer her ID.

"I'll take that," said a voice to her left.

Turning, Callie found herself face-to-face with the girl in charge of the guest list.

Alexis Thorndike.

Damn.

Swallowing an enormous lump in her throat, Callie did her best to smile. "Uhm, hi, Lexi . . ."

"Oh, you two already know each other?" asked Clint. "Well, that certainly makes everything easier!"

Lexi's smile looked faker than a plastic surgery disaster. She tucked a curl of brown hair that had broken loose from her all-too-real-looking tiara back behind her ear and said sweetly:

"Of course, how could I not know her after she's been slaving away so diligently for my *FM* COMP? Welcome to our party."

Lexi leaned in and gave Clint a lingering kiss on the cheek.

"Perhaps you two already know *my* date?" Lexi asked coolly, gesturing toward the crowd. Callie turned and saw a tall, dark-haired guy weaving through the masses to take up his place by Lexi's side.

Gregory.

"Sure we do," said Clint, smiling at Gregory. "Greg's my favorite freshman on the squash team. You should've seen him play in our match last week against Dartmouth! You couldn't have picked a better guy."

A flash of fury flickered across Lexi's face as Clint punched Gregory on the arm. Turning to Callie, she cooed:

"Gee . . . I just love your costume. . . . It's so creative. But tell me: are you a stripper or a crack whore?"

Callie felt as if she'd been slapped in the face. Clenching her fists, she tried to focus on feeling *angry* as an alternative to what she really wanted to do, which was cry. Gregory chuckled as he sipped his drink, but Clint was starting to look uncomfortable.

"Easy there, Lex," he said, handing her both of their IDs.

Lexi smiled angelically. "I was only teasing. Hmm," she said, gazing at Callie's ID and squinting. Then in a voice that could certainly carry to where the bouncer stood she asked, "Marianne Smith? But I'm so confused. I thought your name was Callie."

And just like that Callie's urge to cry disappeared. She was now officially angry.

Snatching back their IDs, Clint shot Lexi a withering glare. "You never change, do you?"

Before Lexi could reply, Clint grabbed Callie's arm and marched past the bouncer into the party, tossing an apologetic "Catch you later, man" over his shoulder at Gregory.

Fists clenching and teeth clamped so hard it hurt, Callie barely registered that they had made it safely into the party. The music swelled around her, and she found her fear of Lexi ebbing away. There would be no more staying classy or pretending to be aloof: if Lexi wanted to play games, then Callie was ready to hop into the ring. Since Lexi was determined to hate her no matter what she did or how hard she tried, she might as well give up and give her something to work with.

All's fair in love and war . . . and *this*—this was war.

"Let's dance!" she yelled at Clint, pulling him into the fray.

What began as a whisper, a tuck of the hair, and a light series of kisses on the cheek, neck, and ears soon devolved into a full-on, dance floor make-out. PDA wasn't normally Callie's style, but as she watched Lexi turn *pink* with envy, a grim satisfaction settled over her.

Mission accomplished.

"Trashy little freshman" makes out with hot upperclassman in front of ex's friends and cohorts . . .

Round one: Callie 1–Lexi 0

After nearly half an hour on the dance floor, Callie felt tired and sweaty, and, in the words of Grandma Andrews, her wig was "starting to slip."

"Want to take a break?" she shouted over the music. Clint nodded and led her to a booth where Tatiana, Alexander, Mimi, and Fahad were seated, enjoying a round of colorful drinks. She spotted OK at a nearby table with a girl she recognized as a sophomore: cute but obviously not captivating enough since OK kept stealing sidelong glances at Mimi and muttering—no doubt issuing a deadly *fatwa* against Fahad.

Mimi seemed too tipsy to notice the heartache and drama unfolding around her and chattered happily with Tatiana about the old glory days while Alexander and Clint started speaking in Man ("football-football-football").

"So, Fahad . . ." Callie started.

"So . . ." he replied.

"So."

"So . . . ?"

"Uhm . . . have you seen Vanessa?"

And then, miraculously, there she was, plopping down next to Callie, a little breathless and uncharacteristically unaware that her Cleopatra headdress was lopsided.

"Where's Prince Charming?" Callie asked, scanning the room for Vanessa's "reputable index fund."

"What—you mean James?" said Vanessa, sounding less than enthusiastic. "He's at the bar getting another drink, though, honestly, I don't see how he can possibly drink anymore. He's already so far gone, I doubt he even remembers his own name. . . ."

"All the more reason for *you* to make sure he gets home safely and that nobody takes advantage of him," Callie joked, nudging Vanessa in the ribs.

Vanessa didn't laugh. She tugged at her hair, looking frazzled. "Me! Take advantage of him? Ha! More like the other way around. That bastard tried to grope me and shove his tongue down my throat!"

"Ew," said Callie distractedly as she caught sight of Lexi dancing with a group of girls. Gregory was nowhere in sight.

Abandoned by her date at her own party . . .

Round two: Callie 2–Lexi 0

Clint and Alexander, who had gone to the bar, returned with two huge scorpion bowls and proposed a race: boys versus girls. Following Mimi's lead, Callie deduced that they were all meant to drink simultaneously using multiple straws. She, Mimi, Tatiana, and Vanessa crowded around their bowl, sipping frantically while Clint, Alexander, and Fahad made the contents of their own disappear.

"Oh, shit, he's back," Vanessa muttered as James stumbled toward them.

"There you are!" James slurred, cramming into the booth so close to Vanessa that he was practically on top of her, his arm snaking around her hips. "Thought you could run away from me, didn't you?"

Vanessa gave him a tight-lipped smile and tried to scoot closer to Callie. Misinterpreting, Callie moved closer to Clint to make more room. Clint smiled and wrapped his arm around her.

Vanessa stood.

"Hey, where are you going?" James cried, immediately standing with her.

"Bathroom," she answered curtly, trying to shake him off.

"Hey now . . . don't be like that. Let's dance."

Callie threw her head back in laughter as Mimi and Tatiana began acting out a scene from one of their European misadventures in which Fahad had been cast in the role of a disgruntled camel. He was rising to the occasion beautifully. Vanessa looked at James, then back at the group, and then over his shoulder, searching for an escape route before James could launch into another monologue about how many houses he owned (the only thing he could talk about) or feel her up again (his idea of "dancing").

"If you'll excuse me," Vanessa began, backing away from him, "I have to go to the lady's r—"

"Shhhhhh," he whispered, wrapping his arms around her and steering her toward the dance floor.

"James, *no*," she hissed, trying to push him away.

"Oh . . . *yes* . . ." he moaned, his hands sliding down, lower and lower.

She tried to break free. "Stop it!" she cried shrilly. "Get the hell off of m—"

"Is there a problem here?" a voice asked, its owner stepping out of the crowd.

"Hey, man, no, there's no problem at all. We're just having a lil fun, aren't we sweetheart . . . ?" James slurred, tightening his grip on Vanessa, who turned and cried:

"Gregory!"

"I think you need to back up, pal," said Gregory, placing a hand on James's shoulder.

"What the fuck's your problem, man?" James yelled, finally stepping back from Vanessa and spinning around to face Gregory. "If I wanna have a lil fun with *my* date, I don't see how that's any of your goddamn business—"

The music stopped. Callie and Mimi, who had finally realized what was happening, came rushing over with Clint and Fahad at their heels.

"Guys like you are my problem," said Gregory, his voice deadly calm. "Now listen carefully: you have ten seconds to leave the party, go outside, grab a cab, and go home. You will never so much as touch, speak, or even *look* at this girl again. Do I make myself clear?"

"Clear as fucking crystal," James muttered, shuffling backward toward the door. But then he paused, and eyeing Gregory, he lunged.

He was so drunk that he missed by about three feet: sucker punching the air. Gregory watched James stumble. He smiled wryly. And then he punched him in the face.

James spun backward and collapsed on the floor.

Somebody screamed and the bouncer came running over. He stared at James for a moment, an oddly satisfied expression on his face. Then, pulling him to his feet, he dragged him out of the club.

"Vanessa, what happened?" Callie demanded.

"I am so sorry—" Mimi started.

"We had no idea he was such a creep—"

"Or that you needed help—"

"Do you need anything?"

Vanessa shook her head through her tears, unable to speak.

"C'mon," said Gregory, sliding an arm around Vanessa's shoulders, "I'll take you home."

"Good idea," Clint agreed. "Vanessa, I'm so sorry. I had no *idea* that guy was such an asshole."

Vanessa nodded glumly, her head on Gregory's shoulder.

Callie stared dumbfounded as Gregory guided Vanessa out of the party. Clint was saying something, but she couldn't concentrate on his words. Gregory—to the rescue? Gregory—and Vanessa? Was this for real?

Apparently, Callie wasn't the only one who had noticed. Lexi was also watching Gregory and Vanessa retreat into the night, anger and disbelief etched across her face.

Publically deserted by her date in favor of another "trampy vixen froshling . . ."

Final round: Callie 3–Lexi 0

The winning point felt far less satisfying than Callie had anticipated.

TWELVE

elections

Matt Robinson

10/22/2010

Crimson Op-Ed COMP Piece # 22

Submitted to: Grace Lee, Editor

Sexism at Harvard: A Psychological Inquiry

The question: why would an intelligent woman willingly degrade not only herself but the entire history of the Women's Movement by entering the doors of an all-male Final Club?

The answer is, simply, that I don't know.

All we have to consider are the facts.

Harvard, Princeton, and Yale, or "the Big Three" as they've been commonly known since the 1880s, continue to dominate in the rankings as the best, most elite undergraduate institutions in the country. Of the three, Harvard University, established in 1636, is the oldest; the nation looks to us to set the precedent for the rest of the academic community.

In 1969 Princeton and Yale both became coeducational. However, the two schools' infamous social clubs (the Eating Clubs at Princeton, the Skulls and Bones at Yale) did not begin admitting female members until 1991.

At Princeton the Eating Clubs went coed as the result of a lawsuit.

At Yale, when the board of trustees for the Skulls and Bones found out that the male undergraduate members had started "tapping" females, they changed the locks to the "Tomb."

As if that weren't bad enough.

Harvard, by contrast, did not go fully coeducational until the year 1999, when Radcliffe (the all-women's college) and Harvard were finally integrated. In other words, women who attended the university graduated with a degree from Radcliffe, not Harvard, up until the final year of the twentieth century.

Today Harvard is the last among the Big Three to remain socially segregated according to the sexes.

Forget for a minute that the all-male Final Clubs promote classism, elitism, and exclusivity; forget that they are the most likely places on campus where a sexual assault will occur; and forget that the fledgling all-female Final Clubs haven't a hope of acquiring property in the Harvard Square area without unimaginable financial backing.

Rather than ask *why* women don't have their own social spaces on campus, I ask you: why isn't anybody *fighting* to make this happen? Why instead do the majority of females on campus subject themselves to this blatantly male-dominated environment, disappearing behind closed doors without a care for their safety or their rights every weekend night?

Ladies? You tell me.

"I'll get it!" Vanessa cried, leaping to her feet and running to answer a knock at the door.

Callie, who was curled up on the couch reading *Madame Bovary*, stayed where she was, wondering why OK or Matt had bothered to knock when they usually just came barging in.

"Flowers! For me?" Vanessa cried, grabbing the large glass vase from a delivery man and returning to the common room, staggering under the weight of an enormous bouquet.

"Oooh, pretty," said Callie. "Who are they from?"

"I don't know!" said Vanessa, leaning in to smell a lily. "Somebody must have remembered that it's my birthday!"

Callie laughed. Nobody could have forgotten that today, Friday, October 29, was Vanessa's birthday: she had been reminding them for weeks. To celebrate, Vanessa, Callie, and Mimi were going to dinner at UpStairs on the Square.

"Oh, wait, look! There's a card!" Vanessa cried, noticing a small white note that had been tucked inside the leaves.

"'Beautiful flowers for a beautiful girl.' Isn't that sweet? 'Congratulations . . .'" Reading on in silence, her face suddenly fell. "Oh, whoops," she said. "I think these are actually for you, Callie."

"For me?" asked Callie. "Let me see it. . . ."

Beautiful flowers for a beautiful girl.
Congratulations on finishing your first round of COMP!
Official Celebration starts on Saturday.
—C. W.

"Wow," said Vanessa. "And at the end of October! Shipping them in must have cost a fortune! I think he really, really likes you."

"They're so . . ." Callie was stunned.

"'Congratulations on finishing your first round of COMP!'" Vanessa read, picking up the card again. "Wait a second: I thought you weren't done until tomorrow?"

"Ugh, don't remind me!" said Callie, blowing a frustrated gust of air through her lips.

"Thank *god* I quit after the first meeting. I cannot believe how hard you've been working!"

"I know, I know," said Callie, frowning. The past few weeks had been absolute hell: staying up until three every morning at the *Crimson*, editing until her fingers felt raw and her eyeballs were popping out of their sockets. "At least this round will be over by tomorrow. Maybe I'll get cut and then I'll have time to spend on my actual assignments," she finished, waving *Madame Bovary* in the air.

"Don't say that!" Vanessa said. "You're not getting cut. The pieces I read were amazing, and really funny, too— Wait, they're supposed to be funny, right?

"Sometimes . . ." Callie laughed.

"Well, whatever. They're great, you're great, and I am very, very proud of you!"

"*Aw*, thanks."

"So, listen, back to me: the reservation tonight is for nine o'clock sharp. I have to run some errands and go to Newbury to pick up my dress, so I'll just meet you there, all right?"

"Got it," said Callie. "And what's on the agenda for after dinner?"

"I was thinking drinks at Daedalus," Vanessa replied. "Where, if all goes according to plan, we will *accidentally* run into Gregory: my knight in shining Armani with his trusty steed, the Carrera."

Callie laughed and shook her head. "All right, nine o'clock sharp, UpStairs on the Square, drinks afterward: we'll be there. Though I probably can't stay at Daedalus for very long because Matt and I are planning to proofread each other's pieces later tonight."

"Good. Well, you have to come for at least *one* drink," Vanessa began, slinging her purse over her shoulder and heading for the door. "It just wouldn't be the same without my best friend!"

Best friend . . . Wait, what? When just two months ago Vanessa had been embarrassed to be seen with her in the dining hall?

But the more Callie thought about it, the more it made sense. Vanessa's main group of girlfriends from school treated her like New Money, and her guy friends . . . Well, seeing as she thought touchdowns were called baskets and beer was synonymous with bloating, she didn't actually have many male friends to speak of.

Plus, what happened in the dining hall had been eclipsed long ago by Vanessa's nobler actions: helping Callie through her breakup, saving her from herself at Calypso, lending her outfits without blinking, and trying to get her punched for the Pudding.

In fact, Callie was certain that if their situations at Mad Hatter's had been reversed, Vanessa would have been there to help her. Even now, a full week later, Callie still felt guilty when she thought about it.

"I can't believe James turned out to be such an asshole," Callie had said the morning after Mad Hatter's, feeling terrible for not noticing when Vanessa was in trouble. "Are you sure you're all right?"

"Yep," Vanessa answered firmly, though her expression had darkened when Callie mentioned his name. "It was basically all worth it just to be rescued by Gregory. . . ."

"Yeah," said Callie, staring at her lap. "He was pretty amazing." She lifted her head but couldn't quite bring herself to meet Vanessa's eyes. As casually as possible, she added: "Did anything happen between you two last night?"

"No." Vanessa smiled. "Though you could tell he totally wanted to make a move but, like, couldn't because of the situation. He was a perfect gentleman."

"Ha!" scoffed Callie before she could stop herself. "Since when has Gregory ever acted like a gentleman?"

"Oh, Callie, he's really not as bad as you think! He was completely wonderful last night. I feel like I finally got to see a side of him that not very many people know. I think we really connected!"

"Really?" asked Callie. "So . . . no good-night kiss? No nothing?"

"Nope," said Vanessa, sounding inexplicably cheerful. "Normally I'd take that as a bad sign, but he kept dropping hints left and right."

"Oh . . . Like what?

"Just, you know, saying how he might finally be ready for something more serious and how it might be nice to have a girlfriend . . . Oh, *and* when we were talking about OK and Mimi, he said that Mimi told him she finds OK attractive and loves his personality but doesn't want to hook up casually with him—because they're such good friends—until she knows if they have real relationship potential. Anyway, the entire time he's saying this, he keeps giving me these looks . . . you know, really long, meaningful ones."

Callie knew it'd be wiser to end the conversation there, but she just couldn't keep herself from asking: "Wait, so how did that topic of conversation even come up?"

"Oh, you know," said Vanessa, "we were just gossiping about all the roommates: saying how funny it'd be if OK and Mimi got together since Adam and Dana are dating. . . . And then I guess he was wondering if you and Clint were officially a couple and I said yes—"

"What?" said Callie sharply, "What do you mean you said yes? Clint and I aren't officially together; we've barely even started dating!"

"Oh— Really? I guess I just assumed you were official already. I mean, why wouldn't you be? He's so into you and he's perfect!"

Staring at the beautiful flowers, Callie almost laughed aloud at the thought that just one week ago, she had objected to their being referred to as a couple. The only reason she'd been able to survive the past seven days was Clint: he had brought her coffee at the *Crimson* nearly every night, massaged her neck and shoulders, and seen her through more than one work-induced near nervous breakdown.

At this point there was only one thing holding her back. And no, despite what you may be thinking, his name wasn't Gregory. (Though did he really like Vanessa? I mean, really? Why did he care if things with Clint were official, anyway?)

This particular issue dated all the way back to the original asshole—no, not Adam—Evan. After what he'd done, when it came to relationships, she really didn't know if she'd be able to trust guys again, ever.

So she should probably stop thinking about Clint that way . . . constantly . . . and stop having fantasies about him throwing her COMP pieces on the floor and lifting her onto a desk at the *Crimson*. . . . Or making another midnight trip to the top of the Astronomy Tower and climbing the ladder to the observation deck . . . Or about him pressing her up against the wall in the coatroom at the Pudding . . . Or . . . Or . . . Or . . .

NO! Sex, as she ought to be doing a better job of reminding herself, could lead to catastrophic unforeseen complications way worse than the usual array of STDs, pregnancy, and oxytocin overdose.

Clint. Evan. Gregory. Clint. Clegorvan—ARGHHH!!! She

buried her nose in *Madame Bovary*, vowing to finish at least this chapter before she returned to the daunting stack of COMP assignments piled high on her desk. Turning the page, she read:

> Before she married, she thought she was in love; but the happiness that should have resulted from that love, somehow had not come. It seemed to her that she must have made a mistake, have misunderstood in some way or another. And Emma tried hard to discover what, precisely, it was in life that was denoted by the words "joy, passion, intoxication," which had always looked so fine to her in books—

Callie was once again interrupted when Dana marched into the room. Her face looked like a five-year-old's face-paint project gone wrong. It appeared she may have been trying to use makeup for the first time. "Dana, what . . . ?" Callie ventured. Dana turned beet red.

"Well, I aced my Physics 15 midterm, but when it comes to this type of thing, I'm like a wild African warthog stuck in the bottom of a muddy watering hole. . . ."

It took Callie a few seconds to process that before she turned to her roommate in amazement. "Dana—was that a joke?"

"Yes," said Dana. "An attempt, anyhow."

Callie laughed. "It's really not that difficult. Here, come into the bathroom and I'll show you."

"Thank you very much," Dana said.

"No problem!" Callie replied. Anything to get away from Emma Bovary and her boy problems . . .

It was 8:55 and they were running late. Mimi had been napping and slept through her alarm, while Callie had spent every possible moment editing her pieces for COMP.

"Hurry up, Mimi. Let's go!" Callie cried, steering her roommate toward the door. It had barely shut when they turned and found themselves face-to-face with Matt. He looked disheveled and unshaven, and Callie wondered guiltily if he couldn't find anyone to hang out with on a Friday night.

"So, are we still on for proofreading later?" he asked Callie, eyeing her dress.

"Yes, yes, of course!" she assured him. The look on his face made her feel like she should have some sort of an excuse for what she was wearing. "It's, uhm, Vanessa's birthday tonight, and just the three of us girls are going to dinner. After that, I'll be there, I swear." She didn't know why she felt the need to emphasize that it was just girls, or omit the part about getting cocktails later. . . .

"Okay, great," he answered, starting to smile. "I'm really looking forward to reading your final drafts."

"Yeah, me too," she said, lying through her teeth. She would die of embarrassment if he actually saw some of the latest things that she had written, like "Top Ten Low-Cal Fro-Yo Toppings" or "How to Wear Your Hair with Glasses." Not that those topics were *her* fault but still . . . "I'll only be out for an hour or so and then I'll meet you there."

He frowned slightly, a dubious expression on his face.

"Matt, I promise. Just one hour and I'll be there."

They were only three blocks away from the restaurant when Mimi's phone started vibrating in her pocketbook.

Callie frowned. Probably Vanessa calling to yell at us for being late.

A strange expression crossed Mimi's face. She stopped walking. Before Callie could ask what was going on, she too felt her phone vibrate in her pocket.

"Hello?"

"Get to the John Harvard statue." The voice was calm and deadly serious. "You have three minutes—or else." Click.

"You got the call?" Mimi asked Callie. She nodded slowly.

"We have to go," said Mimi, making her way back toward the Yard.

"What about Vanessa?" Callie asked, looking hopelessly in the direction of the restaurant.

"I am certain she will meet us there . . . but regardless, we must go *maintenant*."

Callie didn't know what was going on, but Mimi had said Vanessa would meet them there, so Callie followed her down the street, marveling at how fast her roommate could move in high heels.

When they arrived at the John Harvard statue, Callie noticed that they seemed to be among the last to join some twenty-odd freshmen from New York City and abroad. Gregory and OK were standing nearby; they gave the girls a knowing smile, which Callie barely registered. Her eyes scanned the crowd, searching for Vanessa.

Slowly it dawned on her. She recognized the Upper East Side

JAQs, WASPs, NYC Prepsters, Malibu Barbies, Star Athletes, and OPEC Kings. About sixty socialites of the campus elite were there: the members of the Hasty Pudding.

But where was Vanessa? Was she still waiting at the restaurant? Surely she would have known what it meant when she got the call, if she had gotten the call at all. . . . No, that was impossible—there must have been some mistake.

The freshmen rippled with excitement as Tyler Green stepped forward with a giant megaphone and boomed: "WELCOME!"

Everyone near Callie broke into thunderous cheers, hugging each other and shaking hands as if this were a cheesy disaster movie and they had just collectively saved the planet from imminent destruction. Callie pulled out her phone, wondering if she should call Vanessa and what she ought to say. There was a text from Vanessa asking where they were, confirming Callie's worst fears: Vanessa hadn't gotten the call.

Callie felt a physical, visceral ill settling in the pit of her stomach as her phone suddenly lit up with an incoming call from VANESSA V. Callie *knew* she shouldn't ditch Vanessa—and on her birthday, of all days—but she also had no idea what she could possibly say to her. Surely there would be some explanation, but for now the only thing to do was buy some time.

> VANESSA, I AM SO, SO SORRY.
> EMERGENCY AT THE *CRIMSON*,
> HAD TO RUN. HAPPY BIRTHDAY,
> LOVE YOU & I PROMISE TO MAKE
> IT UP TO YOU SOON.

She let her phone slide back into her pocket. The shouts around her faded: the novices of the group suddenly aware that the veterans weren't smiling.

Tyler Green raised his megaphone once more and cried: "Amanda Cooper!"

A tiny freshman girl stepped forward, trembling slightly. Silently Tyler handed her a slip of paper, and then two upperclassman members poured a "welcome" shot down her throat.

"Brandon Huntsman!"

Brandon stepped forward. And so on: each new member-elect called forth until soon enough, it was her turn.

"Callie Andrews!"

She accepted the slip of paper, which bore the heading *A Letter to New Members from President Tyler Green*. She opened her mouth to the alcohol and let the warmth wash over her, hoping to erase her guilt. Clint took a step forward from the crowd, beaming at her and lifting his fingers in a covert wave.

After all twenty-five names were announced, the upperclassmen suddenly broke into wild applause. Screaming words of welcome, they raised their bottles in a toast to the newest members of the Hasty Pudding Social Club.

Callie threw herself into Clint's arms. He grabbed her around the waist and dipped her like a tango dancer before pulling her close and planting a long, lingering kiss upon her eager lips.

She kissed him fully and passionately. Nobody could take *this* moment away from her: not Gregory, not Evan, and not . . .

Wait a minute, Callie thought abruptly, pulling back from Clint. Where's . . . ?

Then she spotted her, talking with a group of newly elected members.

Alexis Thorndike.

She looked perfectly happy and carefree as she threw her head back and laughed at something that OK had just said.

Relieved, Callie turned to Clint. "Ready for some mandatory mingling?" he asked.

"Absolutely."

Ninety minutes of introductions, speeches, and welcome shots later, Tyler was nearing the end of his "anti"-hazing proclamation, *wink, wink, nudge, nudge.* When he finished, Callie turned to Clint and whispered: "So, are you going to haze me now or haze me later—in private?" In the *Crimson*, in the science center, in the coatroom, on a desk, under the telescope—

"You!" he cried accusingly, tickling her sides. "Perhaps I will have to haze you into learning some respect for your elders!" She screamed as he chased her, brandishing a ten-dollar handle of rum.

Catching her, he threw his arms around her waist and said: "Seriously, though. How did I ever get so lucky?" he asked, nuzzling up against her neck. "The coolest, most beautiful girl on the Harvard campus and for some reason she picked me."

Callie leaned into him. *He* was lucky *she* had "picked" him? Clearly it was the other way around. There wasn't a girl on campus who wouldn't kill to be Clint Weber's girlfriend—probably a few boys as well. The word for him, and for the moment, that kept surfacing over and over again was *perfect*. Everything was absolutely *per—*

"And I'm so sorry about Vanessa," Clint added, suddenly somber. "I really did everything I could, but she was blackballed by someone on the board. Something about some girl's boyfriend and the first week of school. I went to bat for her, but there was nothing else I could do. . . ."

Everything went mute. Vanessa. They had abandoned her at UpStairs on the Square, alone, with no explanations, on her birthday. She and Mimi had both assumed that Vanessa was going to meet them there, but still that was no excuse. Biting her lip, Callie said: "Clint, I'm sorry, but I've got to go. I need to find Vanessa—I never should have come without her."

"That's all right," he said. "Dinner tomorrow to celebrate the completion of your first COMP portfolio?"

"Sure," she said, forcing a smile as she realized that Vanessa wasn't the only person she was going to disappoint tonight.

Mimi was completely engrossed in conversation with a group of seniors, so Callie gave Clint a farewell kiss on the cheek and then left the party.

Why me? she wondered as she walked. It was Vanessa who fit the profile of the Pudding, not Callie. Vanessa who had wanted it more. Vanessa who deserved it more . . .

Lost in her thoughts, Callie arrived at Wigglesworth.

Gregory was sitting on the stone steps that led up to their entryway, smoking and staring off into space. He tossed his cigarette aside when he saw her. "Hey."

"Hey," she replied cautiously. "Crazy night . . ."

"I'll say."

"I guess we made it," she said, hovering awkwardly. He wasn't exactly blocking the door, so she couldn't exactly ask him to move.

"So what?" he asked, tapping out another cigarette and placing it between his lips.

Her eyes lingered there momentarily. She shook herself. "So . . . so nothing, I guess."

"You see Vanessa yet?" he asked. "She seemed pretty upset."

"She's— Wait, you saw her?"

"Yeah . . . about ten minutes ago. She was standing right where you are yelling something about a birthday dinner, so I told her about the Pudding, but before I could say anything else, she ran inside." He shrugged.

Callie's face fell.

"You okay?" he asked.

"I—well—ah, I'm worried . . . about Vanessa."

"You should go talk to her," he said.

She stared at him for a few seconds. He stood up to make room so she could pass. It was tactful as far as dismissals go, but the message was still clear. Reaching for the door, she tried to block out the look of concern on his face—concern, evidently, for Vanessa.

"Hey," he said suddenly, his fingers brushing her wrist. "Will you—will you let me know later how she is?"

"Sure," Callie muttered, averting her eyes. Her heart plummeted from her stomach into her knees. Her knees felt weak. As quickly as possible, she climbed the stairs to the second floor.

When she reached the landing, she ran into Matt who, hands full, was on his way down to take out the trash. As soon as he saw her, he turned back toward his room without saying a word.

Oh, crap, she thought. In all the excitement of the Welcome Party, she had completely forgotten to text him and let him know she wasn't coming. Still, she had to at least try.

"Matt, look, I'm so sorry. . . . You can't possibly guess what happened tonight—"

Matt whirled around to face her, his expression furious. She had never seen him even angry before.

"What happened tonight, Callie?" he yelled, throwing the trash bags onto the floor. "What? Did your *fabulous* new friends come up with some *fabulous* new event that you couldn't possibly bear to skip?"

She tried to open her mouth, but he cut her off.

"Whatever, I'm done. I'm so tired of waiting for the girl I met on the first day of school. You know: the one who was smart and ambitious and cared about things outside of events and parties? Do you even remember her or is your head so full of alcohol and air now that you've completely forgotten?"

Stunned, Callie watched as he grabbed the trash bags and stomped down the stairs. It was as if he had read in her heart the very worst things she thought about herself and then said them aloud.

Completely deflated and more than a little upset, she trudged into her common room.

Vanessa was huddled up on the couch shoveling Easy Mac into her mouth. Her dress looked rumpled and she had only bothered to remove one shoe, while dark streaks of mascara formed telltale tracks down the sides of her face.

I am officially the worst person in the world. "Vanessa," Callie started, but Vanessa just shook her head and forced several more spoonfuls of mac-n-cheese down her throat before standing and heading for her bedroom.

The door closed with a slam.

"Please, Vanessa!" Callie yelled after her, making her way toward the door. "Just give me a chance to explain. . . ."

No response.

"Look, when Mimi and I got the call, we had no idea that you—"

"That I what?" Vanessa cried, flinging open her door. "Got rejected?" She shook her head. "You know, you really don't *get it*, do you, Callie? Just this afternoon I called you my best friend, and yet you can't even bother to tell me the truth when you *ditched* me on my *birthday* for the Pudding. Yeah, it sucks that I didn't get in, but what *sucks* even more is that you didn't have the guts to tell me to my face. Instead, I had to hear it from Gregory!"

For the second time that night, Callie couldn't think of a response. Vanessa snorted and slammed the door once more.

Callie walked into her own room and sank onto the bed. She could hear Gregory and what sounded like Mimi with several other new Pudding members talking and laughing outside, right underneath her window. The sounds of a movie playing drifted over from Dana's room, where she was most likely cuddling chastely with Adam. The creak of a door and the slam of another told her that Vanessa had probably locked herself in the bathroom yet again, trying to purge the imaginary damage done by the mac-n-cheese.

As Mimi squealed loudly in reaction to something someone said, Callie wished she were in the mood to celebrate, wished that Vanessa had gotten into the Pudding, or that she'd had the guts to tell her roommate the truth, and wished that she weren't, undeniably, a terrible friend.

She lay back on her bed and stared at the ceiling. She was debating whether to change into her PJs or just go to sleep in her clothes when her phone vibrated once.

She flipped it open to find a text message from Clint.

I MISS YOU ALREADY!

HOW'D IT GO WITH VANESSA?

Sighing, she dialed his number. No matter how low she felt, she knew she could count on Clint.

THIRTEEN

"Three may Keep a Secret If Two of Them Are Dead"

The Harvard Crimson

BREAKING NEWS OPINION FM ARTS SPORTS

OPINION

My Facebook Stalker

The online consequences of a relationship gone awry

Submitted ANONYMOUSLY, Edited by GRACE LEE

It's taken me nearly a year to write this story, and I'm not kidding when I say that sometimes I'm still afraid.

"Dan" and "Alex" (aliases I borrowed from the film *Fatal Attraction*) had been dating long-distance for nearly all of college. He was a senior at Harvard; she went to the University of Wisconsin. Alex was completely in love; Dan, on the other hand, was slightly bored.

That's where I, a naive sophomore at the time, came into the picture: Dan, whom I met during a talk at the Kennedy School of Government, developed unsolicited romantic feelings for me. It was a harmless crush, really—that is until Alex was able to track our flirtation by logging into his Facebook account and reading his private correspondence.

After surviving several months of hate e-mail, angry phone calls, and bitter instant messages from a distraught Alex—who had obtained my contact information via Dan's Facebook profile—they finally graduated, and I thought I was in the clear. Despite everything that had happened, they were planning not only to stay together, but to live together in Chicago, where he was headed for graduate school after college.

I thought it would end there. As it turns out, I was wrong.

At the beginning of my junior year I got a friendship request from a random girl named "Judy Masterson." I didn't actually know her, but I made the mistake of accepting her friend request because we had several friends in common, and hey, I didn't want to be rude, right? Big mistake.

Things were normal at first, and sometimes Judy's online activities would show up on my News Feed (aka Stalker's Paradise). I found it a little odd when she would send me casual "getting to know you" messages, but when I looked closer at her profile, I concluded that she was just a lonely girl living in New York City. She had about 300 Facebook friends and even a couple of photo albums, and even though each photo had a detailed explanation of why you couldn't actually *see* her in the picture, never for a second did it occur to me that the profile wasn't real.

Wrong again: after several months of online "friendship" with Judy Masterson, things started to get a little weird. First there were some strange messages, then a couple of passive-aggressive posts about "Harvard sluts that steal people's boyfriends," which seemed clearly, though inexplicably, targeted at me.

Finally I figured it out: Alex, who must have felt restless at home while Dan was away all day getting his master's in psychology (oh, the irony), spent countless hours creating a fake Facebook profile *all for the purpose of stalking me.*

After a nasty online confrontation she was forced to deactivate her stalker's profile, but from time to time I still get random "friendship" requests from people I know nothing about other than the fact that we have a couple of friends in common.

A word to the wise: *never* accept a request from somebody that you do not know IN PERSON and *never* post private information (phone numbers, e-mails, addresses, photos, etc.) in a public forum on the internet. You should know better—especially if you are a psych major—not to give your passwords to a potentially unstable girlfriend.

In short, you never know who can gain access to a profile or who is out there watching. . . . It might be as harmless as a future employer, but for all we know in this anonymous cyber-world, it could be another psychotic, possibly dangerous Facebook stalker.

On the following Friday Callie was making her way back toward Wigglesworth after class when she ran into Gregory and Clint headed in the opposite direction. They were both wearing athletic gear, squash rackets in tow.

"Hey!" Clint cried, hugging Callie. Gregory glanced rudely at his watch.

"Hi!" Callie answered, disengaging quickly because she was, after all, anti-PDA. Or so she told herself. "I didn't realize you guys had practice right now."

"We don't," said Clint. "But every Friday we stop by the local public high school to hit the ball around with some of the kids."

"Just for fun?" she asked, looking from one to the other.

"Well, it *is* fun," said Clint, "but also their program can't afford a coach, so we divide up their practices among the guys on our team."

"Wow," said Callie. "That's so great."

"It's really no big deal," said Gregory, avoiding her eyes. "Hey, we should probably get going."

"Quit being so modest," Clint said, punching Gregory on the arm. "The whole mentor program was his idea in the first place," he added, turning to Callie. "He organized the entire thing!"

"Did he . . . ?" Callie asked, staring hard at Gregory.

"Just padding my resume," he muttered, shuffling his feet.

"You should see him with the kids," Clint continued. "They love him."

"Speaking of which," said Gregory, "we really do have to get going. We can't be late."

"The man is *dedicated*," said Clint, slapping him on the back. "Anyway, I will call *you* later," he said, pointing at Callie. "Maybe tonight we could all meet up for a drink?"

"Can't—I'm busy," Gregory said at the exact same moment that Callie shook her head and muttered, "I have to work."

Clint gave them a funny look. "Well, you guys are no fun. Guess I'll see you tomorrow?"

"Sure," said Callie, and then she watched them walk away side by side.

Back in Wigglesworth as she stood facing the door to C 24, Callie noticed a large manila envelope sitting in the metal drop box.

It had her name on it.

Her heart started to beat three times faster as she tore it open. Reaching inside, she pulled out a thick stack of papers, recognizing her COMP pieces—or rather what remained of them after the editor's unforgiving pen.

There was also a note.

Dear Callie Andrews,

Congratulations! We are pleased to inform you that your first portfolio has been successful. We have returned your pieces with feedback. You'll have a few weeks to revise these and prepare a new portfolio for the second round.

Keep up the good work!
The Editors at FM

"Vanessa!" Callie cried as she threw open the front door. "Vanessa, I made it! Vanessa—"

And that's when she remembered: Vanessa wasn't speaking to her. A full week had passed, but apart from a "Hurry-up-in-the-bathroom!" and a surprised grunt after a near collision in the hall, Vanessa had been completely silent.

And it's all my fault, Callie reminded herself. Lately she'd become a rotten, horrible person—worse than Lexi, worse than that dude who stabbed Caesar, and almost as bad as Evan.

All week long she had been trying to think of ways to make it up to them: Vanessa and, not to be forgotten, Matt.

Of the two Matt had been slightly easier. After a few awkward silences in the hallway she'd knocked on his door wielding hot chocolate, a giant cookie, and her best sad, puppy-dog eyes. It had been impossible for him to resist.

Vanessa, on the other hand, still hated her guts. Callie had tried everything: cookies, apology notes, little presents, and funny cartoons about Dana and Adam, and she had even asked Mimi to talk to her (which turned out to be a mistake, since Vanessa was none too pleased with her either).

As Callie entered her bedroom, she realized her phone was vibrating in her pocket.

ONE INCOMING CALL FROM . . . Worse than Brutus. Oh, goody.

"Hi, Evan," she said, sitting down at her desk.

"Callie? Hey! How are you? Are you coming home for Thanksgiving br—"

"Save the small talk, Davies," she snapped. "It's been almost a month already. Did you take care of it?"

"Well . . ."

"Yes or no, Evan."

"Yes . . . ," he started, "*and* no."

"What do you mean 'yes and no'? What the *fuck*, Evan?" she yelled, standing up and starting to pace around her room.

"Callie, look, calm down," he said. "I couldn't exactly 'take care of it' because more than one person has a copy—"

"*What*? But you said—"

"Please," he interrupted, "just let me explain. Like I told you back in September, I gave a copy of the file to my big brother because it was worth a lot of points in the scavenger hunt. But I realized immediately what a huge mistake I had made, and that's when I called you—"

"Yes, I know. I was there. And then you swore to explain the situation to him and get it back—erase it—whatever. Which you did . . . you *did*, right?"

Evan was silent. "Well . . . I did . . . try. But he said it wouldn't count unless we showed—"

"'SHOWED!?'"

"Just to the brothers who were in charge of initiation—to prove that I actually did it!"

Callie felt sick. She sank back down in the chair at her desk.

"My big brother *promised* me that it was only saved on his computer and that he would delete it permanently after initiation was over. But, just to be safe, I broke into his room two nights ago and I erased his entire hard drive. Including," he added darkly, "his senior thesis."

"So then it's fine?" Callie asked, gripping the sides of her chair. "It's erased—destroyed—and all of this is over?"

"Well, not quite. I *thought* that'd be the end of it and was about to call and tell you so last night when . . ."

"When *what*?"

"When an e-mail went out over the fraternity list. And the file—it was attached. Everyone in the frat . . . has a copy now."

"How—how—is that . . . *possible*?" Callie's head was spinning so fast she could barely see.

"I—I don't know, Callie. I'm sorry," Evan said, his voice breaking. "I did everything I could. Please believe me. This morning I quit the frat."

There was nothing left for her to say, except: "Evan, I *never* want to speak to you again."

"Callie—"

"And I need to see that e-mail. Send it, and then don't contact me *ever* again."

"All right," he said after a pause, swallowing hard. "I'll forward it to you right now, and I'll call you later to see if there's anything else I can—"

"Don't ever call me again." She hung up the phone.

Callie flipped open her computer screen. Her foot started tap-tap-tapping as she logged into her in-box, waiting for Evan's e-mail to arrive. Angrily, she clicked Refresh, and sure enough, a new e-mail appeared.

But it wasn't from Evan. Instead, it was from the "Hasty Pudding Club; est. 1770":

From:	**Anne Goldberg**
To:	**Callie Andrews**
Subject:	Welcome to the Pudding!

Greetings, neophytes!

Your presence is requested for a mandatory meeting at the clubhouse (2 Garden St.) this coming Tuesday, 2 P.M. sharp. The meeting should not take more than half an hour: we just need a signature from you acknowledging that you have received and read the club's rules and, of course, your installment of this semester's dues, payable no later than Dec. 31st. Details can be found in the letter you received last Friday evening. We are happy to accept payment via credit card or personal check. At the end of the meeting, you will all receive your set of keys to the clubhouse. Please e-mail with further questions or concerns.

Best,

Anne Goldberg, Secretary

Callie had to read the e-mail twice before she understood what was meant by the word *dues*. With a sinking feeling she picked up the letter that Tyler Green had handed her a week ago during the Pudding welcome party.

Sure enough, near the bottom of the page, there was a paragraph about "Club Dues."

Quickly she calculated in her head. Lunch fees . . . guest fees . . . one-time participation fee . . . maintenance fees . . . ONE THOUSAND DOLLARS?

How the hell was she going to pull that off when her entire budget for both semesters was two thousand dollars minus at least seven hundred for books?

What could she possibly say to her parents?

"Mom, Dad: could you please double my budget?"

"Why? Oh, just for social reasons . . ."

It was impossible. They would never understand. Especially when they had just spent so much money on a plane ticket to fly her home for Thanksgiving break.

Tears of frustration and hopelessness started to leak out of the corners of her eyes as she navigated back to her in-box. And there it was.

From:	**Evan Davies**
To:	**Callie Andrews**
Subject:	(no subject)
Attachments (1): C:\Users\Evan Davies\Desktop\Private\Captains'_Practice.avi	

I'm sorry.

She couldn't bring herself to open the attachment. Instead, she flung her head down on top of her desk and started sobbing, beating the wood with her fists. She wished her parents *hadn't* been able to afford to fly her home for Thanksgiving—how could she ever show her face in Los Angeles again?

She barely noticed the sound of Vanessa's heels clicking down the hall, or her voice, which seemed annoyed as she announced, "Callie—I'm just coming in to take back that dress I lent you last month—"

Vanessa paused midsentence as she barged into the room.

"Callie?" she asked.

"Oh! Vanessa!" Callie gasped through her sobs, accidentally knocking over her desk chair as she stood.

"Callie—oh my god—what's wrong?"

Callie collapsed onto her bed, her body shaking with sobs. Vanessa hesitated for a moment but then sat down on the bed and placed a hand on Callie's shoulder.

"Vanessa," Callie said as she cried into her pillow. "I am so, so, *so* sorry about what happened on your birthday—what I did to you. It was unforgivable. I've been so completely horrible lately. I don't even deserve you as a friend—"

"Oh, hush," said Vanessa. "I don't appreciate that you lied to me and I expect you to promise never to do it again in the future, but we can talk about that later. . . . Now, why don't you tell me what's wrong?"

"It's my ex—Evan, from high school. . . ."

"What? I thought you'd be totally over him by now since things are going so great with Clint—"

Vanessa cringed as the mention of Clint sent Callie into a new gale of hysterics.

"Clint! I forgot all about—oh god—if he—never going to speak to me again!"

"Callie, what on earth are you talking about?" Vanessa demanded. "Didn't Clint just invite you to have Thanksgiving at his parents' house in Virginia?" Suddenly she looked sheepish. "I didn't mean to—I mean, I overheard you telling Mimi about it the other night. . . ." Vanessa realized her words were only making things worse. Taking a deep breath, she tried once more:

"Callie, please. You're starting to scare me. What is going on here?"

But by now Callie was sobbing too hard to speak. Pathetically she gestured toward her computer.

Vanessa sat down, clicked OK, and waited for the file to open. Her eyes widened in shock, which soon turned to embarrassment, and then horror. Quickly she closed the window. She had seen enough.

"Callie," Vanessa said urgently, turning to face her. "You didn't—*know*—about this—at all, did you? Even when it was happening?"

"No," Callie murmured into her pillow. "*No*! Of *course* I didn't know it was happening! Do you really think I'd *agree* to something like that? He did it secretly, for some stupid fucking dare—and it wouldn't be a problem now if he'd destroyed it afterward, but then he"—she paused, choking up—"he gave it to somebody in his fraternity—"

Vanessa's horror-struck eyes opened wider still.

"And e-mailed . . . e-mailed . . ."

Callie stopped abruptly, unable to continue.

Vanessa rushed back to her and embraced her as tight as she possibly could.

"Oh, Vanessa," Callie murmured, leaning her head on Vanessa's shoulder. "I'm ruined. . . ."

Privately, Vanessa couldn't help but agree.

FOURTEEN

GO ASK ALICE

The Meaning of Life Is a Rainbow

A poem by Matt Robinson

Lettuce is green
Girls are mean
Bananas are yellow
Boys are mellow
My shirt is purple
Greg's a turtle
Hair that's red
Means crazy in bed
Rhymes with orange?
I'm not blue
I'm a shoe.

There was nothing Callie could do other than try to lose herself in schoolwork, editing her second COMP portfolio, her social life, and Clint—the latter two being a limited luxury depending on if, or really *how quickly*, gossip could travel from California to Cambridge. In the olden days of parchment, wax seals, and men on horses, one could count on news to travel slowly, but now it was no longer possible for people to have hos in different area codes or to do something naughty in one state and expect to be absolved simply by moving to another.

It was Wednesday night: a mere five days since that fateful e-mail, and Callie was sitting in the common room with Mimi and Vanessa as usual, halfheartedly trying to concentrate on Nathaniel Hawthorne's *The Scarlet Letter*: this week's reading assignment for her literature course on the nineteenth-century novel. As she read, a line from the page leaped out and caught her eye.

> "Hester," cried he, "here is a new horror!" Roger Chillingworth knows your purpose to reveal his true character. Will he continue, then, to keep our secret?"

So much for nineteenth-century novels being "irrelevant": was it a coincidence that the books from her class seemed like a mirror for her life, or was this uncanny syllabus clearly the mark of divine intervention—a holy practical joke, if you will. Were there angels up there now having tea and biscuits with Hawthorne, Wharton, and Flaubert and laughing their heads off?

Or was it simply the work of an extremely clever narrator?

Callie hurled her book onto the floor. Mimi and Vanessa stared, obviously still unused to the moody, unpredictable changeling who seemed to have replaced their cheerful, easygoing roommate some time in the past few weeks.

"It's just bullshit, you know!" Callie cried, gesturing toward the novel. "I mean, so she had illicit sex—so what? Who *cares* if it was with a minister? He was hot and you can bet that both of them liked it!"

Vanessa looked concerned while Mimi perked up, hoping to be entertained or scandalized.

"And *now* the whole *fucking* town's making her wear this *bullshit* 'scarlet letter' just because she won't tell them her secret? Well, you know what I say? *Fuck* those guys, man. *Fuck* those *fucking* puritanical Bostonians who can't stop thinking about all the *fucking* they're *not* doing and instead have to *fucking* punish the people who do!"

"Are you done yet?" asked Vanessa.

"No I'm not done yet!" yelled Callie in a mock-irritated-aren't-you-finding-me-so-amusing sort of voice. "I have just one thing left to say about this novel and that is"— She stopped for a moment before breaking into an elongated, deliberate, Tarzan-style yell: *"FUUUUUUUUUUUUUUUUUUUUUUUUUCK!"*

"Bravo!" cried Mimi, clapping her hands. Gravely she picked up her pharmacology textbook for Drugs and the Brain and held it out in front of her. "And to you, my silly textbook friend, I say also: *fuck you!*" she uttered gleefully, giving her homework the middle finger.

"Maybe we should take a break from studying. . . ." Vanessa started, afraid that both her roommates were on the verge of snapping and completely losing it.

"Excellent," said Callie. "Great idea, V."

"Protein bars and TiVo?" Vanessa asked, setting her books aside now as well. (Diet Strategy of the Week: no carbs—"Carbs are, like, totally bad for the environment. Global warming is not a myth.")

"Grand Theft Auto IV!" cried Mimi, rising to her feet. "I would like to shoot things and steal the cars!"

"Great, let's do it," said Callie, starting toward the door. On their way out she yelled, "Hey! Dana! We're going across the hall to chill if you wanna come!"

"That's all right," said Dana, popping her head out of her room. "Adam's going to come over for a movie later so I think I'll just stay here and work until—"

The front door banged shut.

Without knocking Callie, Vanessa, and Mimi barged into the boys' suite across the hall.

Immediately Callie could sense that something was off: the air smelled sticky and sweet, like the odor that often lurked in very special places all over California—near the best surf spots on the beach, in that park behind her high school, spilling out the sides of a foggy-windowed car as four giggling teenagers disembarked on their way to a party, in the bathrooms at the movie theaters, and in every location imaginable across the UC Berkeley campus. . . .

"Tetrahydrocannabinol!" cried Mimi ecstatically as OK broke into a coughing fit and Gregory shoved something under the leather couch.

"It's all right, dude, it's only our neighbors," Matt said from where he'd been reclining on the other couch.

"Matt?" asked Callie. "I didn't know you were a fan of hitting the peace pipe!"

"Peace pipe!" echoed Gregory, giggling in a very un-Gregory-like fashion. "Who calls it that!"

OK, who was looking dazed and confused over on the couch, took a few extra seconds to process the term *peace pipe* before he began mimicking a tomahawk yell and making various gestures that all of us *native* Americans learn at a tender age are blasphemously politically incorrect. "Me-Chief—" he paused, eyes darting around the room for inspiration and settling on an empty can of beer—"Chief Milwaukee's Beast demand passage of peace pipe. Now."

Raising one eyebrow, Gregory handed him the pipe.

"What?" asked Vanessa as she looked around the room. "I don't get it. What's the joke?"

"This is not a joke, Vanessa," OK snapped, suddenly back to his BBC best, attempting to look affronted as he sat up straight on the couch. "On the contrary, this is a very serious effort to engage in some *very serious* relaxation. . . ."

He trailed off as Sublime's cover of "Smoke Two Joints" started to play from the speakers in the corner.

Vanessa rolled her eyes. "Really? On a Wednesday?" she muttered to Callie. Callie laughed and nodded in affirmation: that smell in the room was unquestionably marijuana, and their friendly neighbors from across the hall were stoned out of their minds.

"Well," said Matt, reaching for the pipe, "are you just gonna keep standing there staring or are you guys gonna sit down and chill?"

"I've never smoked pot before," Vanessa admitted to Callie in a whisper. "Because it, like, you know, makes you fat."

"Neither have I," Callie reassured her. "Never wanted to because of soccer."

"Should we leave?" Vanessa asked, glancing longingly toward Gregory as Mimi, already comfortable on the couch, passed him the pipe.

Callie had always prided herself on being the type of girl who avoided using substances to alter her mood. But, then again, until now she'd never suffered from a mood that was in serious need of alteration. Plus, she couldn't bear the thought of returning to her room. . . .

"No, let's stay and try it," she said, taking Vanessa by the hand. "College is supposed to be all about new adventures and experiences, and there's no other person with whom I'd rather lose my pot-smoking virginity."

"Did somebody say 'virginity'?" Gregory asked with a mischievous smile. His pupils were so dilated that they had nearly swallowed the cold blues of his irises. "I didn't know you were a virgin, Callie. I never would have guessed."

Before Callie could respond, Mimi cut in: "Oh no, *she* is definitely not a virgin," she cried, shaking her head at Callie, and then pointing to Vanessa: "but *she* is!"

"Thanks a lot, Mimi," Callie and Vanessa murmured simultaneously, both turning pink.

"Hey, it's all right, Vanessa," OK said as he lit the pipe, inhaling deeply. He exhaled slowly, releasing an enormous puff of sweet-smelling smoke. "Matty here's a virgin, too!"

"That's right," said Matt. "I'm saving myself for someone special."

"What's wrong with me, baby?" OK joked, leaping to his feet and rushing over to tackle Matt, trying to mount him as Matt struggled to resist. "Am I not special enough for you?"

The two boys, both well over six feet tall, wrestled for a few moments in an affectionate tangle of black and white limbs while Mimi screamed. Matt managed to pin OK, who, fighting for freedom, flung himself onto Mimi, pretending to cling to her for comfort.

"There, there," she cooed, patting OK on the head as he tried to nuzzle closer to her chest. "I will protect you, the enormous black man, from the skinny white boy you just tried to molest. . . ."

Gregory looked up from helping Vanessa light the pipe, chuckling appreciatively. Midway through laughing, a confused expression passed across his face: he couldn't remember what had been so funny. He kept laughing anyway.

Callie watched as Vanessa inhaled, expanding her cheeks and furrowing her brow in a way that made her look like a constipated blowfish. Vanessa held her breath for a good ten seconds before she exhaled in a tremendous fit of coughing. Gregory patted her fraternally—or was it affectionately?—on the back.

"Your turn, *Caliente*!" Gregory cried, leaning over Vanessa and brandishing the pipe.

Vanessa succumbed to another hacking fit, tears streaming out the corners of her eyes.

"I'll be gentle, Callie, I promise," Gregory whispered, positioning the lighter. "Just try to breathe slowly and hold it in your lungs for as long as you can."

Callie nodded and placed her lips around the mouth of the pipe. Slowly she sucked the sweet-smelling smoke into her lungs, then gulped a large mouthful of air like a swimmer surfacing from the water and held it for a count of five Mississippis.

Her head felt light, and she, like Vanessa, started to cough uncontrollably, her throat burning.

"Atta girl, *Caliente*, atta girl," said Gregory, patting her on the knee. "Always knew you were a champion."

Meanwhile Matt had leaped up and walked over to the other side of the room, returning with two water bottles. Smiling like a proud soccer mom, he handed them to Callie and Vanessa.

Callie let the cool water soothe her aching throat. "Wow, water bottles and everything!" she said when she had recovered her powers of speech. "Who knew you were such a pro? To be perfectly honest, I never would have guessed that you . . ."

"That I what?" asked Matt, sliding between OK and Mimi with a mischievous look on his face. "Like to smoke pot? Just because

I'm from *upstate* New York doesn't make me a naive little farm boy."

As he said the word *upstate*, Callie noticed him flash a look in Gregory's direction. She was reminded of the time she'd concluded that Matt wasn't going out on Friday night because nobody had invited him to a party. Why do I immediately assume that Matt isn't as, well, *cool* as the rest of us? she chided herself. He was smart, friendly, funny (sometimes unintentionally), and even rather good-looking in certain lighting when he bothered to substitute contacts for his glasses. . . .

Callie suddenly realized that Vanessa, who usually couldn't shut up, hadn't said a word since she'd smoked from the pipe. A dreamy expression had settled across her face: an expression normally reserved for the occasions when they passed by the display window of Finale, the high-end cake store in Harvard Square. Callie wondered if Vanessa was "high." Callie, for one, hadn't started to feel anything yet.

"I'm hungry!" Gregory exclaimed, folding his arms and leaning back.

"I could make you some popcorn!" Vanessa cried, snapping to attention. "It's just across the hall—I'll be right back!"

"Mmm . . . that would be wonderful," Gregory murmured, his eyes half-closed.

"Ew—popcorn!" Mimi said, wrinkling her nose. "The things you Americans like to eat . . ."

"If you could eat anything right now, what would it be?" asked OK, staring at Mimi as if he'd just asked her to fly off to

Vegas and marry him tomorrow and was awaiting her response.

"Hmm . . . cornichon pickles *avec du beurre* and that hot sauce they make at Felipe's."

"Excellent. I'll ring for Babatunde and have him bring it up immediately," OK said, reaching to his left and grasping at some empty air. He looked very perturbed when he realized there was nothing there. "Where's my summoning bell? Did you guys hide it again?"

"Summoning bell!" Callie howled at the joke.

Matt cut in: "I threw it out the window two nights ago—that damn bell was *annoying*, man. If you want to talk to one of us, get up off your ass and come find us."

Matt looked to Gregory for affirmation, but Gregory was busy staring at the enormous poster of a topless porn star that was plastered on the wall opposite the big screen TV: so "college" and so clichéd. "She's always watching over us," he muttered. "Like an angel with giant, giant boobs . . ."

Speaking of boobs—

"I'm back!" cried Vanessa, busting in with a huge bowl of popcorn and sporting an extremely low-cut tank top that she hadn't been wearing earlier. "There you go!" she said, placing the popcorn down in front of Gregory in a way that gave him a full view of her chest.

"Angels . . ." whispered Gregory, reaching into the bowl as Vanessa lingered seductively over the coffee table.

Slut! Callie thought irritably. She watched Gregory stare down the neck of Vanessa's top. Wait a minute, what am I saying? Vanessa's my best friend at Harv—

"Scoot over!" Vanessa hissed, squeezing into the narrow space between Callie and Gregory on the couch.

Slut-faced whore!

Callie suddenly realized that Matt was holding the pipe, looking at her expectantly. Annoyed, she accepted, hesitated, and wondered how you were supposed to light the damn thing before thrusting it in Vanessa's face, which was currently hovering obnoxiously close to Gregory's.

"Oooh, *thanks*!" Vanessa cooed without even turning to look at her. "Gregory, would you do me the honor?"

"Sure thing, darlin'," he answered, holding it for her with one hand and lighting it with the other.

In the meantime things were starting to get a little weird over on the other couch. Matt, who apparently thought he was being funny, cried: "Look, guys! I can breathe underwater!" before submerging his entire head in the gigantic bowl of popcorn, sending buttery kernels soaring around the room.

This sent OK and Mimi into a fit of hysterics until German techno-pop started playing on the iPod shuffle: *Oh, du mein touch privaten Raum, wo ich mein Herz . . .*

Callie was struggling to recall the name of the song when OK leaped to his feet and roared:

"HANSEL EBERHARDT, HOW DID YOU GET IN HERE? WHERE ARE YOU HIDING? COME OUT AND

FIGHT, YOU TIGHT-PANTS-WEARING SEX GOD!" In a frenzy he raced around the room, lifting pillows off the couch and peering under the coffee table, searching, apparently, for the "Techno Prince of Europe."

Amused, Mimi started yelling, "OK! Relax! He is not actually in here. It is just his band—Sexy Hansel—playing on the iPod."

"Oh!" said OK, clapping his hand across his forehead. "I mean, yeah, I knew that. Just don't like this song is all . . . thought I'd change it if nobody minds?"

"Sissy," Mimi muttered wickedly.

"What'd you just say!" cried OK, jumping as if somebody had just shot a surprise enema up his ass.

"I *said* that you are a *sissy*." Mimi laughed. "Similar meaning to 'wimp,' 'fairy,' and 'pussy'? I looked it up today on UrbanDictionary dot com!" she finished proudly.

Shaking her head, Callie regretted the day she had elected to tell Mimi about UrbanDictionary.com.

Still rattled, OK settled back onto the couch. Mimi patted him on the knee and reached to take the pipe from Gregory's outstretched hand. Nobody seemed the least bit concerned that Matt's head was still submerged in the popcorn bowl like an ostrich burrowed in the sand.

Vanessa was swaying to the music, a vacant expression in her eyes until, catching sight of Matt, she started to scream, *"OH MY GOD! Matt! What happened to his HEAD?"*

Gregory started snickering, but Vanessa was on the verge of tears. "What—what happened to it? It's not attached to his body!

Where did it go! Is he still . . . *alive*?" she stammered, recoiling from what Callie realized in some bizarre marijuana world might look like a body without a head. Clearly she wasn't as high as the rest of them.

"Uhguh-chughuh-tawy-aetma-wee-oot!" came Matt's muffled response from deep inside the bowl.

"What!?" cried Vanessa, clinging to Gregory for comfort.

"He said he is going to try to eat his way out," said Mimi, a deadpan expression on her face. "Really, Vanessa, I thought you said you *know* how to speak French. . . ."

"Mais non, elle n'a pas la sophistication," Gregory offered as he patted Vanessa's head (which she was resting on his shoulder), a bored expression in his eyes.

"I thought you spoke Spanish?" Callie shot at him.

"*Oui, Caliente, je parle les deux*. And Italian, Chinese, Japanese, and Arabic, in addition to a perfunctory knowledge of Latin and Greek. What?" he added as she looked at him, incredulous. "Surprised to learn I'm more than just a pretty face?"

"You *don't* speak all those languages, my little California football champion?" OK asked obnoxiously from the couch. "Everybody knows you need at least Chinese or Japanese for business, Latin and Greek to pass boarding school, Arabic if you're ever tapped by the CIA, French and Italian if you're ever in love, and Spanish if you want them to get things right in the burrito you order from Felipe's when you're shit-faced at two A.M."

"Amen to that!" Gregory and OK did a fist pound, and Mimi stared at them in awe, no doubt wondering if she had just witnessed new material to add to her high-five repertoire.

Suddenly Matt's head shot out of the popcorn bowl. "I've had a vision!" he cried, springing to his feet and running toward his room.

"Of what?" asked Mimi, giggling as OK slid his arm around her shoulders. "Trans fats and the color yellow?"

"Need pen and paper!" came the muffled reply. He emerged moments later holding a notebook covered with doodles and drawings. "Sometimes when I'm high, I like to write poetry. . . ." he said, a serious expression settling across his face.

"Sometimes when I'm high," started OK, also looking serious, "I think that I've grown a third ball. I look down and I see three glorious fucking testicles just floating around like I'm the king of the fucking sperm gods. But then," he continued, his face falling a little, "a few hours later I look down again and realize that it was all just a beautiful, beautiful dream. . . ."

Ew, thought Callie as Mimi dissolved into laughter. For some reason Callie still wasn't feeling high at all, and she felt like the only sane person in a room full of idiots. She didn't think she could stand it much longer: Matt's bad poetry, OK's third ball, Mimi's tendency to lapse into French, or Vanessa resting her head on Gregory's broad, muscular shoulder as if she were about to fall asleep—

"I'm leaving," she said, standing up and feeling miserable at the prospect of returning to Hawthorne's *Scarlet Letter* and the odd smacking sounds of inexperienced kissing drifting from Dana's enclave of romance.

"What?" asked Gregory, turning so abruptly that Vanessa's

head fell off his shoulder. "And leave me here to pine for you, heartbroken and alone?" He leaned over the couch, reaching his arms out dramatically as if he were trying to pull her back.

Callie struggled to suppress a smile. "It's not you guys—it's me. I'm just not feeling it. . . ."

"No, no, no," said Gregory, shaking his head. "I know it's been said that not every girl can come during her first time, but *every* girl always comes with me." Mimi and OK started to laugh, and even Matt looked up from his notepad on which he'd been scribbling. Callie did her best to look stern. The truth was, in spite of everything, his words had sparked a tiny fire in the region a few inches below her belly button—a flame that not even Vanessa's sleepy, pouty expression had the power to extinguish.

Even when they were almost entirely pupils, Gregory's eyes still made her feel like she was Alice tumbling down the rabbit hole—especially when they took on that grave expression. "But seriously, Callie," he said, "you should have piped up earlier. There are definitely other ways that we can make it work."

"Other positions we can try," OK chimed in.

"Oh no—" said Matt, biting the edge of his pen. "You guys aren't planning to—"

"HOT BOX THE BATHROOM!" OK and Gregory yelled simultaneously.

"Again," Matt finished feebly. "Last time it smelled in there for days."

"Which would actually be an improvement to its usual smell," Mimi said delicately, "if I might weigh in on the matter."

"Dibs on the Jacuzzi!" OK cried, leaping to his feet. "Care to take a bath, my dear?" he added, turning toward Mimi.

"Veto!" cried Gregory. Standing behind Callie, he placed his hands on her waist and guided her toward the bathroom. "*Caliente* and I reserved it weeks ago. Bad luck, buddy."

"Oh, shut up, both of you," said Mimi, walking into the bathroom. She slammed both the windows shut, ripped back the shower curtain, and turned the water on *hot*. OK, Callie, and Gregory piled in behind her, and Gregory closed the door. Matt stayed on the couch, engrossed in his poetry, and Vanessa had actually fallen asleep sometime between the words *positions* and *hot box*.

Soon enough the room was thick with steam. Gregory repacked the pipe and held it to Callie's lips, tucking a loose strand of hair behind her ear.

"That's it . . . breathe deeply now. . . ," he encouraged. As she exhaled, the smoke mingled with the steam. She didn't cough this time, and her head was actually feeling much lighter . . . maybe it was the heat.

"Another one, just for good measure?" she asked, smiling at Gregory. He grinned in return and relit the pipe.

Meanwhile OK was filling the "Jacuzzi" and Mimi was perched on the toilet, singing Edith Piaf's "Non, Je Ne Regrette Rien" and verifying for them all why singing was not one of her many talents. As she sang, Mimi noticed a bottle of pink bubble bath resting on the side of the tub and lifted it questioningly.

"A gift for the room from Matt's mom," OK explained. Mimi nodded and started pouring the entire contents of the bottle into the tub as she began to hum Simon and Garfunkel's classic ode to cougars.

Callie felt like the fog in the bathroom had moved inside her head: it was as if in slow motion she watched OK remove his shirt, revealing ebony skin and sharply defined abdominals.

"Wahooooo!" cried Mimi. "Take it *off*!"

Obediently OK removed his pants. Mimi clapped her hands. To Callie's surprise—and Mimi's apparent delight—he didn't stop there: in under three seconds his white boxer briefs were lying in a pile with the rest of his clothes. Before Callie could even start to feel embarrassed, he had hopped into the tub: concealed by a sea of strawberry-scented bubbles.

"Your turn, Mimi, dear!" he yelled, suds splashing.

Callie giggled as Mimi also started to remove her clothing. When she was down to her boy shorts and bra, she jumped into the tub. Callie glanced at Gregory and was pleased to find him staring at her instead of Mimi.

"Let's just chill over here," Gregory said to Callie's vague disappointment, spreading a fluffy blue towel across the cold tile floor and motioning for her to sit.

She obeyed him readily and plopped down onto the towel, amazed at just how *fluffy* it really was . . . and how *blue*, too. She ran her fingers over it, up and down, up and down, marveling that her *fingers* were actually attached to her *hands* that were touching this towel that was so *fluffy* and *blue*. . . .

"This is great," Gregory said as Mimi and OK squealed and

splashed, sitting down next to her so that their shoulders were touching and she could feel the warmth of his skin through her thin T-shirt. The little blond hairs on her arm started to stand on end and she suddenly felt cold . . . then shivery and hot. . . . Wait a minute—did he just say something?

"What . . ." she asked, rubbing her arm, "what . . . did you say?"

"Oh," said Gregory, staring at his hands. "I just said that this is great—you know: us getting some time to hang out like this. We should do it more often."

"What—smoke pot?"

"No," he said, "just hang out. Talk about books or something. You know, whatever."

Am I high or is he being serious right now? she wondered. A little shiver ran down her spine.

"Are you—are you *cold*?" Gregory asked as the hot steam swirled around them.

"No . . ." she said, shivering again. Suddenly she felt his arm slide around her shoulders, pulling her close to his body.

"I'll keep you warm," he whispered, and rather than reacting in horror that her mortal enemy Gregory Sleazebag Bolton was trying to touch her, all she could feel was pleasant and content, like this position was totally natural for two people who generally behaved like they despised each other.

In the meantime it appeared that OK had sprouted his "magical" third ball.

"Mimi!" he was insisting, waving aside the bubbles. "Mimi, come on! You've got to take a look at this!"

"Okay, OK." She sighed. "But *only* for clinical purposes." She peered down through the translucent water.

"Well?" he asked.

"Well," she said, waving the bubbles back into place, "I can *see* only two, but that certainly does not mean there is not a third one somewhere else. . . ."

"Oh, shit," said Gregory. "I think somebody got way, way too high . . . damn. I *told* him that if he didn't slow down he was going to green out later on."

"Green out?" asked Callie, blinking and struggling to concentrate on what was happening around her when all she could feel was the weight of him around her shoulders and that *hand* caressing her bare arm.

"Like black out but for weed? That's clever," she murmured stupidly.

"OH, MY SWEET JESUS!" OK roared suddenly, leaping to his feet for the second time that night as Mimi leaned back. "SOMEBODY'S TAKEN MY THIRD BALL AND HIDDEN IT IN THE ALLEY. IF I DON'T GET IT BACK TONIGHT, THEY'RE GOING TO BOMB THE ENTIRE CITY!"

"OK . . ." Mimi started.

"NO!" he cut in. "NO! IF I DON'T GET IT BACK TONIGHT, NONE OF YOU—I REPEAT, NONE OF YOU—WILL LIVE!"

With that he sloshed out of the tub and flung open the bathroom door, giving them all a generous view of his glorious, royal rear. Mimi sighed, stood, and reached for a towel. Turning to Gregory and Callie, who were still sitting on the floor, she said, "Now I am better understanding the meaning of the phrase 'tripping *balls.*'"

Gregory laughed. "I should go put him to bed," he said, getting to his feet.

No, don't go—

"Come on, *Caliente,*" he added, holding out both hands. She took them and he pulled her up toward him. They were only a few inches apart now, and he had yet to let go of her hands—

At that moment Vanessa appeared in the bathroom doorway, rubbing her eyes and looking confused.

"Guys, I fell asleep and had a dream that a large black man was running naked through a field and then there was a big slam that sounded like a door—"

"Oh, putain! Fils de pute! Il s'est cassé!" Mimi cursed, pulling her jeans on over her wet underwear. "I will find him, I will find him," she added, pushing past them out of the room. "He cannot have gone far. . . ."

"What on earth . . . ?" Vanessa asked.

"Don't worry, we'll explain later," Callie replied, repeating Mimi's curses silently as Gregory also walked out of the bathroom.

"All right," said Vanessa. "Actually—I wanted to talk to you about something. . . ."

Oh, shit I'm a bad friend I'm a bad friend—

"It's about Matt."

What?

"Look, I know I've been asleep for a while, but I'm pretty sure that earlier he was hitting on me."

Callie peered out of the bathroom to check on Matt, who at the moment was having what seemed like an intensely philosophical conversation with the fake plant in the corner. "Listen, man, I *know*," she heard him murmur from across the room. "I've had *my* share of bad luck with the ladies, too, but that doesn't mean you should stop putting yourself out there. . . ."

Callie, stifling a laugh, was pretty sure that hitting on a human being was the last thing that Matt had in mind.

"Look," Vanessa started again, "I don't want this to get weird, but I know you guys had your whole geek-crush thing going on before you wised up and found Clint, so I felt I should tell you and say that I don't intend to act on it."

Callie just stared. "I didn't . . . I never liked . . ." She gaped, trying to explain.

"It's all right, sweetie; I won't tell anyone. It's bros before hos, right? Or—er—chicks before dicks?"

Callie continued to stare at Vanessa, who, for all intents and purposes, appeared to be serious.

"Uh . . . thanks," said Callie. "You really are great. In fact, you're the best!" Elated with a sudden burst of affection, she gave Vanessa a big bear hug. As they embraced, her eyes locked with Gregory's. She wasn't sure how—perhaps the pot had made her temporarily telepathic—but she *knew* in that instant that they were both wondering the exact same thing: how to get back to that blue towel and steal a few more precious seconds alone. . . .

OK was back inside a room shaped exactly like his own, only for some reason everything was pink: the bedspread, the walls, the picture frames, the furry pillow resting on the chair at the desk. He blinked and rubbed his eyes, but when he opened them, the objects in the room still appeared just as pink.

He stumbled around as if he was looking for something but couldn't quite remember what it was. He could see that he was naked, and *that* usually only happened right before he went to bed. . . . That was it! His bed: he was looking for his bed. Just the thought of it made him yawn enormously. . . .

He stared for a moment longer at the pink, velour bedspread before shaking his head and stumbling past the Marilyn Monroe poster that Matt's mom must have given him and back into the common room.

There were TV sounds coming from behind the door immediately to his right. He had a television in his room so . . . clearly this was it!

Yawning deeply, his eyelids so heavy they were almost shut, he plodded into the pitch-dark room, pleased to have found it so that he could finally get to bed.

He was asleep before his body even hit the mattress.

There was a loud, girlish scream as Dana reached for the light, certain that somebody was attacking them—

"What the *heck*?" Adam screamed, hitting a high G again.

There was a deep groan and a "Shove off would you—I'm trying to sleep" before Dana found the light and discovered a very large, very naked visitor in her bed. . . .

Mimi, who hadn't been able to find OK outside or on any other floor of their dormitory hurried back toward his room. Quickly she rushed up the stairs and walked into the hallway just in time to witness a livid, bathrobed Dana run out of C 24 chasing a naked, terrified OK back into C 23. Adam cowered behind her, looking almost as scared as OK.

"I swear I just popped in to borrow a cup of sugar!" OK screamed as Dana hounded after him.

Shaking her head, Mimi followed them back into C 23.

Dana was more than a little upset. She was yelling so loudly and so quickly that she was almost unintelligible: Mimi heard something about a "Wednesday" and a "waste of an education" several times, followed by a "don't know what kind of drugs you've been doing" and a "glad you never invite me to these things, anyway." In any event the message was clear: it was time for bed.

Dana stormed back across the hall, and Adam stood helplessly for a moment before evidently deciding that it would be safer to return to his room. Mimi, Callie, and Vanessa bid their farewells and trudged out into the hallway.

At the door to their suite Vanessa hesitated. "Uhm . . . I think I—forgot something. I'm just going to run back and get it. Good night. See you girls in the morning!"

Callie felt a nagging sensation in her stomach as she watched Vanessa, but she knew there was nothing she could do about it. Mimi looked at her and shrugged, then embraced her before entering her room. Callie paused for a moment, and then also returned to her bedroom. It would be a long time before she managed to fall asleep. . . .

Vanessa tiptoed back into C 23, smiling when she realized that everybody except Gregory had gone to bed. He was staring at the porn star poster, looking heartbroken.

Somebody—probably Matt—had written a name across each boob. On the right: Harold. On the left: Maude.

"He's in for a beating when he wakes up," Gregory said, tearing his eyes from the poster and grinning at Vanessa. "What up, V?"

"Well . . ." she started, staring at her hands. "I was just wondering if . . . if maybe I could sleep here tonight?"

"Uh—well, sure," he said, eyeing her quizzically. "I mean, I don't think that the couch will be very comfortable but it's yours if you want it. What happened? Another fight? It seemed like you three were getting along so well?"

"Oh *no*," she cried. She tried to laugh, but the sounds got stuck in her throat. Encouraged by the way his eyes fell on her chest, she took a step closer. "What I meant was: can I stay here tonight with *you*—you know, in your room?"

He was silent, staring at her.

She smiled flirtatiously, trying to disguise her nerves. "My weed-smoking virginity doesn't have to be the *only* one you take tonight. . . ."

Gregory's face changed abruptly—as if a bucket of cold water had just shocked him into clarity through the post-pot haze. Forcing himself to tear his eyes away from Vanessa's chest, he looked up and met her gaze.

"V, I'm sorry, but I can't. You're *gorgeous*," he added as something in her face seemed to collapse from the inside, "but the truth is—"

He paused. This was normally the part where he drew on his arsenal of the usual excuses: *I'm married—gay—have herpes—Value our friendship—Let's just be friends?—It's not you, it's me—Just got out of prison—Only got a month to live—Slept with your sister—Phone fell down a toilet—Thanks, I'd love to, but I have a meeting with my psychiatrist. . . .*

But in the end he broke the mold and, for perhaps the first time, he told the truth. "The truth is I think you're great, but I have feelings for someone else."

She was on the verge of demanding to know *who* was standing between her and the man she'd just offered her virginity when suddenly it hit her like a sack of bricks:

"It's not—is it?"

His glance toward the floor was as good as a yes.

"Oh—silly me," said Vanessa, backing out of the room as fast as possible. "I should've known! Well, see you later!" she managed, turning and slamming the door—lest he notice that the "later" had been swallowed by an involuntary sob.

Once she was safely inside her own common room, Vanessa headed straight for the bathroom. She locked the door behind her and then sank to her knees. Leaning over the toilet, she stuck her finger down her throat and pulled the proverbial trigger. . . .

For a long time after it was over, she stood there, transfixed by her image in the mirror. Then she washed her face, brushed her teeth, turned, and clicked off the light.

FIFTEEN

What Goes Around Comes Around

Dearest Froshlings:

There's an old joke that goes . . .

Private school: $30,000 per annum. SAT tutor: $10,000. College counselor: $15,000. Bribing the authors of your letters of recommendation: $1,500. Final phone call to the Dean of Admissions (aka the promise to donate a new building): $5,000,000+.

A Harvard education: priceless. For everything else, there's Daddy's MasterCard.

But in all seriousness, I know that Harvard can be a little more *expensive* than you had originally anticipated. Whether it's the dues you've got to pay after your unexpected admittance into a Final Club or that expensive dinner you shouldn't have charged to your already maxed-out credit card, no one can argue that sometimes college students just *need* a little extra cash. For some reason I've had an awful lot of blog posts lately asking what students can do around campus for said extra cash, so—by popular demand:

spare change:
Attempting to Narrow Harvard's Socioeconomic Gaps

1. **get a job:** This may seem obvious to many of you, but for those of you who have never really worked a day in your life on anything other than a problem set, try getting off your lazy ass

and GET A JOB! There are ample opportunities for grunt work at Harvard: from grading papers to working the library front desk to calling alumni for donations to working as a barista in Lamont Café. . . .

2. participate in a psych study: Depending on the study, this option can be risky, but there are always eager psych/med students around Harvard willing to pay if you'll let them poke you, prod you, or look inside your brain. Some studies are as benign as clicking a button, but some (and unfortunately these are usually the ones that pay the big bucks) bear an eerie resemblance to Stanley Milgram's Obedience to Authority electric shock experiments. . . .

3. find a patron or a sugar-daddy/mommy: I think this probably works better in the movies than it does in real life, but go ahead and dare to dream. . . . Now I ain't sayin' she's a gold digger, but I'm sure there must be plenty of wealthy, unattractive people lying around at Harvard somewhere just waiting to be exploited. If *The Real Housewives of Orange County* can do it, then so, my friend, can you.

4. hook up with a tf/professor: Now, I'm certainly not advocating *blackmail* per se, but perhaps you might try encouraging them to . . . request your silence. If nothing else, at least you might earn an A for your efforts.

5. start an escort service? No, that's probably bad advice. Starting a fake charity: also bad advice. Seriously, don't do that. (And don't blame me if you get caught.)

Well, those are all of my creative ideas for the moment. Please feel free to write in to the blogs with your own suggestions or any further questions.

Also, I want all of you freshmen out there to please keep in mind: whether you make your own money or were born into it like the best–er, rest–of us, no matter how fabulously "rich" you may feel, you still have to pay your dues to those who are "richer" than you both in knowledge and in years. Contrary to the impression you may have formed, simply having money at Harvard does *not* equal social mobility. No freshman will ever be exempt from paying Harvard's "social taxes," and upperclassmen will always be unshakably–as it should be–at the top of the campus Food Chain.

Go forth and prosper,
Alexis Thorndike, Advice Columnist
Fifteen Minutes Magazine
Harvard's Authority on Campus Life since 1873

Swipe. Stamp. "Have-a-nice-day!" Swipe. Stamp. "Have-a-nice-day!" Swipe. Stamp. "Have-a-nice-day!" Swipe. Stamp . . .

Callie stared miserably at the clock: 6:51.

Only nine minutes left to go until her four-hour shift working the desk at Lamont Library would end: her exhilarating new job that paid a generous twelve dollars per hour to swipe (students' identification cards), stamp (the due date into the library books), and bid a cheerful farewell ("Have-a-nice-day!") even on days like today when she felt anything but cheerful. The combination of virtually no sleep the night before and her "green-over" was making her feel stupid and slow, as if every movement took extra effort and inordinate amounts of concentration.

With every monotonous swipe she pictured another quarter dropping into her imaginary piggy bank, still hundreds of dollars away from being able to fund her Pudding membership.

She glanced across the foyer at Lamont Café, where many fellow members were congregating, sipping coffee, and gossiping. She could see Anne Goldberg at a table close to the counter, always keeping half an eye on newcomers in the doorway or the cute boy a few tables over while pretending to concentrate on her books.

Just over a month ago their lifestyle as Harvard's social elite had seemed so far out of reach; now, miraculously, they had accepted her as one of their own. She finally understood what it meant to belong.

Well, not quite . . . she thought, stamping a library book for a pretty, senior girl whom she had met during initiation. It pained her to let them see her working, but she had no other choice. If she was lucky, after a semester of working four-hour shifts three times a week, she'd be able to afford the price of being popular.

She cringed as she recalled the telephone call she'd had with her mother about the Pudding earlier that week. She should have known that her mom—who had raised her to be frugal and cautious with money—would never understand why she *needed* to belong to this club. She had only been two sentences into her explanation when her mother had cut her off.

"I don't understand why you should have to pay people in order to keep them as friends."

And *that* had been the end of it.

"I like your headband," the senior girl said, smiling as she loaded the books into her tote bag.

"Thanks," said Callie, smiling back and reminding herself that she ought to be thanking Vanessa, who had given Callie the red, oriental silk headband earlier that week because it "clashed" with her own reddish hair.

Over the past several days Vanessa had been truly amazing. She had taken Callie on a Girls Only spa excursion the Saturday after the e-mail disaster, where the pain of getting waxed and plucked for the first time had effectively distracted her. Yesterday morning Vanessa had even insisted on proofreading Callie's pieces for her second COMP portfolio, which were due the following week. In a way Vanessa's sympathy about the Evan Incident and her attitude of total forgiveness made Callie feel even worse about the Pudding. But on the other hand, being able to confide in someone had been such a relief. Two months ago she never would have guessed that Vanessa might be the sole friend at Harvard whom she chose to take into her confidences, but Vanessa had proved supportive and nonjudgmental beyond any of Callie's expectations.

These days it seemed like their bond was stronger than ever before—especially after such a crazy time last night. Especially, Callie couldn't help but think, since I heard her coming back just a few minutes after she left.

Vanessa had been fast asleep when Callie headed to class that morning so she hadn't had a chance to get the details yet, but she had a feeling that nothing serious had happened.

6:57 P.M.: only three more minutes of torture until Callie could grab a bite to eat, finish her homework, and pass out in her tiny twin bed. . . .

Just then a scrawny freshman boy who looked like—and may very well have been—a fourteen-year-old genius approached the counter and whined in a nasal, prepubescent voice:

"Uhm, I'm looking for the Quantum Electrodynamics textbook for my advanced level physics course. According to the library's database, it *should* be located in the stacks on the fourth floor, but I've been up there looking and am certain that it's been misplaced. I already filed a Missing Book form and arranged to pick up a different copy from Widener Library tomorrow, but I really thought you ought to know so you can go up there and verify that it's actually missing before you leave today."

He finished, looking at her expectantly.

Seriously? She stared back at him, hoping he'd be intimidated by the fact that, even as a girl, she was at least a head taller than him.

He didn't budge.

Lucky me! she thought with an aggravated sigh, coming out from behind the checkout counter and heading toward the stairs. She glanced back over her shoulder before opening the double doors. Sure enough, he was still standing there, staring. She had no other choice: he was clearly going to stay put and make sure he fulfilled his vigilante library duties by forcing her to approve that stupid missing book form.

Slowly she climbed the stairs. Having no prior need for a little light reading in advanced physics, she had never been up to the fourth floor stacks. Rumor had it that since so few people cared about quantum electrodynamics, the fourth floor stacks were a preferred destination for clandestine library encounters, usually of an illicit, sexual nature. . . .

Catching two people in the act would certainly be the icing on a fan-freaking-tastic day, she thought as she followed the confusing arrows toward the quantum mechanics section.

Wandering through the stacks was like wandering through a maze, but eventually she found the right aisle. The Q section was low down, close to the floor. As she squatted to search for that little pinprick's textbook she thought she heard voices coming from somewhere in the adjacent row.

She didn't think much of it until she distinctly heard the words *shame*, *COMP*, and *magazine* spoken by a female voice, and then another female voice give a muffled reply.

Holding her breath, Callie inched past the Q and R sections all the way down to the S titles: a point from which the conversation was suddenly far more audible.

". . . a little bit about how the COMP evaluation process works. We cut over fifty individuals during the first round, so now there are about sixty people left to compete for ten coveted spots."

So she'd heard right. They were talking about some sort of COMP! Of course, it could be for a different organization, but she knew there were about sixty people vying for places at *FM*.

"Each of our current editors is responsible for reviewing five portfolios a day, which means that we'll have the results of the second round tallied shortly after we return from Thanksgiving break. Less than thirty people will continue for the third and final round."

Bingo! They were *definitely* talking about *FM*, and this girl had to be one of the editors. Callie strained to hear the voice, grasping for familiar nuances or intonations, but the tone was too muffled by all the dense Erwin Schrödinger books to identify the speaker.

"Competitors' portfolios are supposed to be completely name-blind and anonymous, but it's pretty easy to tell who each person is based on the pieces they've submitted. Regardless, each editor scores the pieces on a scale of one to ten, and then gives the portfolio an overall score before passing it on to the next editor. At the end of the process all of the scores are compiled and averaged. The ten people with the highest scores win a spot on the magazine after the third round, though usually there's a run-off and we all take a vote based on—other qualities."

Callie couldn't believe her luck! *Nobody* outside of the *FM* editors knew the specific details of how COMP selection worked, and yet there these two mysterious girls were, somewhere between *Space-Time Structure* and *Statistical Thermodynamics*, about to reveal it all. . . .

"Now, so far the 'anonymous' COMPer in question has done much better than I'd expected. By some fluke of nature the scores on her first portfolio were actually very high—even a few tens, which are unheard of for a freshman."

Callie's heart stopped. Could it be—was it possible—that these girls were talking about *her*? She tried not to let her ego speed ahead of her as she processed the phrases "even a few tens" and "unheard of for a freshman." In high school, whenever her teachers had announced that the standard deviation was skewed because somebody had outscored everyone by a significant margin, they had always given Callie a significant look, and she knew, just *knew*, that she was the person they were talking about.

As quietly as possible, she crouched and began to pull out one heavy book after another, while the other girl, whose voice was softer and harder to hear, was murmuring something about "read her pieces" and "really talented."

Working quickly, Callie cleared an area large enough for her to poke her head into. She could see through a serendipitously empty space between the books in the adjacent aisle. Cautiously she looked from left to right—thank you again, Advanced Theoretical Physics, for being so boring—before lying stomach to the floor and sticking her head through the gap.

"... too much drama and too much controversy for the magazine. As you might imagine, we have an image to protect, and that image is *crucial* to the success of our publications."

Crap, Callie thought irritably, squinting: all she could make out was a scuffed gray floor and somebody's navy blue Longchamp bag resting against the bookshelves. That bag could belong to anybody in *FM*: you could spot at least eighty of them on any given day during Justice. . . . Did she dare try to shift the position of a book from the shelf in their aisle? It seemed just a little too risky. . . .

She was about to reach out and move it anyway when she suddenly froze.

". . . image: it's the same reason I advocated to keep her out of the Pudding—and unfortunately, we both know how that turned out, don't we? It's a way she has with men: manipulating them and wrapping them around her finger with that bleach blond hair and that whole transparent act about being an innocent little California girl. It's amazing how she had both Tyler and Clint salivating at her heels so that they just *couldn't* say no. . . ."

When she heard "bleach blond," Callie had been ninety-nine percent certain about the identity of the speaker: a fear which was then confirmed as the girl took a step forward and Callie caught sight of the ivory Chanel flats with two interlocking golden Cs and the slim, alabaster ankles that could belong to only one person.

Alexis Thorndike.

Lexi, plotting against her in the Advanced Theoretical Physics section of Lamont Library with an unknown cohort, trying to figure out if there was a way they could keep Callie out of—

"Now, I can't ensure that she gets cut this round if her scores continue to be so high, but we are at liberty to use our discretion when it comes to serious questions of character. If *somebody* can cast a dubious light on another person's integrity, then we can choose to deny her admittance based on the potential for scandal because, like I said, we do have a very important reputation to uphold. Can you think of something?"

The other girl, whoever she was, was silent.

"Plagiarism? Racism? Nepotism? Inappropriate Facebook photos? No? Anything at all?" Lexi prodded.

More silence.

Lexi's flats disappeared from view. "Look," she started again, her tone dropping so that Callie had to strain to hear, "I think we both know what the real issue is here and that's this thing about the Pudding. Now that I know you a little better, I for one think it's a crime against nature that you didn't get in."

Callie felt her heart start to sink in her chest as she realized she *did* know a specific somebody who owned a navy Longchamp bag . . . somebody who also didn't get into the Pudding. . . .

"I'll admit that I wasn't exactly pushing for you during elections, but I can see now that I was mistaken: you fit the Pudding profile exactly. You belong with us. In fact . . . when I think about it, you had a lot of advocates, but then one girl went ahead and blackballed you. I believe it may have been something to do with her boyfriend . . . Jeremy or Jeffrey something? Anyhow, blackballing is such an aggressive, distasteful move that personally I would never make, but as you know, once an individual invokes it, there's really nothing we can do."

"Wait. If you can't do anything for me, then why am I . . . ?" came the sound of a voice that was now painfully familiar.

"Because the girl who blackballed you is a fifth-year senior, meaning she's going to be *graduating*—thank god—at the end of this semester."

"Ahh . . ."

"Exactly. Spring Punch. I can guarantee it for you, just as I can guarantee now on behalf of the club that you really are a perfect fit and we'd absolutely love to have you. That's the beautiful thing about *true* friends, Vanessa: they help each other out with these things. And you: you're a true friend. I knew from the second I read your e-mail that you'd be somebody I could count on. . . ."

"It's just so frustrating, you know?" Vanessa suddenly exclaimed. "I did *everything* for her! It's like she was Cinderella and I was her fairy godmother."

"A social ugly duckling that *you* grew into a beautiful swan."

"Yeah!" said Vanessa with bitter enthusiasm. "Yeah, exactly. I practically made her what she is today: she was just so freaking *clueless* when she first got here! I mean, how can you be from *Westwood* and yet the only shoes you own are a pair of ten-dollar bargain-bin flats? I did my best to include her, I showed her how to dress and introduced her to all my old friends and how does she repay me? By stabbing me in the back!"

"You deserve better from your friends," Lexi agreed. "We all do. I know how it is: I had a friend like that *my* freshmen year, too. She was fun and sweet to my face, but all the while she was plotting how to steal my things—my social life, my extracurriculars, my classes, my boyfriend—she even stole my favorite pair of Manolos, for crying out loud!

"Essentially these people are all the same: they know they can never be like us and that they can never truly belong to our world, so they take, take, take—shamelessly clawing their way up the social ladder because they're so *painfully* jealous. . . ."

"Jealous?" asked Vanessa. "You really think she's jealous—of *me*?"

"Of *course* she's jealous of you!" Lexi replied. "Who *wouldn't* be jealous of you? You're Vanessa Von Vorhees, for heaven's sake! You don't need me to tell you that!"

Callie could just imagine Lexi's sweet smile and large doe brown eyes. Vanessa was probably hanging on her every word, eating it up faster than mac-n-cheese after a party.

"Anyway, it's time for Vanessa Von Vorhees to start thinking about who her true friends really are. Are they the people who use you to get ahead and then leave you in the dust? Or are they the people who promise to go out on a limb and make sure that you get what you want—what you *deserve*?"

Vanessa was quiet. "Okay," she said finally. "All right, yeah. I'll see if I can think of anything that might help you, but you should know that I'm not sure if I'll be able to find anything good. She's very secretive, you know."

"Really, *anything* scandalous will do. . . ."

"I *said* all right," Vanessa answered. "I just need some time to . . . think about it, that's all."

"Good," said Lexi. "And in the meantime I'll be pulling strings for you with the board. And do keep in mind what I said earlier about you being a great fit for *FM*, too: the fewer freshmen that get on the magazine this semester, the more spots there will be in the spring. . . ."

Callie's face was burning. She made her way as quickly—and as quietly—as she could out of the stacks, leaving a pile of books abandoned in the middle of the aisle.

Her head was reeling. She could barely think straight; she could barely *walk* straight. Was Vanessa going to tell Lexi . . . everything? And if she was, what could Callie possibly do to stop her? And *why* had Vanessa suddenly turned on her—just when it seemed like everything was going so well? What about all that bullshit about being "best friends"?

Why did I think I could fucking *TRUST* her? Callie stumbled down the stairs and burst through the double doors.

Thankfully, that obnoxious little child genius was gone; there was no telling what Callie would have done if he had still been there, but strangling him with the front desk's telephone cord or clobbering him to death with the metal date-stamping device both seemed like excellent, viable options.

It was already well past seven o'clock. She hadn't finished her usual clean-up duties, but she didn't care. She rushed behind the checkout counter and started jamming things into her bag, desperate to leave as soon as possible.

What do I do? Confront Vanessa? Bribe her? Lock her in the bathroom and wait for her to starve? Invite her on a walk along the Charles River and then push her off a bridge? Or do I try to make nice: kiss her ass and convince her that I *am* a true friend and that Lexi is a goddamn, mothereffing, two-faced son of a !@#$%^&*!@#$%—

"Hi, you!" a familiar voice called from behind her as she was bending to retrieve her scarf.

Oh no, not . . .

"I made dinner reservations at Casablanca tonight—surprise!" Clint said as Callie turned around to face him.

"Or . . . you're not in the mood for surprises today?" Clint added, catching sight of the expression on her face.

"No—fine—sounds good. Let's get out of here," she replied, throwing her bag over her shoulder and striding ahead of him toward the door.

"Whatever you say, boss!" he said, following her down the steps.

Outside it was beginning to look a lot like winter. The once brilliantly colored leaves decorating the ground had turned brittle and brown, the tree branches bare and skeletal. The sky was an ominous shade of gray. Callie walked as swiftly as she could away from the library—so fast that Clint practically had to jog to keep up.

"I've never been to this restaurant, but I hear it's supposed to be good: really quaint and romantic—"

"Great—fine—whatever," she shot over her shoulder, quickening her pace.

"Hey . . . wait a minute," he said, running to close the gap between them and reaching out to touch her shoulder. "What's wrong?"

"Nothing!" she snapped. "I've just had a horrible day!" She knew she shouldn't take her anger out on him, but she could hardly stop herself.

"What? Why? Was it something I did?"

"Yes! I mean, no! Nothing *you* did. I'm just—I'm just frustrated, that's all!"

"Frustrated . . . ?" he asked, looking confused. "With me? Why? What did I do?"

"It's not you—it's *this*! This situation you've created," she floundered, gesticulating between them. "What we have is so—frustrating—because it's so, so . . . ambiguous!"

"What?"

"Yes, 'what.' That's exactly right. *What* . . . are *we*? What am *I* to *you*? A girlfriend? A fling? Just some freshman you're hoping to bang by the end of this week—"

"Whoa, whoa, whoa, Callie, now hang on just a second." he started. "Slow down."

She knew she was hurtling into the dangerous territory of high-risk relationship behavior, but she just couldn't shut up.

"I should have *known* better and followed everyone's advice about staying away from upperclassmen. You never know what they expect from you. Well, you should know from *me* that I am *not* the type of person who's into drama and random hookups. It's just too complicated and—"

Her speech ended abruptly as Clint leaned in and kissed her on the lips.

"Calm down, Callie. . . . There's no drama or complication here. We're dating, that's all. I like you a lot, and I hope that you feel the same way about me. In fact, I've been wanting to ask if I can call you my girlfriend, but I thought you felt like we were moving too fast when I invited you home for Thanksgiving, so I figured I would give the whole 'official relationship' thing a little more time. . . ."

His voice trailed off as she started to sob.

"Calm down," he whispered, taking her into his arms. "There's no need to cry. If something's wrong—if you're unhappy with me—you can tell me."

"No," she mumbled into his chest. "There's nothing wrong with you. You're perfect." But there is something horribly wrong with me, she added silently, forcing herself to look up.

"Oh no—your shirt!" she cried, realizing that two huge mascara stains had formed on his left shoulder.

Looking down, he broke into a grin. "You know, there are more subtle ways to tell me that you don't like my wardrobe."

She smiled weakly through her tears.

"Come on," he said, "let's get you home."

"I can't go back there!" she cried, shaking her head.

"All right, well, then: do you want to come to my place?"

SIXTEEN

Dangerous Liaisons

twitter

Home Profile Find People Settings Help Sign Out

What are you doing?

Marine Aurélie Clement
265 following 328 followers 548 tweets

Home

MeMe21: Missing my roomie . . . ☹

TripleV: D & G SALE!! Hitting it up on Newbury as we speak . . .

PrinceOK: Is it wrong that I LOVE the new Britney Spears album?!?

PrinceOK: And it's not because I think she's hot . . .

PrinceOK: It's because I just want to dance! Dancing Queen, DANCING QUEEN . . .

MeMe21: @PrinceOK: WTF is up with these tweets mon ami?

PrinceOK: I feel pretty, oh so pretty, oh so pretty, and witty, and GAAAAAAAAAY

PrinceOK: ATTENTION ALL. ACCOUNT HAS BEEN HIJACKED BY G. BOLTON. THIS IS THE REAL OK SPEAKING.

PrinceOK: @G_Bolton: arsehole!!

G_Bolton: @PrinceOK: Aw, love you too, man.

PrinceOK: @G_Bolton: giant, gaping arsehole!

Trending Topics

Hansel Eberhardt
Spee Punch
Brangelina
Thirsty Thursdays!
C&C
IvyGate
Bored@Lamont
Drew Faust
Crimson COMP
HP Social Club

twitter

Home Profile Find People Settings Help Sign Out

Calbear12: Love, love, loving Adams House; @MeMe21: missing you too ☹

MeMe21: Boy next to me in Justice is picking his nose. Ew. Très Ew.

DanaGray: I do not understand what this is for. Why do you all spend so much time on this?

PrinceOK: feeling betrayed by my roommate . . .

TripleV: @PrinceOK: know what that's like

Calbear12: The food in upperclassman houses is SO much better!! How did I survive before?

MeMe21: @Calbear12: Où es-tu, mon amour? Je suis très triste sans toi . . .

MRob: @Calbear12: yeah, dude, where are you?

Calbear12: @MeMe21 @ MRob: kidnapped and held hostage at Adams House!!

TripleV: wondering why some feel the need to brag about their upperclassman boyfriends . . .

Calbear12: oh no! I think I gained 2 pounds this week!

MeMe21: ça suffit, ladies, take it outside

DanaGray: I don't get this. I am deactivating my account. Good-bye, cruel world.

"You know, you look much better . . . *without* your clothes on," said Clint.

"Hey!" cried Callie as she hooked her bra behind her back. "There are more subtle ways to tell me that you don't like my wardrobe!"

"In that case," he said, rolling off the bed and grabbing her top from her hands before she could slip it over her head, "I hate this shirt. It's just so . . . white. And it doesn't have any sleeves. Totally offensive."

"I still have twenty minutes before I have to be in class," she said, leaning into him and placing her hands low on his waist.

"But . . . how . . ."—he moaned as she began nibbling on his ear—"but . . . how . . . will you . . . ever . . . learn?"

"Shhh . . . ," she said, brushing her lips against his neck. "It's okay, I can skip. . . . We're covering *On the Genealogy of Morals* this week, and I already read it in high school."

"Oooh, baby, I love it when you talk Nietzsche to me," he teased her before picking her up and tossing her back on the bed. "I promise I'll make it worth your while."

No thanks to Economics 10, Callie was beginning to discover the true value of prime real estate. For the past week she had been staying at Clint's and had quickly learned the many reasons why

Adams House was to Wigglesworth Dormitory as the Four Seasons is to a broom closet as The Ritz-Carlton is to jail.

Number one: privacy—you don't know what you have until it's gone. Number two: sleep space—after a few months in a twin, a king-sized bed is not to be underestimated. Number three: residential dining halls—where the food is slightly less lumpy and colorless. Number four: cute, popular, male roommates—enough said. And most important, reason number five: no Vanessa.

As far as Callie was concerned, she never needed to see Vanessa again.

Now it was Thursday evening, and she was putting the finishing touches on a paper for Justice discussing the role of autonomy in Kant's *Grounding of the Metaphysics of Morals*. She was nervous about the assignment because she had skipped both lectures that week: the last two before Thanksgiving break. Yesterday she'd had a legitimate excuse: she'd needed to do a final read-through of her second COMP portfolio before turning it in later that day. And on Monday she'd needed to . . . catch up on extra . . . *uh* . . . sleep. . . .

She yawned: a reaction that seemed to be causally correlated with hearing or even typing the word *metaphysics*. She knew that cutting class had been a stupid, stupid decision that she would later regret, but the reality was that—COMP and Clint excuses aside—she'd rather suffer through Kant alone than in a lecture hall full of people like Vanessa.

She looked up as her phone started to ring. It was Mimi.

"Hey, Meems," she answered, her eyes continuing to skim the computer screen.

"Callie, darling, just phoning to say *bonjour*. When will you return to the room? I miss you and Dana is distraught, although I think that might have something to do with you and Clint living wed without a lock, whatever that means."

Callie laughed, but she couldn't help noticing the conspicuous absence of Vanessa's name. Whatever. "You know you can come here and watch *Entourage* On Demand anytime you want, right? Clint's roommates keep bugging me to invite you over: they said to tell you that we have Grand Theft Auto V. . . ."

"Tempting." Mimi sighed. "But I would prefer to have you back here."

"Not yet, Mimi," Callie said quietly.

"Oh, well. I guess it is true what they say: sex really does conquer all."

"I think it's *love* that conquers all, and no, we're not having sex. Yet."

"What? You have been sleeping there for an entire week and you have yet to—uh, what is it you Americans say, 'do it'? *Pourquoi pas*?"

"Just waiting for the right moment, I guess."

"Oh-kaaay," said Mimi. "But I will be seeing you tomorrow, no? Must we really leave at nine in the ante meridiem? I am not convinced I can do it."

"I'm sure you can sleep in the car." Callie laughed. "See you tomorrow."

Rubbing her eyes, she turned back to her paper. It was the only thing left standing between her and one final weekend of freedom and fun before Thanksgiving break. And she needed to finish it fast, because tomorrow morning she and Mimi would be traveling down to Yale for The Game: the one day a year when even the least social Harvard students started drinking and tailgating at eight A.M. All week long the campus had been abuzz with pep rallies, posters, and people making plans about what to do, where to stay, and how to get down to New Haven. In an abnormal display of school spirit—given that 45 percent of students polled were unaware that Harvard even *had* a football team—Callie spotted crimson T-shirts with colorful sayings everywhere: from YUCK FALE to SUCK ON IT, SAFETY SCHOOL and WHEN ALL ELSE FAILS, GO TO YALE.

Callie, however, couldn't care less about a pathetic excuse to drink early-morning beers—ahem, watch a really great game of ball—and was basically holding her breath until she could fly home to California. There she would be in a much better position to do damage control and, say, hire a hit man to deal with Evan, an arsonist to burn his fraternity to the ground, and go shopping with Jessica to provide an alibi while all the shit went down. Then, *maybe* then, she'd feel like it was safe to return to Harvard, where it wouldn't really matter that much if Vanessa told Lexi because Callie could just deny, deny, deny and live happily ever after with Clint. . . .

Trying not to let her homicidal fantasies get the better of her, she forced herself to reread the paper one last time. It definitely wasn't her finest work, but extenuating circumstances surely allowed for a little leeway—or so she tried to convince herself. In any event, there was nothing she could do about the paper now except print it out and turn it in.

She had two options: Lamont Library or the offices at the *Crimson*.

Lamont would be packed at this hour with frantic students hastening to print off their assignments before heading down to New Haven and then home for Thanksgiving. Vanessa was probably in there right now, gossiping in Lamont Café about god knows what. If Callie were to actually see her, there was no telling what she might do, but hair pulling and fist fights both seemed like likely courses of action.

On the other hand, to go to the *Crimson* was to risk the imminent threat of Lexi—except that for tonight, Callie suddenly remembered, Lexi would be at the Pudding board meeting from seven till eight. In other words, the same place where Clint was right now.

Quickly her eyes flicked toward the clock: 7:50. If she hurried, she could make it. She didn't have a flash drive, so she e-mailed the document to herself instead. Grabbing her coat and the maroon scarf Clint had given her after he'd gotten sick of watching her "freeze to death," she rushed out into the common room, past Tyler's porn stash (poorly disguised as a collection of bad nineties music—note to self: take special care to avoid the *Spice Girls Greatest Hits*), out the door, and down the winding spiral staircase.

Three minutes later she arrived at the *Crimson*. Climbing the stairs two at a time, she hurried to the second floor offices, clicked on a computer, and logged into her e-mail account. Swiftly she downloaded the document, scanned it once, and then clicked Print.

The printer, it seemed, was taking a while to warm up. She began tapping her foot impatiently as it whirred into motion, glancing over her shoulder and half expecting Lexi to explode into the room and attack her at any second. The sudden, loud burst of sound from her cell phone almost sent her into cardiac arrest.

"Hey, gorgeous, it's me." Clint's voice came over the line.

"Hi," she said, smiling in spite of her nerves.

"Great news: the meeting let out a few minutes early." *Oh, shit.* "You know how usually these things can run over for hours. . . . Anyway, I was just wondering: what are you doing right now? Are you in the room?"

"No, actually I'm rushing to print off my paper and then I have to walk all the way to the law school to turn it in," she said distractedly as the printer *finally* started to move. "It's not due until tomorrow morning, but I want to finish it now so Mimi and I can get an early start. . . ."

"You're *sure* it's all right that I'm driving down on a party bus with the Fly?"

"Yes, yes, of course. Mimi's arranged for Gregory to drive us so we'll be fine," she said as the second page printed out more slowly than a tortoise's crippled geriatric grandma.

"Great!" said Clint. "You really are the best. Which is why . . . I have a surprise for you! Make sure you stay away from the room for at least fifteen minutes, okay?"

"Okay," she said as she slammed the stapler down on the pages of her mediocre paper and threw it into her bag, anxiously checking the clock. "It'll take me at least twenty minutes to get there and back."

She flung her bag over her shoulder and rushed toward the stairs.

"Wonderful. I'll see you in twenty, then—"

"Great, see you soon!" she cried, hanging up her phone. She entered the main foyer and began picking her way through the extra newspapers that were stacked against the wall. She was about to reach for the door when it opened and in walked—

Three guesses:

Ali Baba and the 40 thieves

Lulu the inflatable monkey

Alexis Vivienne Thorndike.

"Aren't you worried that coming into this building during an evaluation period is *almost* as tacky as a groom asking to see his bride's gown before the big day? Bad luck, too—" Lexi began with a wicked smile on her face.

"The editors at large said we can use the resources here whenever we want," Callie said shakily. Did Alexis know—well, everything? Was it worth it to try to be nice?

"My mistake," said Alexis sweetly. "You should definitely feel free to use our resources as much as you want—for the limited time that they'll be available to you."

Callie swallowed. "I guess we'll see about that," she said, forcing herself to return Lexi's gaze. "Hopefully the quality of my work will speak for itself."

"You know," said Lexi, taking a step forward, "that sometimes it's not just your *Us Weekly* rejects that count. I can assure you that the editors care about certain *other* things beyond the quality of your work. . . ."

"Oh?" Callie asked, fighting to keep her voice even as she added: "Like what other things?"

Lexi was silent, but a tiny downward twitch near the corner of her mouth gave away her hand: no aces, no nothing. Because, as it suddenly dawned on Callie, Vanessa hadn't talked.

Too shaken to feel triumphant, Callie turned her back on Lexi and practically ran all the way to the law school, her heart pounding in her chest.

As soon as Callie was out of sight, the mask of composure melted off of Lexi's face. Turning to the neat stacks of newspaper that lined the walls, she traced her fingers over the piles delicately as she made her way down the hall. At the last second she turned and, seizing a fistful of papers in hand, she screamed and flung them across the floor. Whirling around, she kicked the nearest stack: cursing as pages from the *Crimson* shot into the air and then floated back toward the floor like ugly, gray snowflakes.

Then she took a deep breath and pulled out her BlackBerry, quickly drafting an e-mail message to some of the COMPers.

> SOMEBODY LEFT A HUGE MESS
> IN THE OFFICES AT THE *CRIMSON*.
> THIS IS SIMPLY UNACCEPTABLE.
> I EXPECT IT WILL BE GONE BY
> THE MORNING.

Keeping her cell phone open as she mounted the stairs to the second floor offices, she thumbed through her most recent messages, pausing on the latest from Vanessa.

HAD SO MUCH FUN SHOPPING THE OTHER DAY! WANT TO DO COFFEE OR LUNCH NEXT WEEK!?

Lexi snorted contemptuously and clicked Delete. Obviously Vanessa hadn't been paying attention in Ec 10 during Feldstein's lesson on quid pro quo. No such thing as a free lunch, sweetheart.

Lexi sighed as a familiar image materialized on her BlackBerry's screen.

It was a photo of her and Clint, a self-portrait taken with his cell phone during their freshman year. Her hair was messy and she'd been wearing a pair of boxers and his Harvard Squash polo—the one she couldn't seem to bring herself to throw away, just like she couldn't manage to erase her background photo. They were smiling. A happy smile. They were happy once, before the Class of 2014 infested campus like rats carrying the plague. . . .

Lexi leaned against the doorframe of the *Crimson*'s computer lab. Shaking her head, she clicked back into her phone's message center and drafted a new text to Vanessa.

COFFEE AND, MORE IMPORTANT, GIRL TALK—SOUNDS GREAT! WHAT DAY WORKS BEST FOR YOU?

Somebody had left a computer on in the corner of the office, and Lexi's face twisted with rage once more.

After all, how would it look to her fellow co-chairs of the Harvard Green Initiative if *her* magazine were wasting half of their funding on electricity bills?

As she moved the mouse to turn it off, the screen lit up and displayed:

Callie Andrews
11.18.2010
Justice

Autonomy in Immanuel Kant's
Grounding of the Metaphysics of Morals

Lexi frowned and blew a frustrated gust of air through her lips. As she shut the document, her phone vibrated with a new message from Vanessa: SOUNDS GREAT! HOW'S TUESDAY?

Slowly Lexi raised her eyes back to the computer screen. She blinked twice. It was just too good to be true.

INBOX [Archive] [Report Spam] [Delete]

11/18	candrews@fas.har . . .	**Justice Paper Attached** Hooray! All done ☺
11/18	zanderwurst@hls.har . . .	**Section Canceled** Hi all! Unfortunately, section to . . .
11/16	Theresa.Frederickson@cd . . .	**Are you alive?** Hey honey, haven't heard from you . . .
11/14	libraryservices@fas.har . . .	**Completed Request** Ms. Andrews, your book is re . . .
11/14	mrobinson@fas.har . . .	**NYTimes Article** Cool Op-Ed in today's paper, yo . . .
11/12	goldberg@fas.har . . .	**Dues?** Hi Callie, my records show you haven't paid . . .
11/10	vonvorhees@fas.har . . .	**BORED IN CLASS** Omfg could this prof be any m...
11/7	Facebook@facebo . . .	**Facebook** Clint Weber has Poked you. To view...
11/5	Evan.Davies@ucl . . .	(**no subject**) I'm sorry.

Callie made her way up the stairs toward Clint's suite in Adams House. Even though she should be able to relax now that all her work for the week was done, standing up to Lexi had somehow been more terrifying than empowering. . . .

She walked into the common room and found Clint waiting just inside the door. He took her bag from her and helped her out of her coat, then guided her toward his room with his hands over her eyes.

"Don't peek," he warned, opening the door and nudging her inside.

Immediately her ears filled with the sounds of soft, smooth jazz music. Clint walked her a few more steps and then uncovered her eyes.

On the floor was a white sheet surrounded by a border of soft pillows and covered everywhere with rose petals, which Clint had also scattered across the white down comforter on his bed. A bottle of champagne, a plate of dark chocolate–covered strawberries, and a picnic basket rested on the makeshift tablecloth, illuminated by the dim glow of tiny tea lights that he had arranged on the coffee table over by his couch.

"The other night," Clint said, "you mentioned that one of the things you missed most about California was being able to eat outside. Well, since we didn't have time to go somewhere warm for a picnic, I thought I'd bring the picnic inside for us!"

Callie was speechless: there was only one thing to do. She kissed him, flinging her arms around his neck and running her hands through his hair.

He kissed her: gently at first, then with greater urgency.

Wrapping his arms around her, he pulled her as close to him as possible, caressing the small of her back.

Her hands slid down over his chest and then behind his waist, reaching beneath his polo shirt and over the warm, smooth skin of his back. Her fingers traced the upper rim of his boxers.

Grinning, he dipped her down suddenly and slid his free arm under her knees, lifting her and carrying her toward the rose-petal-covered bed. He lay her down and climbed on top of her, lifting her shirt and kissing her belly button before moving upward to kiss her collarbone, her neck, her cheeks, and then her lips.

She guided his shirt up over his head and pulled it off, throwing it across the room and taking a moment to admire, as she'd been doing every day that week, his body: toned from so many years of squash. Smiling up at him, she ran her fingers through his hair again. She *loved* that light brown hair, so shabby and *sexy* when it fell across his eyes. . . .

Before she knew it, they had removed his pants as well and he was working to unclasp her bra, her shirt having already joined her jeans in a pile on the floor. Her fingers lingered on his lower abs. She hesitated, but as her bra slid to the floor and he started kissing her chest, she began to pull his boxers down.

His hands rested on her hip bones, fingers tracing little lines beneath her belly button. He looked up at her, a silent question in his eyes. She nodded, arching her back as he slid her underwear down over her legs.

Suddenly they were chest to chest, their two bodies nearly one. He kissed her on the mouth and then tilted his face so that it was a few inches away from her. "Are you sure you're ready for this?" he whispered.

"Yes . . . ," she replied, pulling him back to her. She ran her hands over his chest, across his shoulders and down the lengths of his arms, her body aching for him.

"Sex is a big deal; I just want to be absolutely certain that you're ready. . . ."

"It's not my first time, you know," she said, trying to smile as thoughts of her first time—thoughts of Evan—wandered into her head.

"I know," he said, kissing her forehead. "I mean, I didn't *know*, but I assumed since you mentioned having a long-term boyfriend back in high school."

Stop talking about it! He felt heavy as he continued kissing her cheeks. Images of Evan began flashing through her mind.

"I just wanted to make sure that you were ready with *me* . . . for *us*. . . ."

"Uh-huh," she mumbled, trying to move. He was suffocating her.

"Because I don't want to rush you if you're not feeling ready," he pressed on, reaching out to move the hair that had fallen across her eyes. "Our first time should be special—"

"I think I know a way we could make today extra *special," Evan said, waving the keys to the soccer team's locker room with a mischievous smile.*

"But it's Senior Week!" she protested. "We were supposed to turn the keys in already . . . and everyone's on campus—we could get caught!"

"—and I want you to feel totally comfortable and safe—"

"Don't worry, it's totally safe," Evan insisted, taking her hands in his

and kissing her on each cheek. "We'll lock the door, and no one will be able to hear us because I brought my laptop"—THE LAPTOP THAT MUST HAVE HAD A BUILT-IN VIDEO CAMERA—*"and I can play loud music, just like this—"*

"Callie?"

"Callie, come on: one last Captains' Practice, for old time's sake. It'll be our little secret." And back then she'd assumed that by "secret" he'd meant, "hooking up in the soccer team's locker room during Senior Week"—completely unaware that he had also been *secretly* filming them on his laptop the entire time—

"Callie! What's wrong? Why won't you talk to me?"

And then Evan had shown that tape—a video file saved on his computer—to all the seniors on the team right before graduation to prove that what he'd been bragging about all semester was true—she could finally understand why for the rest of the summer they had all smiled at her with that funny look in their eyes.

"Goddammit Callie, why won't you *say* anything?"

And he had never *said anything* until after he shared the tape with his big brother at UCLA—since "Make a Sex Tape" was worth a "gajillion points" in his fraternity's initiation scavenger hunt. Did they think she'd made the tape voluntarily—that she was a dirty, freaky, exhibitionist, nympho, slut? Weren't there laws against this type of thing? Against filming people doing private things without their consent, without their knowledge?

"Callie," Clint started, trying again, his voice steady now but clearly alarmed. "*Please.* Tell me what's wrong."

"Can't do it!" She gasped suddenly as she noticed that Clint was gripping her shoulders looking bewildered and distressed.

Who had a copy of that file now—besides every single member in his frat—and where was it going from there? YouTube? MySpace? Facebook?

"Can't do it—" she managed to choke out again through strangled breaths. Clint finally realized she needed some air and moved aside.

And what if Clint ever saw it? Or if anyone at Harvard ever saw it? And what about life after college, for that matter? Would a newspaper ever hire her? And her parents—oh god, her parents: if they ever knew, she would—

Clint returned from his bathroom with a glass of water, but she just shook her head and mumbled, "I have to leave," reaching for her clothes.

"No—don't go. Stay, please, and *tell me* what's going on," he pleaded as she yanked her shirt on—backward and inside out—and started jamming her legs into her jeans. "Was it something I did? Did I go too fast? Please, just come sit back on the bed and relax. . . . You're safe with me—"

"Safe?" she cried, wheeling around and accidentally kicking the plate of chocolate-covered strawberries across the room. "There's nothing *safe* about having *sex*—"

"Really, Callie, it's all right. I understand that you're nervous—" he tried again, standing up and pulling on his boxers.

"No, Clint, no you do *not* understand!" she cried, refusing to meet his eyes. "You couldn't *possibly* understand!" She darted around the room, gathering her things.

"All right, Callie, you know what? You're right: I *don't* understand." He pulled on his jeans. "I don't get you—at *all.* One minute you seem totally excited and then all of a sudden you're seriously freaking out! What's the deal? Why can't you just *talk* to me about—"

"I don't want to talk to you about it, okay!"

He hesitated for a moment, watching her search for her shoes and then:

"Fine . . ."

His tone made her pause, one shoe on and the other on the floor. She kept her eyes on her feet, knowing that if she looked at him she would surely start to cry.

"You don't want to talk to me? That's fine. That's your decision. But I can't have a *girlfriend* who doesn't feel like she can tell me things. It's just not fair—to either of us. So maybe you should take some time to think and figure out what you want."

He pulled on his shirt. "I'll be here waiting when you're ready to talk, but *this,*" he added, gesturing toward the space between them as Callie continued to stare at the floor. "This type of behavior, without explanation, is completely crazy and totally unacceptable."

She nodded slowly and pulled the straps of her duffel bag over her shoulder. She glanced at him briefly and muttered, "See you when I see you," then made her way out the door.

She was half expecting him to follow her—to call out to her or at least offer to walk her home—when she heard the door to his room shut with a slam.

Outside it had started to snow.

SEVENTEEN

Beer, Sex, and Football

The Game

Dear Froshies:

Well, the secret's out: Harvard has a football team! For those of you boys who didn't already know: shame on you–get out of the library and get a life! For those of you ladies who did: great job–now stop screwing that football player and get back to the library!

But in all seriousness, they say that beer, sex, and football are the three things that no college student (i.e. heterosexual dude) can live without. That's why the Harvard-Yale football game (read: "tailgate") is most students' favorite event of the year–a magical time when they can usually manage to satisfy all three of these primal collegiate desires consecutively, if not simultaneously. . . .

for your football: Take the Mass Pike heading west, then I-84 and I-91 to New Haven, where the murder rate in the city is higher than the average Yalie's SAT. Game starts at noon on Saturday. Tailgating starts at Toad's on Friday evening and continues when you wake up on Saturday morning (if you even sleep at all). As soon as you open your eyes and recover from the unexpected shock of a) where you are sleeping and b) who is sleeping next to you, you'd be well advised to keep drinking–a mimosa or a Bloody Mary is the *best* way to cure a hangover. . . .

for your beer: The Harvard undergraduate tailgates–including trailers, BBQs, and DJs courtesy of the Final Clubs and Upperclassman Houses–will be located adjacent to the field, next to the alumni tailgates (sneak in for some quality food and booze) and of course the enemy territory. No need to BYOB: the house tailgates and the Final Clubs will have as much Natty Light, Budweiser, PBR, and Coors as your little hearts can possibly desire. Shotgun at will, but remember the importance of knowing your own limits: the "drunk tanks" at Yale-New Haven Hospital tend to fill up pretty quickly with stupid, overzealous freshmen.

for your sex: Well, against my better advice, you *can* decide to hedge your legacy bets and attempt to procreate with a Yalie instead of a fellow Harvard peer. Just be warned that, in contrast to Harvard, requirements for admittance to Yale do *not* require being good in bed. . . . But fling away if you must, little froshies! Just remember that those two minutes of ecstasy may come back to haunt you when Yale comes up to Harvard for the game: 2011. . . .

As always, when engaging in these hedonistic pleasures, aspiring future leaders of the world ought to keep in mind the following three words: decorum, decorum, decorum.

As you shotgun that beer: always have an eye on the individual behind the camera as it snaps your picture, always know where–and on whose Facebook profile–that picture is going to go. In your drunken stupor you may not even notice as an acquaintance's digital camera snaps a photo of you making out with your roommate or takes a short video of you doing a keg stand and accidentally flashing the world. Just remember: once it's on the internet, there's no telling where it might go.

I know you all paid close attention during the college's various lectures about online privacy, but I'll repeat my warning once more: it's the times like these when we think we're the safest to really let loose and get wild that require our greatest vigilance. Get ready for the scandals and get ready for the fun. . . .

Hang on to your hats–it's HARVARD-YALE!
Alexis Thorndike, Advice Columnist
Fifteen Minutes Magazine
Harvard University's Authority on Campus Life since 1873

"SWALLOW! SWALLOW! SWALLOW!" the crowd chanted before erupting into a roar.

"Come on, girls—one more time!" Bryan yelled above the cheers, holding two cheap plastic bottles of gin in each hand at the top of the ice luge: a large block of ice tilted at a forty-five degree angle with two miniature "riverbeds" carved into it so that two young coeds could place their mouths on the lower end and receive a long stream of freezing-cold hard alcohol.

Mimi shook her head from side to side as Bryan screamed encouragements, motioning to Callie that she couldn't handle any more booze. "Shoulda flowed your a'vice and spit insteada swallowed," Mimi mumbled drunkenly, stumbling off to the side.

Thus abandoned by her partner in crime, Callie was about to back away from the luge when Mimi's vacant space was suddenly filled.

"Okay, let's go!" Gregory cried, smiling at Callie.

For a split second Callie hesitated, wondering if this was a very bad idea. Deciding that yes, it was a terrible idea indeed, in the true spirit of college she bent over and did it anyway.

As she stood up a moment later, gin punch trickling down her chin, she searched for Mimi—relaxing when Callie spotted her wobbling toward the DJ near a table for the Fly.

It was Game Day and the tailgate was raging. The morning sun shone brightly over the massive fields adjacent to the Yale Bowl, which were currently overflowing with endless rows of trailers and cars decorated with banners and balloons, beneath which students and alumni clustered, barbecuing and drinking beers. It was freezing cold in spite of the sun, but most were too intoxicated to notice, stumbling from table to table and sampling the food and drink while the trampled grass grew muddy beneath their feet.

Callie and Mimi had already gotten lost three times on their way to find the Harvard undergraduates' section, surviving catcalls and mock death threats from Yalies who spotted their crimson sweatshirts. Finally they had happened upon a crowd of familiar faces. Banners for some of the upperclassman houses fluttered in the breeze next to tables full of booze and bagels that had been set up in front of trailers painted with logos: the Fly, the Delphic, the Isis, and the Bee. The Final Clubs had pooled their money and rented a DJ. Music blasted from the nearby speakers, and a dance party was quickly materializing—the wildest ever to occur before noon in the history of the Ivy League.

"I had fun last night," said Gregory, speaking over Callie's shoulder.

Callie ignored him and continued to scan the area, looking for Clint and wondering what he might think or say if he spotted the two of them together like this. She couldn't see him and . . .

. . . *if* $a = b$ *and* $b = c$, *then* $a = c$ *so* . . .

. . . he must not be able to see her either.

Turning to Gregory, she met his eyes, remembering the events of the previous evening all too clearly: how by the end of the night, she had ended up in his arms . . .

. . . where Clint had practically pushed her. She had been trying to dance with Clint, trying to apologize, when he had stormed out of the bar and left her there, alone, saying: *"Callie, I thought I told you I need a break."*

All night long the words had played to the DJ's soundtrack, over and over again in her head.

"I need a break" as she started dancing with Gregory and—

"I need a break" as their sweat began to mingle and—

"I need a break" as he pulled her closer and closer—

What did it mean: "*I need a break*?"

She felt Gregory's hand on her shoulder and realized that he was still looking at her . . . and Clint still wasn't speaking to her . . . and Gregory's eyes were still just as blue, just as beautiful . . . and Clint still wasn't speaking to her . . . and maybe being on a break meant that it was all right to give in to gravity and lean forward and—

"Bad, *bad* neighbor!" Mimi cried, rushing over and stepping in front of Callie. Glaring at Gregory, she made a fist. *"Laisse-la ou je vais te faire mal!"*

Before Gregory could respond, Mimi grabbed Callie's hand and dragged her off into the midst of the dance party, now packed with hundreds of students. Gregory quickly disappeared from view. Mimi began to move to the music, but Callie froze—for there was Vanessa not ten feet away, dancing up a storm with some prep school girls. She had driven down in their car and was also sharing a room with them at the Omni New Haven. Good for her. Have fun guessing whose jeans cost the most or plotting how to ruin my life.

Suddenly Vanessa waved. It was a tiny, weak wave, but it was still a wave and Callie felt her heart soaring just a little. As far as Callie could tell, Vanessa hadn't told Lexi about the video. Right now she could really use a friend. Her best friend.

"Come *on*," Mimi cried, tugging Callie's hand. "Need foods." She gestured toward a nearby table filled with what looked like boxes of donuts. "Forgotta eat this morning . . ."

Callie nodded and followed Mimi through the crowd. Suddenly she stopped walking. Clint was over by the Delphic's trailer. He had definitely seen her, and he definitely still had zero interest in talking to her. She watched him shotgun a beer and "whoop": drunker and rowdier than usual because—*hopefully*—he was upset about her. A girl walked up to him but he ignored her, high-fiving the guy who had just handed him another beer.

Better than I can say for myself, she thought. From across the way Mimi held open an empty pink box and mouthed: "*No Donuts*," pouting with great exaggeration as she headed back toward Callie. "LET US TRY THE PUDDING TAILGATE!" she screamed.

"OKAY!" Callie screamed back. "BUT YOU DON'T HAVE TO YELL!" Arm-in-arm, they wove their way through the crowd. Unfortunately, instead of food, the Pudding's folding table was lined with bottles and bottles of booze.

"Neos!" cried a bunch of older girls.

"Initiation time!" one of them screamed as another picked up a handle. "Now, drink!" she yelled. Mimi shrugged and opened her mouth. Callie clamped her lips and shook her head. *No way* was she participating in any form of *initiation*. . . .

She turned around and saw Lexi smiling. Smiling? Yes, smiling—

at her, a *knowing* expression in her eyes. Still smiling—*creepy*—Lexi started making her way toward Callie.

"Hi!" she said, pouring some Bloody Mary mix into a plastic cup and selecting a piece of celery. "Are you enjoying your weekend?"

Callie simply stared at her.

"I'd make the most of it if I were you. . . ." Lexi continued, taking a sip of her drink. The bloodred color and her pale, smooth skin made her look a bit like a vampire, and Callie was about to open her mouth and say just that when somebody stumbled into her from behind—

"Hey, watch—" Callie snapped before she realized that Mimi was literally collapsing into her arms. "Whoa there, drunkie—"

"Je dois sortir. Je vais être—être—MALADE!"

"What?" yelled Callie, shepherding her to a less crowded area.

"I said—" Mimi sputtered, tripping over her own feet, "ThatIamgoingtobe—SICK! PUKE! NOW!"

"Oh!" cried Callie. Then: "Not you too! What's wrong with the pair of you—YOU'RE NOT FAT!"

"NO, YOU IDIOT. I MEAN—" and then Mimi barfed—all over Callie's ten-dollar, bargain-bin flats.

"Well, I guess *that's* why I don't buy nice shoes!" Callie mused with cheery matter-of-factness, grabbing Mimi midway through her descent earthward. "Feeling better?" she asked, her concern mounting as Mimi continued to sink downward: limbs like a rag doll's, eyes half closed.

"Nah . . ." Mimi mumbled. "Shtill shfeeling shick . . ."

Callie guided Mimi away from the crowd, past rows and rows

of cars, and toward a grassy knoll. Mimi sank onto the ground. Callie cursed herself for worrying so much about Clint, Gregory, Lexi, and Vanessa that she hadn't paid closer attention to how much her roommate had been drinking. She was trying to figure out what to do—leave Mimi there and go get her some food?—try to see if she wanted to throw up again?—find Vanessa and ask for help?—when all of a sudden, a man in a golf cart zoomed over in their direction.

As he got closer, Callie realized that he was a cop. "*Shit!*" she muttered. Then: "Mimi, we've got to move!"

"Blerg . . ." Mimi mumbled, closing her eyes and leaning her head against Callie's chest. A disturbing-colored spit bubble formed around the rim of her mouth.

Shit.

"You girls look like you could use a little help," said the cop, parking the golf cart and making his way toward them.

"Oh no, officer," Callie said, trying to sit Mimi up straight. "We're doing fine . . . just fine—"

"Dandy!" Mimi opened her eyes and yelled happily, "Peachy keen!"

Nudging Mimi in the ribs, Callie continued, smiling: "Yep, just fine and definitely not in need of any assistance. But thank you very much for asking!"

The officer didn't budge. "Your friend looks very, very drunk," he said.

"Define 'drunk,'" Callie said slowly as Mimi groaned and her head dropped between her knees.

"How old are you girls, anyway?"

"Twenty-one, officer" Callie offered at the exact same moment Mimi cried: "TWENTY-FIVE!"

"Right," he said, staring down at them. "Well, in that case, you don't have a choice. I'm going to take you to health services so they can get you to a hospital."

Head still sunk low between her knees, Mimi lifted her hands as if she were waiting to be cuffed: "Take me away, officer."

"Uh—no, Mimi—HOSPITAL," said Callie, trying to lift her to her feet. The officer bent to help.

"L'hôpital? Oui, bien sûr . . ." Mimi murmured as he scooped her up and carried her to the golf cart.

"Can I come, too?" asked Callie.

He surveyed her skeptically. "Usually it's not allowed unless—"

"*Please*, sir," Callie interrupted, starting to panic. "She's not a U.S. citizen, and I don't want to leave her alone—"

"All right. You can wait in the lobby at the hospital—but don't cause any trouble!"

Seven hours later Mimi was still asleep, hooked up to an IV while Callie waited in the lobby. Numbly Callie had watched many of her fellow freshmen being wheeled in on stretchers. She had watched the football game on a static-ridden TV in the corner. She had watched the clock tick away the hours. And at around noon she had watched her cell phone lose its final bar of battery power as it beeped its way to a tragic, untimely death. . . .

The nurse who had been updating her on Mimi's status walked through the double doors. Mimi was fine—lucky, even, to have escaped a stomach pumping—but she was still very weak.

"Is she awake yet?" Callie asked, standing as the nurse approached her.

"No, not yet darlin'," the nurse answered in a sedate, maternal voice. "We need to let her hydrate and sleep for at least another twenty minutes. In the meantime ain't there anyone you can call to come pick you gals up?"

Callie's eyes widened despairingly. "My cell phone," she whispered, "it—died."

"And I s'pose a landline ain't any help to you kids these days, mmm?" the nurse said, sounding more weary than judgmental.

"Yeah," Callie admitted, "that's right. I don't have any of our friends' numbers written down or memorized. . . ."

"And your girlfriend—she don't have a cell phone?"

Callie shook her head. "I couldn't find it anywhere. . . ."

The nurse sighed. "I s'pose y'all are just gonna have to pay for a cab, then. I'll write down the number for you soon as your friend wakes up."

Callie watched her amble back through the double doors. She didn't have the heart to cry out and explain how they'd left all their cash, wallets, credit cards, clothes, and *everything* locked in their room back at the hotel—the keys to which she had for some reason stupidly entrusted to OK.

Shit, she thought miserably for the ten thousandth time that day. She didn't know if she could think of a way to euphemize the phrase *stranded at Yale-New Haven.* Slumped low in her uncomfortable plastic chair, Callie watched a dark-haired man with the collar of his coat pulled high against the cold sweep through the sliding glass doors, a look of panic in his eyes.

"Gregory?"

"Callie!" he cried, hurrying toward her and locking her in a fierce embrace. After a few moments he pulled back, looking embarrassed.

"How did you . . ." Her head was suddenly heavy with exhaustion.

"It took me a while, but after talking to a couple of people who saw you leaving the tailgate, I was able to piece it together. I already checked the other two hospitals and this was the only one left. Is Mimi okay?"

"She's fine. Still sleeping, but they said she'll wake up soon," Callie said. She sank back down into her plastic chair, finding that her feelings of gratitude were too overwhelming to put into words. "I just can't . . . Thank you so—"

"I'm just glad you're all right," he cut in, sitting down beside her. "I need to text Clint and tell him that I found you," he added, pulling out his phone. "He's been really worried, trying to reach you all day, but he said you'd turned off your cell phone. Since I was the one with the car, I offered. . . ." He looked up from his phone. "Unless, do you want to call him?"

Slowly she shook her head. His eyes lingered questioningly on her face.

"I'm just so tired," she offered lamely.

Gregory shrugged and clicked Send. Five seconds later his cell phone vibrated in response. "He says he's glad you're okay and that you should call him after Thanksgiving break if you're ready to talk."

Ready to talk about why I freaked out on Thursday? thought Callie, shifting in her chair. *After Thanksgiving break? How about more like never?*

"Do you . . . want to tell me what that's about?" Gregory asked, holding up his phone.

"No, not really," she said. "What I actually want—more than anything—is a sandwich."

"A sandwich? Why? When was the last time you had something to eat?"

"Mmm . . . breakfast?"

"You mean, the mimosas we drank before we left the hotel? That doesn't count."

"I see your point." Her stomach rumbled. "Too bad my wallet's been locked in the hotel all day."

"Hang on," said Gregory, standing and walking toward the vending machines over by the TV. In a minute he was back holding a candy bar and a bag of chips.

"Not quite a sandwich, but I did the best I could under the circumstances."

"Thanks," she said, accepting the chips. "You really are a lifesaver."

They were quiet for a moment as she ate. Then: "What was that in your back pocket?" she asked.

"What?"

"When you stood up to go to the vending machines, there was something in your pocket."

"What were you doing staring at my back pockets?"

She was too exhausted to blush. Instead she glared. "Are you going to tell me what it is or not?"

"Fine," he said with a sigh. Then he pulled something small and slim out of the back of his jeans. It was a book: *Persuasion*, by Jane Austen.

Callie grabbed it, her eyes growing wide. "You brought *this* book—to the tailgate?"

"So?"

"To the *tailgate*?"

"I usually bring a book everywhere I go—in case I get bored."

"Yes, but *this* book?" she repeated again, mostly to herself rather than to him. He actually *liked* Jane Austen? Meaning he *hadn't* made it up all those weeks ago just to torment her?

"I understand it's not your favorite. . . ," he began.

What? There was *no way* he could have remembered!

"Maybe I judged it too quickly," she said.

"Yes," he agreed with a smile. "Maybe you should give it a second chance."

"Maybe I will," she said, opening it. He had scribbled all over the pages: the marginalia almost as extensive as the notes in her ancient copy of *Pride and Prejudice*. Her head felt light—with hunger, surely—as he leaned in to read the first paragraph over her shoulder.

They were only three pages in when a very pale, very embarrassed Mimi shuffled into the lobby.

Immediately they stood and Gregory shoved the book back into his pocket. Callie gave Mimi an enormous hug. "Feeling better?" she asked.

Mimi nodded.

"Let's get you to the hotel," Gregory said, throwing a protective arm around her shoulders. She nodded again and allowed herself to be led out to the parking lot.

"Callie . . . ," she started, fumbling for words.

"Don't mention it," Callie reassured her, patting her on the back. "It could have happened to any of us."

"Yeah, but not everyone—"

"*Shhh* . . . We can talk about that later," Callie said. "We're just so glad that you're safe."

"Yeah," said Gregory as they all climbed into his car. "*I* wasn't *that* worried because you know I don't really like you . . . but my *roommate*! Man, if you've ever seen a large emotional African on the verge of tears, then you *know* it isn't pretty."

Mimi smiled feebly from the front seat.

"I practically had to chain him to the radiator before he agreed to wait by the phone in case you called!" he continued.

Calling the hotel? thought Callie. Why didn't I think of that!? Stupid, stupid, stupid!

"He'll be feeling happier now," Gregory added, the gray, darkened streets of New Haven whizzing past. "In fact, he just texted me a few minutes ago to say he ordered from room service: 'everything that the buggers had on their menu' in case you're feeling hungry! Including," he added, glancing in the rearview mirror back at Callie, "a sandwich."

"Thanks," Mimi whispered. Callie smiled.

Several minutes later they were handing the car keys to the hotel valet and piling into the elevator. Callie wondered if she ought to get in touch with Vanessa, who she thought was staying either on their floor or a few floors above. Was she worried? Did she even know what had happened?

Better to let Gregory or OK tell her, and then maybe when they all got back to school, Callie could find it in her heart to forgive Vanessa for the Lamont Library Conspiracy.

As soon as they got off the elevator, the door to Gregory and OK's room burst open and OK ran toward Mimi, folding her so tightly in his embrace that she actually squealed.

"Ah! LetgooFMe!"

"You're *alive*!" he boomed, holding her back from him at arm's length and studying her as if eight years had passed, rather than eight hours.

"Of *course* I am *alive*," she snapped. A tiny hint of color had sprung into her cheeks. "Know anywhere that a girl can get a decent meal around here?"

"Right this way, mademoiselle!" OK cried, flinging open the door to reveal five carts of food. Mimi shook her head and smiled before following OK inside.

"Still hungry?" Gregory asked, turning to Callie instead of heading into the room.

"Actually, no."

"We should probably let them be alone, then," he murmured.

She could feel his eyes on her as her fingers fumbled with the key to her room. It slipped twice before the lock opened with a click.

"Do you mind if I smoke?" he asked when they were inside, gesturing toward the balcony.

She shook her head. Despite Callie's protests Mimi had been quite firm about reserving a luxury suite and charging the entire bill to her mother's credit card, assuring Callie that to let her do so was a "tremendous favor" in service of the great, ongoing goal to "*exaspérer ma mère*."

Silently Callie followed Gregory onto the balcony. She settled down in the wooden lounge chair next to him, propping her feet on the built-in footrest. The night was dark and it had started to mist. A cool wind danced through her hair. She shivered.

"You cold?" Gregory asked. Before she could reply, he had disappeared into the room, returning moments later with an ashtray and a soft fleece blanket. He wrapped the blanket around her shoulders, then settled into the other chair and lit his cigarette. Inhaling deeply, he stared out into the night.

"Can I have one of those?" she asked.

"I didn't know you smoked."

"I don't." She sighed. "But I think I could really use one right now."

"It's a bad habit, you know," he said.

"Well, I suppose it's the bad habits that are often the most tempting," she ventured, meeting his eyes.

He looked away, staring off into the distance for a few moments as if he hadn't heard her.

"So, what's up with you and Clint?" he asked suddenly. "Why isn't he here with you?"

"Not sure . . ." Callie sighed. "I guess we're not really together anymore."

"Really? That's interesting," he said quietly, extinguishing his cigarette in the ashtray.

"Interesting?" she asked as her heart began to pound like a bass drum. "Interesting to whom?"

"To me," he answered, and leaning toward her, he kissed her.

She was drowning in the sound of her thundering pulse, her head dizzy. She felt as if a rug had been pulled out from underneath her feet and she was floating upside down in the misty rain, kissing him like she had never kissed anybody in her entire life, wanting to go on kissing him for hours, for it to never end.

He pulled her to her feet. The mist turned to a drizzle and then into rain, but they kept on kissing, oblivious to the world—to the storm, to the blaring horns and shouts from the streets below, and to the ashtray that had fallen unnoticed into a puddle. They were oblivious to the horrified face of a girl who was leaning, her wet hair plastered against her cheeks, over the railing of a room that must have been only several doors down the hall: watching their every move.

Finally Gregory broke away and gazed at Callie intently. Then he led her back inside.

There were no hesitations—no questions, no conversations. There wasn't anything at all, in fact, except bliss.

As the story usually goes, things were decidedly less rosy in the morning. Gregory was gone, and Mimi, who must have come back sometime after dawn, was hovering near the other queen-sized bed, muttering and flinging her clothes into an oversized duffel bag.

"Morning," Callie mumbled, squinting her eyes against the sunlight filtering through the curtains. She was still completely naked.

"Er, Mimi? Did you happen to see my—"

The pair of underwear in question flung through the air and landed on her head.

"Uh, thanks," she stammered, diving back under the covers.

"It is nothing, darling. Happens to me *tout le temps*," Mimi chirped, happy that it was somebody else's turn to feel embarrassed after last night's adventures. "My favorite leopard-print thong *and* my hot pink spanky shorts are *still* MIA, even after I posted lost underwear flyers all across campus. . . ."

"What!" Callie cried as she wrapped herself in a sheet and ran across the room toward her bag. "Are you still drunk?"

"No, just bitingly witty and exceedingly hilarious as usual."

There was a loud knock on the door and the muffled sound of OK's voice.

"Shit!" Callie cried, dropping the sheet and yanking on her clothes.

"Coming, coming," Mimi called. She opened the door to find OK waiting in the hall, his bag fully packed and ready to go.

"Where's Gregory?" Callie asked, trying to keep her voice casual.

"Oh—didn't you know?" asked OK, stretching out across the bed and watching Callie pack. "He had to get up early to drive back for squash practice. They have a big match coming up." OK yawned.

"Anyway," he continued, "I think he would've stayed behind to drive our lot home if he hadn't already promised a bunch of guys on the squash team that he'd give them a ride back."

Callie froze.

She had ruined everything. Clint . . . Vanessa . . . If they found out what had happened, she'd be lucky if either one of them ever spoke to her again.

Her mind was racing as they left the hotel and hailed a cab to take them to the New Haven train station. Mimi and OK slept the whole way home, but Callie stayed wide awake. . . .

The weirdest part was that the one person she wanted to talk to the most *was* Vanessa. Were they even now? Did flirting with the possibility of betrayal in the library equal much more than flirting with Vanessa's crush?

Probably not, but as they stepped off the T at Harvard Square and trudged back in the direction of Wigglesworth, Callie decided that she would find Vanessa and make things right. How exactly and *what* exactly she was going to tell her, she wasn't sure: she hadn't figured out the details yet, but she knew that somehow things would work out in the end, with both Vanessa and Gregory—no, wait, Vanessa and *Clint*. Clint was *perfect*. But Gregory was . . .

She said good-bye to Mimi and OK, who had decided to play Grand Theft Auto IV, and, too scared to see if Gregory was home, Callie flung open the door to C 24.

"Vanessa!"

"Vanessa?" she called again, more tentatively as she pushed the door to Vanessa's room open a crack.

No one was there.

Sighing, she walked into her own bedroom and plopped down on the chair in front of her desk. She stared out her window and watched the dusk begin to creep across Harvard Yard. Over the weekend the white blanket of fresh snow had turned to gray slush.

Her eyes fell upon a handwritten note resting to the left of her laptop. It was from Vanessa. She began to read:

> Callie—
> After I heard about what happened to Mimi, I stayed at the tailgate looking for you guys for hours. I thought maybe you weren't answering my calls because you were upset we haven't been speaking, but now I know it was only because you wanted to hook up with Gregory behind my back, you HEARTLESS, TRAITOROUS BITCH. How could you do this to me—and with the one guy you KNEW I actually cared about? I guess you really are a slut. I can't believe that I ever defended you or called you my friend. You are the WORST person I have ever known, and I am going to request a room transfer just as soon as we get back from Thanksgiving break.
>
> —V

Callie's hands were shaking and her eyes began to fill with tears as she reached for her phone to call Vanessa. It was still dead. She plugged it into her charger and opened her computer instead. Maybe e-mail would be better: maybe she'd have a shot at forgiveness if she could explain it all in writing first—how she had liked Gregory since the beginning of the year and how everything had happened so fast. . . .

She logged into her e-mail account and was about to click on Compose New Mail when a new message caught her eye.

From: **Alexis Thorndike**

To: **Callie Andrews**

Subject: Does the girl in this video look familiar!?

Attachments (1): C:\Users\Evan Davies\Desktop\Private\Copy_Soccer_Initiation.avi

Just writing to wish you luck in the second round of COMP!
Have a lovely Thanksgiving Break, and I'll see you afterward—
If you decide to come back, that is.

Cheers,
Alexis

6/11, 11/12, 9/15, 4/17, 12/17